GW01338947

FRANKENSTEIN'S PRESCRIPTION

Frankenstein's Prescription

Tim Lees

Tartarus Press

Frankenstein's Prescription by Tim Lees

This edition is published by Tartarus Press, 2010 at Coverley House, Carlton-in-Coverdale, Leyburn, North Yorkshire, DL8 4AY, UK.

Frankenstein's Prescription © Tim Lees, 2010.

ISBN 978-1-905784-29-5

The publishers would like to thank Jim Rockhill and Richard Dalby for their help in the preparation of this volume.

Printed in Great Britain by the MPG Books Group, Bodmin and King's Lynn.

Frankenstein's Prescription by Tim Lees is limited to 300 copies.

My eyes opened. The world began.

Chapter One

'Blessed. Blessed, blessed, blessed.'

His voice is soft, and almost musical: a chant, a lullaby. He lifts the hammer, holds a moment . . . strikes.

'Are they that mourn. For they shall be comforted.'

There is a little, stifled mew of pain.

Another blow.

'. . . the merciful. For they shall receive mercy.'

No sound comes from the house, nor from the woods; even the birds are silent now. Only the ring of steel on steel, seeming to shiver in the air, long after the blow's been dealt, shaking my bones, setting my teeth on edge.

'Blessed . . . are they that hunger after righteousness. For they shall be satisfied.'

It's like a toy, that hammer, wrapped up in his massive fist. It rises, falls. Rises, falls.

The cross is on the ground. The figure on it whimpers, muscles jerking uncontrollably.

'Blessed. Blessed, blessed are the pure in heart, for they . . .'

Once more, he pounds the nail. The body spasms, torso leaping up as if to break the bonds, the spine arched horribly.

I can no longer watch. I curl into a ball. I put my hands over my ears. But nothing can shut out the cries . . .

Germany

Chapter Two

1901. It was the worst year of my life: the year I saw my dreams of fortune tumble in a rout of shame and scandal; the year I suffered exile, poverty, and learned to fear the law. In retrospect, given my actions and proclivities, it may be such a fate was more or less inevitable. At the time, it rather took me by surprise.

I had been born to privilege, and privilege imbues its own specific cast of mind. Yet privilege is relative, when all is said and done, and the protection I enjoyed at home extended but a small way in the outer world. I was a little slow to realise this.

I had been studying at Heidelberg, intent on a career in medicine. My lifestyle was flamboyant, dashing and, I need hardly add, outrageously expensive. Twice I had fought duels, triumphantly on both occasions: the first, inflicting a small flesh wound on my enemy; the second, magnanimously firing in the air, a stylish piece of swagger that won toasts in every hostelry I entered for the next few days. I hosted lavish drinking parties for my friends. I loved to see them raise their cups and cheer my name; as if a bright new sun had risen in the sky. Even the gratitude of strangers filled me with delight, so much that I would sometimes pass a few marks to a beggar just to witness his astonishment, receiving such a princely sum. The trick, of course, was to affect a carefree manner, utterly unruffled by the fear of consequence. The fact that I would wake tomorrow with a headache and a raging thirst, and creditors pursuing me for money I no longer had—these details must be cast quite out of mind. Posterity would pay my debts. Ahead of me I had a great career. Within a year of graduation, my income would be such that all these petty tradesmen who now hunted me would beg me, literally beg me for a glance, a kindly word, the scrapings from my table. So I assured myself, at any rate; especially when drunk.

Thus, my public life. But I enjoyed too a more private world, which proved if anything more costly still—and certainly more time-consuming. Here, as before, I wined and dined, though now as prelude to more intimate associations; on occasion, too, I made a trip to the apothecary, for the women of the city were neither quite so clean nor pure as they might claim. It was an irony my chosen field of study should be medicine. I was, you might say, exploring the trajectories of illness at first hand.

In short, I had become the thing my father always feared: a debauchee, and proud of the achievement. Other aspects of my life—the gloomy moods and doubts that nagged me if I spent too long alone, the clawing panic that would wake me in the small hours, desperate for some distraction—these were matters I preferred not to consider, nor to question, lest they lead me to conclusions I did not enjoy.

Soon, it seemed that every other week I would dispatch a letter to my father, begging for a few more marks, protesting some enormous, unforeseen expense—a broken microscope, a rise in rent, assistance to some poor but honest fellow student fallen on hard times. My father's letters, which accompanied these sums, went in the bin, half-read. Their querulous tone and constant threats were marks of his controlling nature, and the insistence this would be 'the last time' was not at all a thing I wished to see. So long as, folded in the letter, I found money, and enough to match my debts. . . . Until, of course, there came a day I found no money. I tore the envelope apart, thinking his gift might somehow have been caught up in the folds. The single sheet of notepaper, written in my father's large, excessively neat hand, I ignored. I chased the postman, calling him a thief, a churl. We almost came to blows. Only then, I thought to read my father's note, which I had stuffed into my pocket without so much as a glance.

Frankenstein's Prescription

'. . . even in this distant province, my dear Hans, we cannot escape news of the regrettable habits into which you have fallen, nor the dissipation which has come to characterise your life in that unholy town. My dear child . . .' I skipped his imprecations to attend a church, to pray, to mend my ways, etc. The final paragraph seemed burned like acid in my soul: 'Until that day, I regret no further monies can be sent to you. If you wish to return home for a period of relief from your studies, you would be greatly welcomed, and your mother, for one, would be most relieved . . .'

I screwed it up and flung it in the gutter. This wasn't what I needed! I raged, I swore, I cursed the world! Yet in my anger, I hatched a plan, bold to the point of genius—or folly. I would solve my problems on my own, without my father's help. I would succeed in spite of him. I knew a girl, the daughter of a wealthy family, a plain girl, true, yet one who blushed if I so much as looked on her, whose merest glance spoke of idolatry, whose eyes could never bear to meet my own. . . .

But let me skip ahead a few weeks, to the grim and grisly outcome of my scheme.

Chapter Three

I had a brandy headache like a thundercloud behind my eyes. The sun was not yet up; the landscape had a washed-out look entirely suited to my mood. A line of bare, dark trees split empty ground from empty sky. Small figures shuffled here and there, performing their small, sullen rituals. We were not the only duellists out that day. I kicked a tuft of grass, digging at it with my boot toe. I had taken against it, for some reason; this simple clod had started to annoy me.

'God's bollocks. Can't they hurry up with it?'

'Duel of honour, sir, eh now? Can't be rushed.'

My servant shrugged. I shrugged as well. We shrugged together. Some way off, my opponent, Herr Grundig, was convening with his party. They huddled like conspirators. Even at this distance I saw their frowns. They took the whole thing far too sombrely. I resolved to lighten the occasion, if I could.

I drew myself up, called out to him. 'Grundig! Grundig, old chap! Can we not speed this business on?'

Grundig, with a shake of his shoulders, turned his back on me.

'Fine morning, eh?' I yelled.

My servant took my cloak. The cold air seeped into my bones, but I clapped my hands, I stretched my arms. Should I affect a little yawn? No, not yet; best not to overdo things. Rather late, I saw my second, a young law student named Milch, approaching with his party. There were a dozen of them; they looked as grey and miserable as I.

At that moment, a pistol shot rang out, followed by another. Thus those before us in the roster were all done. Neither participant, it seemed, was hurt. The whole thing was a bit of hoo-hah, really. With greatest ceremony, their seconds produced flasks from which they all swigged copiously. Indeed, it would have been hard to say who were the duellists, who the onlookers; they all seemed equally in need of calming fluids.

My friends surrounded me. I, too, took a little refreshment, purely to warm myself. Then I squared my shoulders and I strode across to Grundig's mob.

'Well,' I said. 'Not changed your mind, have you?'

He looked at me. He was a tall young man, with squarish jaw and cropped blond hair. A toy soldier. He surveyed me up and down, his top lip twitching in contempt. I rather basked in his disgust.

'Schneider,' he said, 'you are a perfect swine.'

'Ah! So that is what I am. I've often wondered.'

He glared at me with icy, Prussian eyes.

'I do this for the honour of the Fräulein Henriet. An honour which you—which you—'

'Have purloined most heinously. Yes yes yes. Though I'll admit, it was a treasure she seemed glad to lose.'

His neck grew pink, the only spot of colour in the world.

'Is that a blush? Or has the sun come up?'

I nodded to our predecessors as they left, heading for breakfast in the town. They wished us both good luck—something of a pointless exercise, I felt, since only one of us should really come out tops. Then pistols were produced. I took my weapon. It was a little heavy in the hand. Not my ideal choice. I sighted at a tree stump.

'Hm. It will do, I daresay.'

'If you live,' he said, 'you will regret this day. Had we fought with rapiers, I'd tear your pretty looks till no woman would glance at you again.'

'However,' I reminded him, 'your words were, "Choose your weapons." As I have.'

Frankenstein's Prescription

Throughout my time in Heidelberg, whatever provocation I endured, I had been careful not to be the challenger in any duel; rather, the challenged. It gave advantages, in chief the right of picking arms with which I had a certain competence. Indeed, I was a crack shot, though scarcely clever with the rapier. Rapier duels, moreover, might go on indefinitely, opponents dropping from fatigue as likely as from wounds—tedious events for public and participants alike. Forget the rapier. The scalpel, as I liked to say, was more my tool; though even that, in truth, came second to a winning smile, a wise nod of the head, an outwardly trustworthy (if inwardly duplicitous) demeanour. My future was mapped out, clear and plain in my own mind. Not for me the drudgery of a provincial medic, nor the long hours of the hospital ward. No; let me cater to the wives and daughters of some prosperous commercial city—München, say, or Köln. A life of cushioned ease would stretch before me, sumptuous and sure, spiced only by an intermittent brush with death—as now.

Grundig signalled to his party, and as one they dropped down on their knees upon the frosty ground. As he intoned his pious orders to the Deity, demanding justice, I called loudly for another drink. I was rapidly rewarded. I'd grown bored. It was a question now of merely putting on a show. I could no longer even claim that I was nervous; my head hurt far too much for that.

Grundig and I stood back to back. The ritual commenced. We paced. We turned. He did not, I admit, look quite so far away as I'd have liked. Nonetheless, I held my pistol lowered, showed him the palm of my left hand, inviting him to fire. At the same time, I mentally picked out my target on his person. A little wound around the left upper arm, perhaps; debilitating, painful, but not permanently crippling. It does no good to let such people simply get away. One must either fire into the air, displaying one's contempt, or else come close enough to really frighten them. Besides, Grundig irked me. If there is one thing far more hateful than hypocrisy, it's true, untrammelled piety. A precious, trembling thing. It made me altogether ill.

I felt my body stiffen as I peered into his gun muzzle. I saw the smoke of discharge long before I heard the shot. I registered, in the bare fraction of a second, that I was safe. Then my arm was up, levelled, and aimed. I began to squeeze the trigger—and at the same moment, something dashed into my face. Off-balance now, the recoil spun me round. I batted at a mass of feathers flopping round my head, I stumbled, and was free. A lone pheasant, startled by my foe-man's shot, had leapt out blindly from its hiding place and, by unfortunate coincidence, discovered me where it expected only air.

My clever shot, of course, was ruined.

More than that, my enemy seemed to have vanished. Only when I saw his party running to the spot where I had last observed him, did I realise he was sprawled upon the ground, a bullet in his side.

By one o'clock that day, poor Helmut Wilhelm Grundig was stone dead, and I was in a very large amount of trouble.

Chapter Four

Duelling, while a long and honourable tradition, had always posed a problem for the University. Not only were there implications with the law, but scandals had arisen, attracting much unwanted public interest. Into these ranks I found my own case duly marshalled.

In addition, practical concerns were raised. Dead students seldom paid their fees, a matter of considerable importance to the academic authorities; and Grundig's fees would now be permanently overdue.

My tutor tutted, frowned, as by convention he was bound to do. Herr Doctor Müller had the face of a thug and the hands of an artist, neither of which seemed very useful to me in my present circumstance.

'A sad, sad loss.' He shook his bullet head. 'So very sad.'

I was about to agree, and remark, for form's sake, on Grundig's great potential, his chivalric nature, and so forth, when the true meaning of Müller's comment hit me. It was not of Grundig that he spoke, but of myself.

'I,' I said.

He raised his brow.

'I, I—'

'Yes?'

'But I'm a gifted student. You told me so yourself!'

'Oh, indeed.' His slender fingers settled on an antique globe, turning it slowly, as if to check his place upon the world. 'Also a wastrel, a libertine . . . and now a murderer.'

I protested. He silenced me. 'Grundig's family has influence,' he said, 'unfortunately greater than your own. In addition, there was a girl involved, was there not? The girl's father has petitioned us for your expulsion. The University, while preferring that no charges should be pressed, feels an example must be made . . . to dissuade others.'

The room grew small. The walls pushed in on me.

'I have, of course, despatched a letter to your father.'

'My father!' The feeling of oppression grew to one of terror. This I had not expected; Heidelberg to me was an hermetic bubble, sealed from my past, my home. Whatever stories reached my father I had always had the option to deny, rebuff, or brand as jealous gossip; but not this, a letter from my tutor. 'You had no right!'

'This was not the only message I despatched.' In the face of my increasing panic, Herr Doctor Müller remained calm and solemn. He watched me from beneath his heavy brows, intoning words that sounded like the slow beat of a funeral liturgy. 'A message to a certain . . . *friend* might be too strong a word. A certain colleague or acquaintance, then, who may prove useful to you.'

'But my father!' I was on my feet. 'Can the letter not be stopped? When did it go? Can we retrieve it?'

'Dear boy.' Müller's voice was like a knife blade scraped on glass. 'I am already trying to salvage your career. And possibly your neck.' He spun the globe. 'I believe that the authorities—not to mention the family Grundig—may be placated with a period of rustication. If we're lucky. A year or two. . . . It may also prove of benefit to your character, of course. If we are . . . unusually fortunate.'

'A year? A *year?*'

'Or two. I don't think we can get away with less.'

I looked about myself. The book-lined walls, the surgical instruments immured like hunting trophies in their great glass cases . . .

My knees were weak. My voice was weaker.

'Rus . . . rustication?'

'Out of sight, out of mind. As you have seen fit to remind me, my dear Hans—I may call you Hans?—you are indeed a gifted student. Over-fond of the drink, and of the ladies, true. Never my own vice, I'll admit. If I help you now, it's to preserve that still imaginary future in which you may, perhaps, do some good for this wretched, wayward human race. God knows, even a half-way decent doctor is a rarity. And let me say, I understand the nature of . . . let's call it youthful indiscretion. It need not prove the doom it seems. Many—indeed, some of the greatest—do survive . . .' He came round from behind his desk. 'I can assure you, Hans, even the darkest folly may be forgiven and forgotten, and the flower once seemingly extracted by the roots may blossom again.' He was behind me. I did not turn round. 'You take myself. I am esteemed throughout all Germany, and far beyond. I have healed kings and statesmen. I have dined with barons and with earls. My reputation is the envy of my colleagues. And yet I, too . . .' His voice dropped. He placed his hands upon my shoulders, gently kneading at the flesh. 'It's so long ago. I must have been about your age. A little youthful foolishness, a little sin too lightly covered up . . . a sneaking, envious little creep who whispered cruelly to the Dean. . . . I believed my life was over. Yet now. . . .'

His fingers, long and cold, like sticks of wood, traced their way along my chin, then rose to touch my cheek. His breath was in my ear, loud and throbbing like a steam train.

'Thank you,' I mumbled. 'Thank you, thank you . . .'

'I offer you this refuge in the hope that one day . . . one day you might return the favour, in some form . . . ?'

'One day,' I assured him. 'One day,' and I bolted from the room as quickly as I dared, ran to my quarters, and began to pack.

Chapter Five

The asylum at M—— squats upon the hilltop like the nipple on a scarred and ulcerated breast. Were I to describe it, with its ravaged pines, deep cuts and tumbled rocks, the high, frowning walls of the building itself, you would no doubt conjure up an image of the sort of ruined grandeur popular amongst Teutonic folk, a melancholy beauty suitable for brooding and lamenting, and indulging the most pleasurable self-pity. Well and good in art and poetry, perhaps. In truth, the place was dreary beyond words, so utterly devoid of promise that it seemed to deaden all emotion even as I looked on it.

The coachman left me at the crossroads. I entreated him to take me further. He merely laughed. Such behaviour, contrary to what one sees on stage, is neither sinister nor frightening, but merely rude. My bags were dumped beside me at the roadside. I watched my driver urge his horses on, abandoning me there. I glanced round at the bleak and lonely spot where I was meant to spend my 'quiet' year, then sprinted after, calling, 'Wait, wait!' and brandishing my purse. He did not wait. He did not even slow. I cursed him, as he dwindled in the distance. And I had nothing left to do but stay.

It must have been a mile to the asylum walls, all uphill. I started ferrying my luggage up the path, taking two cases, depositing them, going back to fetch another pair, dragging my two large trunks as far as I could. But it was hopeless. My fine clothes, my medical equipment, my books. . . . All I could do was leave them, piled up by the roadside. I would go to the asylum and commandeer its servants to collect my goods, trusting to luck no ill befell them in the meantime.

I was not entirely happy with the plan. I have always taken pride in my appearance, acknowledging the value of a serviceable wardrobe when presenting oneself to the world. My books and equipment, likewise, were tokens of my stature as a man of learning. It was hardly right to leave them in the woods like this. But what else could I do? Had I the choice, I would have turned around immediately, gone back to the railway station and awaited the next train, no matter how long it might take. Yet I could never move the luggage on my own. As I trudged on up the path, my anger wilted, giving way to something like despair. I felt I would have suffered any torment not to have been sent here, not to have killed Grundig, never to have fought that stupid duel! Still—as I consoled myself—it had been Grundig's fault, not mine. He had been the challenger, not I! Grundig, that sanctimonious fool! Should it not be Grundig, then, dragging himself so slowly up this godforsaken hill, here in my place? (And somewhere in the depths of Hell, perhaps he had his own steep hill to climb. I hoped so, anyway.)

At last I reached the entrance. It was a great, stout door, almost twice my height, the planks worn smooth with age, the iron bindings fit to hold an elephant. I determined: I would not announce my business. I would insist a carriage be prepared at once to take me back to town. I would request—no, no, *demand* a meal, for I was hungry, and it might be that the cellars were not totally unstocked with decent port or schnapps or other liquor, and I would insist on warmth, a chance to change my clothes, a good cigar—

Something caught my eye. A movement, deep amid the woods. It was only for a second, but it seemed a darkness passed across my view, a shadow almost like a man, yet far too large. I peered into the trees, the gloomy stretch of pines, wondering what sort of creature I had startled there. A big one, certainly. Oh, not a bear, please God. Please no. To have come here to this pit of misery, to be immediately savaged by a bear—I turned back to the door, no longer thinking about food and drink. I raised a hand and hammered, furiously.

Nothing happened for a time. Then, plop! Something fell into the bushes on my left. Looking up, I saw the bleak stone walls in silhouette against the sky. I pounded on the wood. There was an odour now, a foul stench of manure. I stood on one leg, inspecting the sole of my boot, then did the same with the other.

Plop!

It hit my shoulder, splashed my face. Christ's balls! The stink! I jumped back. I stared up at the walls. Hard to believe, but somebody was throwing shit at me!

I yelled, I swore—and barely dodged another missile. It splashed upon my feet, with the consistency of raw egg. 'Hey!' I called out. 'Hey, hey! In God's name—'

And the door opened.

Chapter Six

I barged my way inside. I didn't stop to look around, barely even registered the skinny little figure I had brushed aside.

'My luggage is some half a mile along the road,' I said. 'Be good enough to send someone to fetch it for me. I should like a bath prepared. I want food—but first, before that, I want drink. And furthermore,' I rounded on the fellow, and found myself faced with the stark, angular contours of a skull, jutting cheekbones, peg-like teeth and pale, sunken eyes that peered out from their sockets like mistrustful, burrowing creatures. 'Furthermore,' I yelled, to overcome my discomposure, 'someone has been throwing *shit* at me!' I tugged my coat collar, presenting it, so that the filthy stain was almost in his face.

He didn't flinch; he scarcely even blinked. His eyeballs swivelled in their caves. His brow creased, and the furrows stretched up through the thin grey fuzz upon his scalp, almost to his crown.

'Are you listening to me? Do you understand? Are you an idiot or something? Someone's been throwing—'

And I stopped. Ah! Of course he was an idiot! Of course he was. I had come here, to this home of idiots, and what did I find? An idiot! I saw the logic instantly. Indeed, it was quite beautiful. I have never, I may say, been unappreciative of logic.

'Hello? Hello? Do you have a name? Do you have a master here? I need to talk to your master. Go fetch your master, will you? There's a good chap.'

He looked at me. Eyes of an extraordinary paleness, drained of colour.

'Master's dead.'

His voice was soft, like velvet rubbing velvet.

I confess that I could not suppress a smile. If the master here were dead, then surely, I'd no need to stay. The University could have no claim on me. Rusticated I might well be, but I could rusticate myself to somewhere far more tasteful, to Marienbad or Baden-Baden, to Paris, or Berlin. . . .

The pale eyes twitched. The creases in his brow rumpled and shifted, as if his skin were over-large for him. 'Master's dead,' he said again, head on one side. 'And you're dead. Everyone's dead. Come, come.'

He tugged my sleeve. My glimpse of freedom wavered.

'Dr Lavenza,' I said, hopefully. 'He's dead, you say?'

'This way. Quickly please. This way.'

'Is Lavenza here? Is he alive?' I sought to penetrate the veil of lunacy. 'If so, then I must see him, urgently. I am an important person, come here at his invitation. If Dr Lavenza finds I was delayed, or improperly treated—I have luggage down the road a way—it must be fetched at once. Dr Lavenza will be very, very cross—'

'Yes. Dr Lavenza wants you. This way, please. Come.'

'I urge you to despatch someone to fetch my luggage. Instantly. Or it will be the worse for you.'

'Come. Come!'

There was nothing I could do. I let him lead me on, through a succession of peculiar stone rooms. It was like passing through the chambers of a nautilus. Here, two men played chess; one had his head bandaged. He started talking as we passed, addressing me, I think, gabbling incoherently. We hurried by. A woman sprawled upon a couch, clutching a rag doll as if giving suck. Elsewhere, a thoroughly gigantic fellow, his hair as shaggy as a yak's, invited us to join him in a feast, yet the table where he sat was empty, no matter how enthusiastically he spread his hands. Elsewhere, assorted invalids and madmen, several dressed in little more than bedsheets, sat upon their bunks, lolled or cavorted, and the sounds of laughter, cries and conversation echoed and re-echoed through the air. Only then, amid the chatter and the general gibbering, I grew aware of something new.

Someone was screaming.

The little man produced a bunch of keys, trying one after the other in a heavy wooden door.

'Not this one. No. Not this. Or this. . . .'

The screams came from the far side of the door.

They had a most unfortunate effect on me.

I shuffled backwards. My feet moved, without volition, carrying me off. I had heard screams before, of course, in surgery, but that was different; that was in a place I knew and understood. But here . . .

The little man tugged at my hand. He seized my fingers, pulling with surprising strength.

'This way, this way!'

He had happened on the proper key. The door swung open. Ahead, a flight of stairs. A dreadful, high-pitched wailing burst upon my ears. It was the time to run. Instead, I found myself thrust forwards, his little hands pushing and pulling me. I was climbing through some sort of tower, my fists clenched, sweat already dripping from my brow. And when we reached the top—oh! It was a scene from Dante. No other way I might describe it. This was a vision out of Satan's pit, a Black Mass; and I was hurled into the midst of it. The black priest welcomed me. His robe, his face, even his hair was smeared with blood. I was in Hell. I was in Hell and—strangely—I accepted it. I was a murderer, a libertine. What else did I deserve? I stepped towards the priest. I swallowed. I raised a hand in greeting. So this was rustication! To be trapped in some appalling backwater, apprentice to a surgeon scarcely better than a witch doctor!

'Here,' he gestured, hand slick with blood. 'Quick now!'

Approaching him was not, in fact, an easy task. It was a smallish room, with great high windows, and cluttered full of clamps and surgical devices, with trays and chairs and this and that; and people. Yes. Truly, an astounding crowd of people.

First and foremost, I suppose, there was the woman on the table; though at the time her gender scarcely registered with me; she was a supine figure in a soiled robe, nothing more. Her ankles and her wrists were held by leather straps, padded with cloth, and further straps embraced both chest and pelvis. Yet these could hardly keep her still. Around her, half a dozen big men stood, ready to grasp her and immobilise her if she struggled. The most complex of restraints was on her head—a padded clamp that fitted round her skull, adjustable with screws, a further strap across the forehead; a second strap, presumably to hold the chin, hung down, broken and useless.

'Hold her, hold her,' cried the witch doctor. It was a moment till I realised it was I whom he addressed; and even then I found it hard to move. The details of the scene were slowly becoming clear to me. The ragged, filthy wig that dangled from the woman's head revealed itself abruptly as a peeled and bloody flap of scalp. The doctor shuffled it aside. Against the naked brain box he positioned a device which, in the heat of the moment, I took to be an egg whisk. Here was madness at its height. 'Hold her.' He was nodding to the woman's head. I tentatively reached out. 'Firmly, you fool! It's vital she stay still!' When I hung back, he ordered, 'Chin and forehead! Press down hard! Keep her there! And don't get in my way!'

I did as I was bidden, pressing down with all my might on the poor woman's face. She whimpered under me. There was a stink of sweat, and blood, and ether, used for the feeble anaesthesia in which she floundered like a victim in a nightmare.

'Now,' announced the doctor. Around me, the orderlies took hold of their charge. The witch doctor pushed forwards, leaning his weight upon the handle, and began to turn the egg whisk, jamming it into the pale bone of the woman's skull. At which she screamed, and screamed.

'Ether,' he called. A man with arms like a gorilla's unstoppered the bottle, doused a rag and pressed it to the woman's nose. The fumes were so intense I feared I might collapse myself. 'Enough,' the doctor cried, and bent back to his task.

I felt the grinding of a drill-bit cutting bone, vibrations trembling through my hands. My arms began to shake in sympathy.

I watched the fellow as he worked. His hair was wild, his thick moustache untrimmed; his brow was creased with concentration. Yet it occurred to me, despite his wildness, he could be no more than a few years older than myself.

The screaming died, replaced by semi-conscious gasps and grunts. I pressed and pressed, the focus of my task eclipsing now all thought, all feeling, blotting out all rationality. As such, it was a mercy. The witch doctor, his task complete, presently straightened and stood back. He passed his egg whisk to an aid, took swabs, and dabbed the wound.

'Ah-ha,' he said. 'A few quick stitches, and we're done.'

The woman shivered. It was like a minor fit. The doctor bade me hold her once again, and with a loving delicacy, like a spinster seamstress, took up a needle and began to sew her scalp back into place.

His fingers, their nails crusted in blood, moved quickly, and with a grace the more remarkable for the brutality preceding it. The flap of skin was quickly back in place. He sighed, he straightened up. And then his shoulders slumped. He seemed to age; worn out by labour, drained by effort. He caught sight of me, and frowned, as if observing for the first time I was not one of his usual assistants.

'Schneider,' I informed him. 'Hans Mitton Schneider, medical intern. You would be Dr Lavenza, I believe?' I held my hand out. We each looked at our soiled and slippery fingers. We did not shake.

He stripped his apron. He led me back downstairs, into an annexe where towels and water bowls had been laid out. Here, we washed, as best we could. He said nothing. I wondered what I had been party to; was it surgery or torture? In truth, I had often found it hard to tell the two apart.

Lavenza raised a hand to indicate I follow him. He seemed too shattered to form words. He led me through yet more rooms, up a second flight of stairs, along a corridor. My hands still shook; my head was in a daze. At last we reached a locked door. He took a big, black key, inserted it, and gestured me inside.

The late sun thrust its rays through leaded glass. Here, in what were, presumably, his private quarters, I found at last some semblance of a civilised existence. My host collapsed upon the davenport. I took a chair beside the book case, glancing briefly at the spines; medical texts, chiefly in Latin and German. Few were known to me.

'Heidelberg . . . ?' he said. I nodded. He reached into a cabinet, produced two glasses and a large bottle of cognac. He must have seen my look, because the slightest glimmer of a smile lit on his face.

'The woman,' he explained. His voice was almost empty of expression. There was a hint of accent—Swiss, perhaps, or Austrian? 'Her name is Fleischer. Bourgeois stock. Some years ago she began to suffer headaches, conjoined with fits of violent rage, quite foreign to her character. It was felt to be a form of women's illness, somewhat like hysteria. Her husband spoke with many doctors. In the end, a ferocious assault—I believe upon a tradesman—led to her imprisonment. She was considered to have become, through means no-one could easily identify, a violent and aggressive criminal. And thus, after some years, she was referred to me.' He sipped from his glass, holding the liquor in his mouth a moment before swallowing. 'I have performed a simple trepanation. I have, as you observed, drilled a hole into her skull.'

My mind was much confused. Adrenalin still shivered in my system; I have at other times had cause to notice how its residue depletes the power of reason. All I remembered were my first impressions, blundering into the operating theatre—certain I had stumbled on some vile Satanic ritual.

'And that allowed the—the bad things out?'

'Sir?'

'The, the . . .' I could not find the words. 'The evil spirit?' I said presently.

He peered at me.

'That's what they teach at Heidelberg these days?'

'I'm sorry—I—I was—'

'I determined she was suffering from a tumour, Herr Schneider, and I relieved the pressure of it on her brain. As you should, I think, be well aware.' He downed his glass in one, and was already reaching for the bottle. 'Or was it an attempt at wit? If so, then you must notify me when to laugh. I have no sense of humour, sir. None whatsoever. Nor have I ever felt its lack.'

Chapter Seven

I glanced out of the window. Day was fading; there was perhaps an hour of light still left. As I recovered something of my senses, a matter of great urgency began to press upon my mind.

'Herr Doctor,' I implored. 'Forgive me if I beg a favour, but my luggage—my life's possessions—I was forced to leave them on the road. They are not far. If you would have some servant prepare a carriage, I would be greatly in your debt, sir.'

His eyes were glazed, focused on nothing. He seemed fatigued beyond endurance, almost ready to collapse.

'Sir? You do have servants, sir?'

'Of course. Many, many servants. . . . Have Karl sort it out. Karl! Karl!' He began to shout, and reached for a bell pull.

A moment later, a small, thin figure scampered into view. I was not best pleased to see it was the idiot who had first admitted me into this world of madmen.

Lavenza clapped his hands, commending me to the little chap, and tendered his apologies for not accompanying us. So I set off with Karl, once more into the bowels of the asylum, and yet again explained my needs.

He nodded, muttered, 'Yes, yes, yes.' I had Lavenza's stamp of approval, transforming the relationship between us; indeed, the idiot seemed willing to do anything I wished.

Karl. Karl, Karl. I would befriend Herr Karl. I looked in my purse for a few pfennigs to offer him. If Karl were a servant, he might as well be my servant as anybody else's.

I knew the art of winning loyalty from those of the lower orders, even if most other wisdom had, to date, eluded me.

Frankenstein's Prescription

❦

Riding an ancient trap, pulled by an almost equally decrepit horse, we retraced my steps. Dark trees loomed over us. I, too, now suffered from fatigue, and it seemed delirium might overwhelm me, as the branches turned to spiky fingers, poking at me, jabbing and accusing. I forced myself to rationalise; remembered all I had to do was find my luggage, get it to safety, and devise my exit from this dreadful place. Already I was plotting my way out. The coach ran without schedule, but it seemed to me, with Karl's help, I might gain wind of its passing, and be ready to join it on its next run through. At no point did the option of staying, accepting my punishment, seem in the least bit viable. The crowding trees, the dimming sky, my own awareness of the madhouse at my back— these were depressing circumstances; yet my heart grew light. No circumstance so dark that one could not escape. Why, only days ago, I had imagined ruin, even prosecution; and this, as ugly as it was, was certainly not that.

Ruin, I regret to say, still lay ahead.

For now, I daydreamed: Vienna, Paris, London. . . .

And we reached the coach road.

'You've brought us the wrong way.'

Karl, the imbecile, swivelled his eyes at me.

We had not come the wrong way. Indeed, there was no other way. Had my goods been stolen in the brief few hours since I abandoned them? I made Karl turn, go back along our route. There were landmarks here I recognised; I remembered struggling to drag my trunks around the knobby stub of an old fallen tree, for instance. I could not be sure of the exact spot I had piled my possessions, but, after a moment, I signalled Karl to halt. In the fading light, scattered by the roadside, I gradually made out some items which had not, to my memory, been present when I first traversed the ground. At this distance, their nature was obscure;

items of clothing, possibly, as if some careless laundry-woman had let slip a few small items from her basket on her way to the asylum. But of my own luggage, the two trunks I had left so neatly side by side, and my accompanying bags—I saw not a thing.

A nasty thought crept then into my head, but I rejected it. A crow cawed in the treetops. I dismounted cautiously, stepping in among the shadows of the woods. I had not, after all, mistaken the place. Oh no.

My clothes—my beautiful clothes! My books! My papers! They lay scattered at the roadside like the debris of a shipwreck. I could do nought but stare. It was incomprehensible. For while the bags might well have been torn open by some vagabond, the trunks were of stout oak rimmed with iron, both firmly locked; I had the keys upon my person now. A gang then, a gang who had most assuredly carried off my stout oak trunks, who had—

I wandered, dazed. And here and there I came upon so many items that I knew for fact had been locked safe inside my trunks. My spare coat, my boots of fine Moroccan leather, a heap of beautiful silk shirts . . . I began to gather them up, until my arms were so full I could hold no more. Yet also, there was something else here, which confused me mightily.

Repeatedly I stumbled over lengths of broken wood, and twisted iron, and . . .

Someone—some force—had smashed my travelling trunks.

Smashed them? No. Blown them apart! Nothing else could have performed such wholesale, such complete destruction. I had chosen them specifically for strength. They were as tough as safes. I recalled the blacksmith in my home town, a huge man, muscled like a Michelangelo, and his assurances that no-one, nothing, not even an elephant could put a dent into his work—

I felt a plucking at my sleeve. It was the imbecile, Karl.

'Master.' (It seemed I had gone up in his esteem; before, only Lavenza had merited the title. I wish I could announce that this promotion pleased me, but it did not.) 'Is this the reason why we're here?'

I merely nodded, and stood there while he went about, collecting up my clothes, the scattered pages of my books, my toiletries and personal effects, from among the bushes and the trees, the ditches and the mire, and all the filth and dirt and cold of this disgusting outcast realm.

Two things he did not retrieve: my microscope, and my set of surgical knives. I sent him on, further afield, but he came back, shrugging his shoulders, looking at me like a puzzled dog, wondering why I should be so much out of sorts.

'We must go to the police,' I said.

'Police . . . ?'

'The law! Even out here—for God's sake. There must be—I don't know. A sheriff, a marshal—someone—?'

Karl considered this. He scratched the faint grey bristles on his chin.

'Police,' he said.

'That's right. Police.'

'Ah-hah.' He nodded, comprehending me. 'Police are dead,' he told me. 'All dead. Each and every one.'

Chapter Eight

I hammered on Lavenza's door. I waited, and the longer I waited, the angrier I became. When the man at last appeared, his hair was hanging in his face, his eyes puffy and swollen. He was dressed, but had clearly been asleep. I pushed by. His quarters stank of liquor. I addressed him forcefully.

'Who's the authority in this place? Does the town have a mayor? A governor?'

He said nothing.

'I've been robbed! Is that the sort of welcome you give guests?'

The cognac bottle was still out. I didn't wait to be invited—I seized it, poured myself a glass and knocked it back.

'If someone had been sent to meet me, as the laws of hospitality dictate, I should hardly have to suffer this.' I poured another drink. 'I have seen my whole life—all my achievements—scattered down the highway. Thrown about like trash, like dirt—'

He sat down, still without a word. I poured myself another glass, then one for him. He sipped like an automaton. He was a man quite burned out, utterly exhausted.

'They threw my clothes about the woods! I had the finest tailors in all Heidelberg, and they, they—they stole my microscope. My surgical tools. They smashed my trunks to matchwood! That ought to be impossible! What barbarians do you have here, for God's sake? What kind of savages? I would be better off in darkest Africa than, than—'

'Trunks,' he said.

'The pair of them! Smashed, shattered! Not simply levered open but destroyed! I believe explosives were involved. Yes. Explosives of some kind, and—'

'You saw signs of combustion?'

'What?'

'Combustion. Burning. From the explosives?'

'I know what combustion is, God damn it!'

'And there was evidence?'

I gestured furiously, trying to get my meaning through to him. 'My clothes, my books, thrown in the mud! My medical equipment gone! I—no. I saw no burning. But how else could such a sacrilege be carried out? My trunks, sir, were the finest ever built. How do you suggest they were destroyed? By bare hands?'

Lavenza's voice was very small. He had paled visibly under the candlelight.

'Yes,' he said. 'By bare hands.'

And he would say no more.

Quarters were prepared for me, adequate enough, though far from luxurious. But I slept little. Come morning, I availed myself once more of Karl's assistance. He proved both placid and extremely keen to please. Lavenza was now shut up in his quarters; I had been unable to rouse him. Karl drove me to the town—it was scarcely more than a village. The buildings were of wood; even the church was of wood. A few small scrawny hens went scuttling from our path as we approached.

Enquiries found me what I sought—at least, its nearest local version. Soon I was conversing with an aged man who seemed to be some species of official. His exact title eluded me. His eyebrows sprouted white and bushy, like the snow on pine trees; as we spoke, he chewed a strip of leather, threading it into his mouth, extracting it between his fingers, quite unselfconsciously, as if this were as natural as lighting a pipe. The leather was an ugly, slimy thing, disgusting to behold. I found my gaze drawn to it, though much against my will. It was a most distracting item. I carefully explained my case. The officer took pen and paper and produced a few vague, scratchy lines. I suggested I write my account up for him. He acquiesced to this, then fell asleep, his snores wafting around me like the flies upon a summer's day.

It was apparent how much justice I would come by here. I finished my account, threw down my pen, stormed out onto the street. I glared this way and that. A lazy trail of smoke rose from the chimney of a nearby hovel. It was all too much. First Grundig, my exile, that dreadful scene in the operating theatre yesterday; then the loss of my two trunks, and now, my helplessness, my impotence before the forces of stupidity . . . I stood beneath the grey sky and my eyes filled up with tears. I would have wept, I would have fallen on my knees and begged the God I had abandoned to have mercy on me; but I saw Karl watching from his seat upon the trap, and steadied myself. They say that lunatics possess perceptions lost on most of us, for they see the world unfettered by convention. It would not do, I knew, for him to see me weep.

I coughed. I blew my nose to hide my face. I pulled myself up to my full height, took a little time to straighten out my coat collar, then called to him, 'We're done here. Let's go home.'

My cheery smile did not disguise the misery that crept into that final word.

⁂

Lavenza was awake. He had washed, I think, though certainly not shaved; his chin was dark with stubble, moustaches hanging down like dead things.

'These trunks, you say. Stout, you say?'

'Of course.'

'Stout as, say, that door?'

'I hardly see the purpose of comparison.'

'Please. Was the wood as thick? The iron as strong, as well-cast? You must be able to make some manner of estimate.'

'Alright. Stout as that door.'

'I had that door designed especially. It separates my quarters from the rest of the asylum. If he could shatter that. . . .'

'Who?'

'Who?' he echoed me, as if I'd introduced some wholly new dimension to the talk.

'You said *he*. If *he* could shatter it.'

'Ah. Did I? Figure of speech. Yes. But the power involved. . . . Sweet God. . . .'

I looked at him. His face was drawn; there were bags under his eyes, a wildness in the way his pupils darted, even while his body seemed near-stiff with nerves.

There was a matter which had troubled me since yesterday, and, though I had resolved to act where possible with courtesy, I found I could no longer hold from broaching it.

'Herr Doctor. You have been here some years now, am I correct?'

'Hm? Oh . . . three years. Three or four. Yes. I could find no funding for my work . . . research, you understand. I needed some form of employment. The position here . . . in many ways ideal, I must admit. It much appealed.'

'To be stuck here with the peasants and the lunatics?'

He sighed, and settled in his chair. 'One has to understand.' He gave a nervous glance towards the door. 'The nature of insanity . . . with these people, it's as if each one dwells in a separate world. All different, all unique. To speak with them, communicate—to understand—it's like travelling to the furthest outlands of the world, seeking for tribes so strange no white man could have dreamed of them. One has to place oneself upon the very borders of those worlds, upon the frontiers, as it were. . . . One grows accustomed to their ways. Fond of them. In so far . . . that is to say . . .'

'Upon the frontiers.'

'Yes. But tell me. These trunks of yours. Are you quite sure—'

'Herr Doctor.'

He seemed distracted by my interruption. He reached out for the cognac, poured himself another shot; but I, in what I felt was a particularly manly move, placed my hand over his glass and halted him. I peered into his bloodshot eyes. 'My dear Lavenza. It seems to me you are no longer on the frontiers. That you have passed those frontiers long ago, yet to return. Has it not crossed your mind that you, much like your charges, have become quite mad?'

He peered at me. For maybe half a second I saw anger there, and prepared to defend myself. Then he relaxed. His shoulders slumped, and something vaguely like a smile strained at his face.

'Oh yes,' he sighed. 'It's crossed my mind a thousand times. You need have no doubt there.'

He seemed amused; even, I thought, peculiarly flattered. And looking back, I do believe this was the moment when our friendship first began.

Chapter Nine

'Think of the basics, to begin with. Not medicine, but mathematics. Nought to one. Nothing, and then something. How? By what means? Where does the difference lie?'

'I don't follow your argument.'

'*Heidelberg*,' he moaned.

'I was considered very promising. Herr Dr Müller—'

'Is an old queen. Yes, we've met. I myself was at Ingolstadt. There is a family tradition in this. I had hoped to gain the kind of knowledge so important to my forebears. But even there, it seems, standards are scarcely what they were. . . .'

He seemed to drift a moment, lost in thought, then looked up sharply.

'When were you first aware of death?'

Grundig's face flashed in my mind's eye. I blocked it out.

'Come, come!' Lavenza cried. 'There has to be a moment. Suddenly—and contrary to all that one might think or feel, one realises one is as fragile as a candle-flame, to be snuffed out by a simple accident, or by some petty act of malice, or else to gutter and expire the moment its allotted share of wax is done. When did you recognise your transience? That all your striving, all your efforts in the world amount to nothing? That your finest thought will vanish, as if it never was? That you yourself, your very substance, will rejoin that great cycle of Nature, will go to worms, be shat out, grow up in grass to be devoured by cattle, and in turn, perhaps, devoured by man? When did you realise that?'

I said nothing.

'For me,' he said, 'it was an early lesson. For all my family. We are born into the shadow of death.'

'As are we all,' I said. I had enjoyed our conversation in its early stages; now, I grew discomforted. I took too great a draft to drink.

'Most people speak of birth as if it were the miracle. But surely, surely, death is more miraculous. Two living things combine to make a third; that's merely sensible and right. But when a living thing ceases to live? What happens then? What process is at work? One moment, we have a functioning, reacting, sentient, responsive creature, and the next—dead meat, no different from the meat upon a butcher's slab. And there exists no science which can measure the small difference between one and the other; the living and the dead, to scientific eyes, are both the same. And yet the first may speak and laugh and love, the second merely lies there without motion. Where do we find the difference? What difference is there?'

'None,' I said, 'but for a bullet in the chest.'

'I'm sorry? Was that humour? Perhaps you could arrange to smile, or laugh a little, just to let me know.'

I neither smiled nor laughed.

'Ah. Well then.' He nodded to himself. 'Bullets, of course, cause catastrophic damage to the body's mechanism. Quite true. Bullets are the Luddites of biology. But, barring such an injury, what are we left with? A man may die without violence. If he's lucky. And what then?'

Some remnant of Philosophy came back to me.

'I believe,' I said, 'that Plato had his Socrates propose the same enquiry.'

'So I am in the company of Socrates. Well then. Do go ahead.'

'His conclusion, I recall, was that some essence must depart the body, leaving it inert. Some animating power. He deduced that it would be the last thing to escape the flesh, and must, therefore, be present in the body's final exhaled breath.'

'The soul, no doubt.'

'As good a word as any.'

'And could he demonstrate this? Could he describe this soul? How long is it? What does it weigh? What is its colour, or its odour? Does it speak?'

'The man was going to be executed. It's not surprising he sought comfort, in the circumstance.'

But Lavenza still would not be stayed. 'Above all else,' he said, 'above all else—if Socrates were able to deduce the difference between life and death, did he not see living as by far the preferable state? The chance to move, and speak, and act upon the world? Is that not blessed?'

'No doubt.'

'Then why,' boomed Lavenza, rising to his feet, 'why is this *Socrates* not with us yet? Why, supposing that he knew so much, did he not choose to live?'

This seemed to me so thoroughly nonsensical that I excused myself, returning to my quarters, where I lay for some time fully clothed upon my bed. Yet sleep would still not come; and so, in time, I went to look for Karl, instead.

※

Karl's posture mirrored mine of minutes earlier; curled upon his bunk, eyes shut yet wide awake. I strolled into his room. I had a quantity of tobacco with me. I placed a part of this upon the table by his bed, to win his interest.

'The coach,' I said. 'The big coach, on the big road, yes? Do you know when it's due?'

'Due.'

'Yes. When it comes along the road. Going either way, I don't mind which. How often?'

He merely stared. And then, it seemed a light dawned, as if a cloud had shifted in his brain. 'I was a coachman once.'

'Yes, yes. We drove down to the big road. But I mean the *big* coach—the coach that doesn't come up here.'

He stirred, sat up. 'I drove to Leipzig—and to Hamburg once. And—'

'No. I mean the coach that runs by here. The coach I came on. How often does it run?'

But he grew animated. He beamed at me. What teeth he had were brownish and misshapen, like rocks eroded by the sea.

'Every day. I drove it every day, sometimes all night as well.'

And then a thought occurred to me. 'To Hamburg?' I said.

'Once.' His hands came up; he shook them with excitement. 'The man I carried—he was a diamond dealer. I wore a pistol. But we saw no thieves, no highwaymen. There was a village where we stopped, I don't recall the name . . .'

'You were in Lavenza's employ?'

'Oh no. This was before . . . long, long before. It was my work. I loved to be alone, up on my driver's seat, to watch the world roll by. . . .' He made an odd, apologetic little shrug. 'I wasn't mad back then. Or perhaps . . . only a little.'

This last surprised me; I had expected no such insight from the man. Yet I was not concerned with that. I stared at this peculiar little fellow. Was it possible? I tried to picture him, a young man, dressed in livery, perhaps; clean, shaved, coherent.

'You were a carriage driver?'

He smiled proudly.

'Sir,' I said. 'I have underestimated you, for which I very much apologise. And while I remarked your skill with a horse, I hardly thought . . .' I leaned close. 'Will you take a fare? To wherever you think fit. The nearest city. Even a sizeable town would do. I can see you have it in you still. The open road—eh? Can you remember that sensation? The wind upon your face? The landscape, unfolding all around you? Remember it?'

He beamed. He stood, he did a little dance for me, clicking his heels together proudly.

'Right,' I said. 'I'll get my things together, and we'll be off.'

The trap was small, but it would do. Tomorrow, or the next day, I would be back in civilised society, my sojourn in the madhouse no more than a jolly tale to liven up an evening's festivities.

But Karl no longer danced. He looked at me. His eyes were solemn.

'Master. . . .'

'You'd like to be a coach driver again?'

A single tear slid down his cheek. I do confess, I was moved by his expression, though not enough to take my mind from my own plans, nor to stop me from exploiting his brief moment's pain.

'Yes, yes.'

'And make a few marks for yourself?'

'Oh yes. But, but. . . .'

I was stern. 'Well? What's the problem?'

'Oh Master. Forgive me, Master. . . .'

'Get on with it.'

He reached out, and his rather unhygienic fingers tugged my sleeve. He took my hand and pressed it to his bony forehead.

'I did a bad thing, Master.'

'Well, no matter. Now you can make up for it, uh-hm?'

'Oh, Master. You see—I lost my way. A long, long time ago. I lost my way, and now it's all changed. That's why I'm here.' A second tear gleamed on his eyelid, ready to fall. 'My other Master—he explained it all. I lost my way, and now I can't go anywhere. I'm sorry, Master. I'm so, so sorry. . . .'

Chapter Ten

Seeking solitude—and God knows, it was hard to find, outside my own small room—I tried a small, unmarked door, and found myself beneath the open sky.

It was an unexpected sight. Here I was, upon the roof of the asylum; here were battlements, though their intent was surely decorative rather than defensive. A little courtyard spread below me, and across, I could identify the tower up which I climbed on my arrival, with its great windows to illuminate the surgery within. Adjoining it, I now saw, though at lower elevation, was a large, dark structure which I took to be a chapel; at least, I could make out the stained glass in the windows, though the light was now too poor to guess their subjects or their quality.

Instead, I turned my interest outwards. I leaned upon the battlements. Here, I was high above the highest pines. Their tops spread out below me, points of colour beneath which lay only deepest blackness. The sky had cleared a little since the afternoon; indeed, the sunset was a lovely thing, with ribbons of pink cloud that stretched across the firmament like some celestial safety-net; one might imagine angels tumbling from the sky, to be caught within its web and saved.

I only wished that someone might save me.

It was now the ending of my second day, and I was no nearer departure. I had my hopes of Karl, but they were hardly high hopes; trusting the whims of lunatics has never been as sound a plan as trusting to a good steam locomotive. I was trapped here, and, for the time being, saw no escape.

Frankenstein's Prescription

I stared over the pine-sea, wishing I could follow my own gaze, bodily soaring like a bird over the treetops; though even then, it would be hard to tell which way to go. The coach road was invisible from here. After a time, I concluded that a plume of smoke rising a few miles hence must mark the town where I had had such fruitless business earlier that day. In the distance, there were low, grey hills. But bar these things, there was no landmark, nothing by which a man might gain his bearings. I felt truly lost—like a shipwrecked sailor, staring out across an ocean everywhere the same.

I sank deeper in my gloomy meditations. I was half-tempted to fling myself over the battlements, just like the hero of some cheap romantic novel. Yet amid such thoughts, I grew aware of a most curious sound; a distant rumbling, steady and continuous, as of machinery. In my two days here, I had heard no such thing. Now, I looked about. I had a moment's hope—soon dashed—that I was listening to a motor car engine, improbable as that might seem, and I would ride off with its occupants the moment that their business here was done. But this was not the sound of anything approaching. It was a constant whirr, as of machinery *in situ*. Baffled, I shrugged my mental shoulders, sank back into my misery; at which point, an extraordinary thing took place.

I have mentioned the large, chapel-like structure crowning the asylum. The sky had darkened now into a deep, impenetrable blue. Yet as I watched, a light rose, deep within the edifice itself, a gentle luminescence that grew, flickered briefly, and then held. The windows blazed, a mass of colours; iron bars behind the glass cut images of saints and clergy into vibrant geometric shapes, a quilt of reds and yellows, emeralds and purples. A web of colour spread across the paving of the courtyard, and grew stronger, stronger as the light of day declined.

I could not explain the uplift that I felt at such a sight (indeed, in retrospect, I was even mildly ashamed at it, like weeping at a sentimental stage show), but I found myself at once much heartened; I would hit upon a way out of my troubles, not a doubt. I would fight, I would struggle, I would have my will. A sudden confidence swept over me—a sense that, after all, I still had some control over my life.

I slept well that night, for the first time in a long while, and the morning was already far advanced before I rose.

Chapter Eleven

'You see the scarring, here, and here?' Lavenza gestured with a large pipette he happened to be carrying. 'The entire front of the skull had to be sawn through and then lifted off. The operation took six hours. The delicacy of it—the sheer difficulty involved, can scarcely be described.'

'You think this a success?'

He caught my doubt and palpably resented it.

'The man before you,' he said coldly, 'went by the name of Alphonse Vogel. More often known, I think, as the Beast of Bremen.'

I looked at this emaciated figure, with his patchy beard, his rheumy and unfocused eyes.

'He was driven,' said Lavenza, 'by a lust to kill. I mean that literally; while he was in my charge, I was able to run certain . . . tests. Only at the sight of blood was he able to produce the normal male response to sexual stimuli. Blood, and, I am much afraid, the sight of suffering.

'He worked in a slaughterhouse. It was the ideal occupation for him. Had he remained, it may be those he later slew would have escaped their fate. As it was, he was dismissed for acts of an unsavoury, even inhuman nature. After a time of rootlessness, he took to killing human beings, which had always been his fantasy. He made few attempts to hide his tracks. He was soon caught, and sentenced to die. I saved his life,' added Lavenza, with a certain pride.

'A matter of opinion,' I said.

I noticed how this figure blinked: long intervals between, and then the eyes would close with a near-painful slowness, like machinery run at the wrong speed.

'I thought that I could cure him. Cut out the centres of aggression, violence . . . make him docile. . . .'

'Well, he's that, alright.'

'The process is phenomenally difficult, for God's sake! The theory is correct, I know, but—you must understand. The width of a blade—once you cut into the brain, the tiniest miscalculation—it would take superhuman skills, Herr Schneider. Superhuman. Yet without me—this man would be dead.'

'Yes. Well.'

'You have a narrow view. You think of pills and potions. But at this level, I tell you, medicine is never *safe*. It is never without risk.'

'He's wet himself.'

'Yes. That's frequent, I'm afraid. I'll have him changed.'

'He is a rat, perhaps, to be experimented on?'

Lavenza said, 'Forgive me. I don't follow.'

I cast about, trying to frame my thoughts. 'This man, whatever guilt he carries, surely is deserving of some dignity, some justice, even if the meagre dignity of death—'

'There is no dignity in death, Herr Schneider.'

Lavenza turned and strutted off. I looked upon the Beast of Bremen. He seemed so frail, a single push might topple him, just like a wooden mannequin. Was this life, then? Dead while his heart still beat, his chest still rose and fell?

He blinked. Slowly, slowly. Or did he wink at me? Suddenly cold, I hurried off, chasing Lavenza, but could not resist a backwards glance; I had the sudden, nervous notion that the Beast would suddenly awake, and follow me.

When places grow familiar, they grow smaller. So with the asylum, which proved less the labyrinth I had first imagined, more the cosy safety of a walled village, or perhaps a monastery.

I grew bolder as the days went on. I took to roaming through its rooms and hallways, or going once again onto the roof. If I could simply have ignored the noise—the laughter and the cries, the chatter and peculiar ululations—it might have been a perfect place to stay and contemplate my sins.

The inmates were an odd lot, as might be expected. Yet knowing them better seemed to make them more, rather than less human. Supervised by orderlies, I saw that it was they, the mad, who ran the place, sweeping its corridors and courtyards, cooking its meals, tending its gardens which extended down the sunward slope of the hill, from which a portion of the forest had been cleared. Those more capable might put themselves at the disposal of less able colleagues, and, like true monks, seemed to gain some pleasure from the service.

It was a strange society, for sure, but I began to see how one might make his home here, abandoning all higher aims and hopes. It did not seem a bad life. I was tempted, certainly. For maybe ten, or twenty seconds. After which, reality returned.

Meanwhile, I accompanied Lavenza on his rounds. We quarrelled now and then, but seldom with much seriousness. He knew his charges each by name; he was called on as a kind of arbiter to settle disputes, make rulings and give counsel. Doctoring, it seemed to me, was seldom part of his agenda.

'Lord knows,' he owned up, 'there's little can be done for most of them. I use herbs—valerian to calm, St John's wort, to lift the spirits. . . . Mostly, I talk to them. They are my dearest friends.' And, as if to demonstrate, he greeted a woman of extraordinary thinness, passing with her arms full of firewood. 'Good day, Frau Rosen. And how is baby Jesus today?'

She placed her fingers on his wrist. 'He's very pleased with me today, father. He says it's going to be a lovely day.'

He smiled, waited till she was out of earshot, then he said, 'You see? When I first came here, I found her racked with guilt. She thought God hated her. She thought He filled her life with obstacles, He persecuted her. And now. . . .'

'Your treatment?'

He shrugged, modestly. 'As I said. I talked to her. I let her speak of her delusions, without requiring her to rationalise. And slowly, slowly, bit by bit . . . ah. Not all my cases have gone quite so well.'

'You have cells here.'

'Sadly, yes. I visit daily, hoping . . . well.'

'You also,' I said, 'have a generator. I couldn't help but notice.'

He nodded his assent.

'It would be possible,' I said, 'to do away with candlelight. Surely, if only for safety's sake?'

'Resources here are limited,' he said, and, walking on, began to discourse on the histories of this patient and that. But I was not paying attention.

❦

Once, when I strolled out on the rooftop, I met a woman there of middle years, a plump creature attended by an orderly. She was wrapped in heavy blankets; even her head was shrouded in a cloth, like a Mohammedan woman. She spoke about her childhood, her family, the little dog she had once owned; she told me she looked forward to meeting her husband and her children once again. There would be grandchildren by now, as well, she said.

'I've been away so long. . . .'

She was Frau Fleischer, the woman I had held down on the operating table, in the hour I first arrived.

She looked into my face. 'Do I know you? Are you new here?'

I could only nod, for once deprived of speech.

It is a shock, perhaps, to anyone who has attended physical, invasive surgery, to realise that the lumps of meat and bone carved on the table are still living, thinking, feeling folk, and scarcely too much different from oneself.

✦

'You claim that you enjoy your life,' Lavenza said, over a meal of boiled potatoes and dried beef. 'How then, can you bear for it to end? Even the knowledge that it must, at some time, cease—surely that must cast a shadow, tainting everything?'

'This dinner casts a shadow,' I complained. 'Can you find no boar, or venison? The woods here must be stocked with game. Is there no hunter who can track it down?'

Lavenza was dismissive. 'There is protein here. A little roughage. The requirements for a healthy life.'

'Good God. Is that all food is for you? Mere fuel, to take you through the day?'

'The body,' he gestured vaguely with his fork, 'requires nourishment. Food, air, water. We are in constant interaction with the world, absorbing it into ourselves. The Bible tells us Adam was created out of clay, and so, daily, we re-create ourselves, taking in the world's clay, hoping to rebuild those portions which, through wear and tear, the world takes from us—'

'And clay is right,' I said. 'Have you never had a proper meal? A steak, cooked with peppercorns, served up with sauerkraut and potatoes? A fine spiced sausage? Is this your favoured diet, sir?'

He shrugged.

I said, 'You will permit me, then. I am a fair shot. I think I might augment our meals with a little game. If not venison, possibly duck or goose. And then, if you will let me give your cook some lessons, we might have some prospect of a decent dinner. Yes?'

He shook his head. 'It would be . . . unwise to go into the woods.'

'Ah yes. The bandits who made such work of my possessions. In truth, I think I look forward to meeting them. Especially with a loaded pistol close to hand. I think that would be very satisfying. Yes, indeed.'

So I began to roam the woods, though all I came by was a wood pigeon, and that not of the largest size. With something almost like acceptance now I passed my days, my 'rustication'; until one morning, when I set off, I found the front door barred, and locked, and was informed that I was not to be allowed outside that day. Not I, nor anyone.

I fumed. I raged. And then I took my fury to Lavenza. And he met it, head on.

Chapter Twelve

'Did you bring him here? Is that it? Did you bring him?'

Lavenza leapt at me. He seized my shirt front in his fist (my fine silk shirt, of delicate pearl-grey—one of the last remaining to me!). I pushed at him. Liquor fumes enveloped me. Behind him towered four big orderlies, like a bestial version of the Pope's Swiss Guard. They moved in, to either side, ready to intervene. I saw I was outclassed.

'What do you mean?' I shoved at his chest. 'You keep me like a prisoner, like, like—like one of your damn lunatics! What is the meaning, what right have you—'

He thrust his chin out, and his hair fell over one eye. 'If you brought him here,' he said, 'I promise you: you'll learn the difference between life and death, alright. Oh yes. For you, the mystery will finally be solved. You understand? For all of us.'

The man was mad. I had been half-convinced before. Now I knew it. Yet he stepped back, released me, made some effort to smooth out the creases in my shirt.

'Sir,' I said. 'I take offence, not merely at this unprovoked attack, but at the manner in which you seem to want control of my life, as if I were another of your charges. Let me assure you, sir, those who threaten Hans Mitton Schneider do so at their peril. I demand—*demand*, you hear—to be released from this place immediately. Do you understand? Do you hear me, sir?'

His body craned up. It was as if he wrestled with some torment deep within himself. He turned away a moment; produced a handkerchief and dabbed his face.

When he looked at me, his lower lip still quivered.

'Do I have your word,' he said then, 'no-one accompanied you here? No-one followed you? You gave no-one directions, or names? You were alone?'

'Yes! Of course I'm alone! Don't be ridiculous! And I gave directions to the coachman, and the station master, and—'

'Ah. Ah.' He did a strange thing: he put his hands up, one on each side of his head, as if to steady himself. 'Quite so. Quite so.'

I took a step back, out of his reach, and brushed my shirt down. I was about to complain again at my confinement when Lavenza, his madness seemingly at bay, looked at me sheepishly.

'Herr Schneider. Forgive me. My nerves. . . . There's been an incident. We were on our way to investigate. I'm afraid . . . the whole thing has unsettled me. If you would care to accompany us? We go into the woods. I think that's what you wanted? Best we stay together. Yes. Definitely best.'

It was cold out in the woods. I had left my coat behind. Crows wheeled above us, harsh cries nagging at my ears. Lavenza seemed quite nervous; at one point, he halted, and had his orderlies stand around him while he peered into the darkness of the trees about. His features twitched. The slightest sound could make him start like a deer. Only after several moments did he signal to go on.

We followed woodland paths. He seemed to know where he was going. And despite his outburst earlier, I think I understood why he wanted me beside him. His servants were—well, to be kindly, they were lumps and morons, nothing more. He had me walk with him. Like gravitates to like, and we were both, each in our own ways, men of science. That he was, it seemed to me, quite thoroughly unhinged, did not mean he had fallen to their level.

He babbled, whispered in my ear. Mere kitchen gossip, as I saw it; late delivery, he kept repeating. Then he looked at me, weighing me up, and curled his lip.

'You come, he comes. Coincidence?'

I shrugged, refusing even to demand the explanation which was clearly due me. To do so would have played into his madness.

He stared about him, taking in the trees, the sky. Once he said, 'Alright. Let's see. Let's see what happens.' Was he addressing me? Or himself? Or some third party, yet unseen? In truth, I could not tell.

He was, in certain ways, pathetic. He behaved as if he knew himself already doomed; like Goethe's Werther, he peered up wide-eyed at the pines, and trembled with self-pity.

For this, I had left Heidelberg? The drinking dens, the gambling clubs—the girls?

He stopped us, then. He indicated something lying on the ground, amid the pine trunks. A rag of some sort. Perhaps a shawl. Yes, a shawl; indeed, there was a head protruding from it, grey hair poking from a dark scarf that had slipped a little, covering one eye. The person seemed to be asleep, perhaps buried in pine needles, or . . . in the ground? Or . . . ? I could not make it out, the angle of the body. It was as if this person had been buried to the neck, and . . .

Lavenza ran ahead. There was something else, a little further down the path. It was a handcart, such as peasants use. A pattern had been daubed along the sides, a crude design of flowers. An object hung upon the handle. Its shape appeared to change as I moved forwards. My perspective re-adjusted, and I saw it plain. It was a hand. The fingers were still clutched around the handle in some post-death rigour. Scattered here and there were other items. I was reminded of the devastation of my own belongings, hurled about the woods as if caught in a whirlwind. Here were clothes, and scattered bric-a-brac. A milk churn, turned upon its side, the contents drained. And body parts. Moving on, we saw them; so many, many body parts. The ants and beetles were already on the meat. I saw fox prints in the dirt. The crows were picking at the flesh, squawking as we came close. . . .

At this point, Lavenza did the first sensible thing that I had seen him do all day.

He turned tail, and he ran.

Chapter Thirteen

'You know what this is all about, don't you?'

I interrogated him. I strutted back and forth while he sat quivering before me. His brandy glass shook in his hand.

'You *know*,' I said again.

He said, 'I thought that you knew, too. I thought that's why you came.'

'I came, sir, in the gravest error. Though it seems now graver than I ever dreamed.'

'Grave? Oh yes. We shall all be in our graves before too long.'

'Sir.' I paced the room, then spun upon my heel to face him. 'I insist that you facilitate my exit from this place. You may also wish to inform whatever passes for the judiciary here that you include a homicidal maniac among your charges. Another reason for me to be gone.'

'Did he follow you to me? Is that it?' This was nonsense, and yet earnest nonsense. 'But—no, no. I see it.' His hand made fierce, flapping motions, as if to beat some vision from the air. 'He took your medical equipment! Of course! He sees I've an assistant. He might even have been watching me for days. But now he thinks—'

'And who, exactly, would this person be? If someone here has my property, whom do you propose we search?'

'Search?'

'You have a household full of lunatics. You have an act which only a true madman would commit. Are you blind sir? Or else mad yourself?'

'My charges,' said Lavenza, and there was a certain dignity in the way he drew himself up in the defence of others, 'are incapable of such behaviour. They may grow agitated or distressed at times, but they would never—no, no, no. They are unfortunates, sir. They are the world's victims, not its malefactors.'

'The Beast of Bremen,' I said.

Lavenza remained silent. And a plan formed in my mind.

I poured myself a drink.

'Well then. Well then,' I said. 'You must permit me, sir. Let me borrow your horse and trap, and your fellow—Karl is his name—and let me go at once to some large town or city and seek a full defence for you against this, this monster. Perhaps even the army should be called in. I can arrange this, sir, if you but permit me. I'll ready my things.'

Lavenza said, 'I've not shown you my real work yet, have I?'

'I think, sir, I have seen enough of your work. In God's name—'

'Oh, not God's, sir. Certainly not God's.'

•.

We drank. We went on drinking. When he spoke again, it was as if in the middle of a conversation; a conversation to which (contrary to his apparent belief) I had not, of course, been party.

'Müller told you nothing?'

'He told me that I must be rusticated for a year. Frankly, that seemed bad enough.'

'He propositioned you?'

'He . . . hinted at . . . certain arrangements. Which I refused.'

'Yes, yes, yes. I had asked if he might find someone to help me here. Trust the fool to take advantage.' Lavenza shook his head. 'You know, I really did believe it was your choice to join me. Your choice, because you were aware. Because you sought me out. It seems I flattered myself.'

'More than likely.'

'And were you really, as you said, so promising a student?'

I thought about this. Promising enough, at least, that my professors had turned blind eyes to my tardiness with their assignments, my out-of-school activities, my presence in their lectures with an ice-pack clamped upon my forehead to relieve my hangover. I had been forgiven much, I saw that now. And I had been very promising indeed, it seemed, for so long as my father paid my fees.

'Of course,' I said, in answer to his question.

'Müller is competent. I'll give him that. Competent, but uninspired. Like all of them.' He leaned towards me, grabbed my wrist. I wondered for a moment if he, too, might be of Herr Doctor Müller's persuasion, given the eagerness with which he gazed into my eyes. 'Tell me, Hans. Are you willing to depart their trivial orthodoxy? To cease from treating meagre symptoms, and delve into the mystery of life itself?'

'Oh, I daresay.'

'Good. I'll have my man fire up the generator.'

I would have much preferred him to have said, 'prepare the horse and trap'. Still, it would be morning then, before I might depart, so I steeled myself to indulge him, hoping to further win his confidence; and little realising the next few hours would change my life.

Chapter Fourteen

'Wait,' he said. 'Wait here.'

We were within the chapel. I recalled the almost holy thrill I'd felt that night, now many nights ago, to see illumination streaming from this very structure. The interior was a disappointment, then, cluttered and functional; an engineering works crossed with a medical laboratory. Stout iron scaffolding had been erected like a skeleton inside the building's skin. From this depended pulleys, chains and hoists, as well as flights of shelving, many of them stacked with bottles and with demijohns in which amorphous shapes had been suspended. Indeed, the stink of formalin was everywhere. I waited while Lavenza strolled around, scrutinising this and that; to be honest, I no longer paid him much attention. He had left me with the bottle, and I must have filled my glass two or three times in the space it took him to inspect his paraphernalia. My mind drifted to other things, a drunk nostalgia for the blissful, carefree life I'd led, oh, three or four weeks earlier. Now ancient history. I warmed to the memory. I hummed a little tune. I waltzed across the floor, my arms around my love—the luscious Liesel, possibly, or the mature charms of Bianca from the Scholar's Rest, a house which had, to date, offered me no rest whatever—anything but. Bianca was a tall, plumpish woman of some years, but when you held her, it seemed that her entire body rippled with delight, and when you kissed her, her response was seasoned with the wisdom of experience. I poked my tongue out, imagining her sweetish schnapps-and-sausage taste. I whirled her round, I pressed my manhood to her belly, while she wriggled with delight—

'Herr Schneider!'

I looked up, startled. I had quite lost myself for a moment. I straightened, cleared my throat. Lavenza was regarding me from down the hall. And he was no longer alone.

There had been a canvas screen draped before the far wall. Now this was gone. A fellow stood there. He was . . . he was hard to make out properly, for Lavenza's lights illuminated only patchily, and the hall was large; vast shadows loomed across the scene, masking the man's face and upper body. Although even then it seemed that there was something odd, something my eyes could not make out. . . .

It struck me he was naked.

Lavenza made a movement, adjusting switches on an apparatus at his side. There was a click, a clatter and a squeak of pulleys. At the same time—though I confess, my mind made no connection—the naked man began to stroll towards me. Lavenza merely lounged against a shelf, and watched.

I was reminded of a scene at the theatre. I forget the play—some melodrama, quite inconsequential. A single light, shone upon the face of an actor dressed in black, had contrived the notion of a severed head, bobbing about like a balloon as it delivered chilling speeches, premonitions, omens, doom and woe. A harmless little game, of course, and nothing more. Yet it seemed to me that something similar was happening here. The fellow strode towards me. Yes, he was naked; his penis swung with every step. He was no doubt some lunatic, some fellow who would shun his clothes, casting them off, as certain of his kind were wont to do. I raised my gaze, seeking a glimpse into his face. It was as if I could see through him. As if, as if. . . .

There was no face. What I saw instead was a cascade of wires and tubes that followed with him, pace by pace, swaying gently, rustling at each move. Looking higher, I observed a kind of trolley, suspended on a rail, up in the shadows overhead. Yet even now, my brain would scarcely process what my eyes beheld. And all the time, the fellow came towards me, at a leisurely, insouciant pace.

'Hello . . . ?' I said.

And stepped back, suddenly.

It hit me all at once, a sudden shifting of perception, as if my brain abruptly jumped a gear. I reached behind me for support. My chest was tight and I could scarcely breathe.

I could make out neither this man's face nor torso, nor his arms or hands, and not through any trickery of lighting, but because *these things did not exist*.

I was looking at—it seemed to be a kind of puppet. The legs moved, the hips were clearly well-articulated. The feet—I noticed this especially—the feet were quite astonishingly flexible, and sensitive to variations in the floor, which was quite uneven. They were both balancing and weight-bearing—exactly as in ordinary human motion. I realised at once that, unlike the string puppet which it resembled, the thing was not supported from above, but moved of its own volition. The tangle of lines above was slack and bore no weight.

As it came close, I heard the squeaking of the trolley wheels above me. The thing—this half-person—walked by, carried on a few yards, and then stopped.

The trolley had run out of rail.

I moved forwards cautiously. The prodigy had stuck in mid-stride, right foot extended, heel of the left just raised a fraction from the floor, the calf muscle quite clearly clenched. I reached out my hand. . . .

I had had experience of corpses. I knew the touch of dead flesh. I knew the arts of preservation, and of peeling back the dead matter to show the organs and the vital parts nestled beneath.

The touch of the skin was cold, and soft, and smooth.

'You're right,' agreed Lavenza, as if I had already made my verdict. He had come up behind without my even noticing. 'It's a toy, and nothing more. Simple animation. What it is not,' he sighed, 'is life.'

Chapter Fifteen

I was sober. I was completely, utterly sober, as if I had been drinking water all night; and was continuing to drink it now. I had acquired a strange immunity to alcohol. My heart beat, racing in my chest. My mind reeled. Yet I endeavoured to appear composed, solemn and scholarly. I felt that he deserved no less.

There is a quality, sometimes called genius, which is distinct from skill or talent and from simply being 'good' at something; it involves a vast and seemingly unprecedented leap in human knowledge and ability, and is possessed by people of such single-minded focus that their actions otherwise appear eccentric and inept near to the point of lunacy. I had glimpsed it once or twice in others, in its mildest forms, enough to know that it was something I did not possess myself. But I had never, never seen it in such force as I believed I saw it now.

We sat once more in Lavenza's room. Another bottle had appeared, as if by magic. I would not sleep this night. Nor would I leave tomorrow. That was plain now. We had a great deal to discuss, Lavenza and I; bargains to make. Not that he knew it yet.

'My family,' he said, 'are . . . somewhat preoccupied with death. We have a shadow hanging over us, like an hereditary illness. We die young.'

I expressed my sympathies. I made a mental note, too, of the urgency of formalising any business deals we might arrange—just in case, as it were.

Aloud, I said, 'Well, we all must die. Let's not think of that at this juncture.'

'I think about it all the time.'

'What you have done—this is a miracle. Truly astonishing! I have seen nothing like it, not in all my time at Heidelberg, nor heard of such a thing. This is your own work, sir? You are alone in your discoveries, or do you have a colleague, an assistant of some kind? Leaving aside myself, of course,' I added, prudently planting the idea in his mind.

'It was my father's work. And his father before him. I scarcely knew my father. I recall his death . . . but there are papers. He left records at the family home. And others elsewhere. These others, I believe, may hold the true secret. I have yet to see them.'

'Well, then we will find them at once! Are they near?'

'In Italy. In a monastery. He was a travelled man. A man perpetually in flight.'

'Italy. Well, we can have them sent, I'm sure. That won't be hard.'

Lavenza shook his head. 'I would not trust them to the mail. I must take hold of them myself. Nothing else will do. But I—it's a long way. I fear to travel. Especially . . .'

His voice trailed off. I clapped my hands.

'Well then—well. Never fear! Arrangements will be made. Now I understand the—forgive the word, sir, I do not wish to bruise your modesty—the magnificence of what you do, I put myself at your disposal. Heart and soul. We shall have the documents drawn up. You are saved, sir! You have a partner in this lonely work, someone to share your struggle! Why, together, we can—'

'I told you. What I have is failure. What I have are toys, playthings. Clever tricks. That's all.'

Nonetheless, there was a certain smugness in the way he spoke; a certain pride. His words spoke failure; his small, sly sideways look sought praise. This was a man unused to compliments. I resolved to compliment him every chance I got.

Meanwhile, I reached out and quietly refilled his glass.

'Failure,' I said. 'If this is failure, I must ask: what constitutes success?'

He said nothing for a while. I prepared a pipe, as much to give my hands something to do as any other reason; my body was electric with excitement. I could scarcely stop myself from twitching.

Then he said, very quietly, as if he hardly dared to voice the words, 'Success would be the absolute, complete conquest of death.'

'Oh, of course. Nobody trains in medicine without at least imagining such things. The prolongation of a life, certainly. That's our role, our work. That, and the relief of certain trivial ills. As students, we have all considered, wondered where such tasks might end, but—'

I looked at him. In the lantern light, his face was hard to read; he stared into the middle distance, quite absorbed within his thoughts.

'Sir,' I asked him, 'are you serious?'

※

'Consider now. Consider this.' There was a mad look in his eye, the look of a fanatic. 'The body is—let's say for argument—a bag of fluids, is it not? Blood and bile and water, held in by a sheath of skin. Suppose I cut myself. Perhaps a little cut, here, upon the finger, hm? The blood should drain, as from a punctured bladder. Yet in minutes, it will cease to flow. Within the hour, the tissues have begun to knit together. In a day or little more, the wound is fully healed. A week and it is scarcely visible. Do I suffer dangerously from the loss? Only if the wound is severe, and even then, the bone marrow is working furiously to replenish it. The body constantly adjusts, grows, renews itself. What an extraordinary mechanism! Imagine a clock which, when overwound, immediately sets about doing its own repairs!'

'Of course, but—' It was like the drunken debates in which my fellow students had indulged, before the liquor fully took away their senses. But this was no debate; Lavenza was in full flow, and it seemed that—unlike blood—nothing would staunch his outpouring.

'Basics, basics,' cried Lavenza. 'Cells divide. All goes well for many years. From conception to maturity, let's say. But then, at some point, errors appear. Small ones, in the main, but over time . . . The cells are like those manuscripts copied by monks, year after year, century on century. Faithful copies. Yet there comes a point—an old monk, eyesight fading, a careless or a lazy monk—mistakes creep in. So too with our bodies, sir. They renew themselves, and yet in time accumulate so many errors that the processes of life become deranged. Homeostasis is no longer possible. Senescence follows. Then—'

I was confused. 'Monks?' I said. 'The monks your father left his papers with . . . ?'

'Listen to me. Listen. Pay attention now! Cancer is a plain example. Cells which replicate in error. If we all lived long enough, we should all develop the disease.'

'However—'

'No! Forget however! Suppose each cell had a corrective mechanism, like the governor of a machine? A regulator, ensuring constant uniformity, no matter how long such an organism might endure? What then?'

'Then I would say that you had made a miracle. And current thinking about miracles, sir, notwithstanding what you showed me earlier, is that miracles are fairy tales. Fisherman's yarns.'

'Medical orthodoxy,' said Lavenza, and there was such intensity about him now that I grew quiet, and hunched up in my chair, clutching the brandy bottle like a comforter, 'is the voice of capitulation. The slave's small squeak before the master's brandished whip. It is the voice of cowardice.'

'In Heidelberg—'

'In Heidelberg, you learn to think like slaves! I spit on you! I spit on your views! I spit on your professors' views! I spit, I spit, I spit!'

'In that case,' I remarked, 'you will end up with a very dry throat.'

He had said he had no sense of humour. Yet this one remark appeared to stop him in his tracks. He threw his head back and guffawed. I was unsure of what had tickled him; perhaps merely my correct citation of a physiological phenomenon. In certain ways he was astonishingly literal-minded.

'What I have seen tonight,' I said, 'is miracle enough, and will astound the medical world, for which you have such small regard. You will be proved correct, a giant among dwarfs. But to imagine that one might go further . . . might take the power of God into one's own hands, as it were . . .'

'It can be done, sir. It can certainly be done.'

'There must be proof, then. There must be . . . some substantial evidence. . . .'

'The evidence, it's my belief, now roams these woods. The "evidence", as you describe it, killed a woman here, not twenty hours ago. Is that sufficiently substantial for you, sir? Or do you still require more?'

Chapter Sixteen

It was dawn before I reached my bed. I lay there as the room grew brighter and the birds began to call. Each time I shut my eyes a new thought would occur, levering them open once again. My mind turned circles on itself. The matters of the past day stretched behind me with an almost epic grandeur, wonderful and terrible, till I could barely contemplate them. I recalled—as if it were a lifetime gone—my anger of the morning. That anger now seemed like the anger of another man, incomprehensible to me and long, long over. In the hours since, I had witnessed the results of an horrific killing, and a show of medical and technological initiative that must mark Lavenza as the greatest practitioner since Koch or William Harvey.

I did not trust him. Nor did I believe that he should trust himself. As I have noted, genius will often leave a man with flaws, since it focuses the character with such a narrow intensity. In Lavenza's case, these flaws were well pronounced. At first light, he had peeped out of the window, crouching like a thief, and beckoned to me.

'Do you see something? A movement?'

I saw only blackness, and told him so. But he was not relieved; he strained, peering out into the dark, and once ducked down as if in fright.

'We're being watched,' he said.

He was, I still believed, half mad; cagey, secretive, his talk all hints and intimations. Yet I saw, too, that quality of greatness in him; and greatness was a thing of which I very dearly wanted part.

Frankenstein's Prescription

I woke in the early afternoon, hungry, thirsty, with a throbbing, swollen head. Conditions scarcely unfamiliar; yet now, and in addition, I possessed a sense of purpose, and an optimism unknown since my days in Heidelberg. I must become my host's disciple, learn the fullness of his work, his methods, his theories—in short, uncover everything. The man was wasted here. Could I remove him, then, to some more civilised environment? He had mentioned Italy. Not my first choice, to be sure, but certainly a start. We would present the Pope with a resurrection of the flesh which he would not forget! I arranged my toiletries. I peered into my room's small, spotted mirror, shaved away my last night's depredations. I slapped my cheeks to give them colour. I found my shirts, though washed, were all in need of starch and pressing. No matter. I was unlikely to find company of much sophistication through the day.

And nor did I. Though visitors we did indeed receive, and one of them was not entirely unfamiliar to me.

I made my way towards Lavenza's quarters, armed with a full array of propositions. An equal partner, certainly—though I knew my limitations; I could no more perform his work than fly. Rather, I would involve myself with fund-raising and publication of his findings, with writing papers and establishing the necessary contacts in both academe and finance, building a platform for the reception of his work. I doubted he could even sober up enough to give a properly coherent lecture. Yet once I had his notes, once I had studied them . . . (I looked forward to the prospect far more eagerly than I had ever to my former scholarly endeavours.) There was also, of course, the question of the legal ownership of such materials. Which I would no doubt come to in good course.

My job now was to sound him out, determine how best to approach him. One thing I knew: Lavenza could no longer languish here at M——, and nor could I. They could throw me out of Heidelberg, but I would be back to mock them—Herr Doctor

Müller most of all. Let him drool at me as I drove past in my coach and four, or—better yet—a brand new Daimler motor car, its engines roaring on the little country roads. I was a man of the twentieth century, when all was said and done, and I would ride in style.

I heard voices as I drew near Lavenza's quarters, and not the banter of the lunatics, but the low, sombre sounds of men talking to men; then Lavenza's voice, emphatic, stern: 'Bandits, sir. Plainly passing through en route from one crime to another. They travel with the seasons, I believe, like shepherds. This dreadful situation—I may say, it wrings my heart even to think of it. . . .'

I knocked. I entered. 'Hans! My good friend!' Lavenza greeted me, I felt, with rather overblown enthusiasm. He had an audience of three; foremost was an old man in what seemed to be a comic-opera uniform: a jacket with a great many fastenings, and rather ostentatious epaulettes, the left one come loose from its stitching, curling like a Turkish slipper. The outfit was too tight under the armpits, too slim to fit around his bulging belly, and clearly tailored for a younger and quite differently-proportioned fellow, no doubt many, many years ago. In his hands this old man clutched a broad, black hat, and from his mouth dangled a string of leather, waggling as he chewed on it.

Beside him stood two younger fellows, tall and strapping, though neither showing any great intelligence. Creatures replete in beef, both in arms and brains, no doubt.

We greeted one another formally, the old man and myself, clicking heels and bowing.

'This is my colleague,' said Lavenza. 'He too has suffered at the hands of these marauders. Isn't that right, old chap? Herr Schneider is from Heidelberg, from the University, at present acting as my intern. You had a terrible experience yourself, is that not so?'

I nodded, but did not reply.

'Your cases blown apart,' Lavenza prompted. 'Possessions stolen.'

At which the white-haired man said, 'No.'

Lavenza looked at him, then shuffled, somewhat awkwardly, from foot to foot.

Out of his hat, the man produced a notebook, and with a bureaucrat's efficiency, read off the tally.

'Two items stolen. Microscope. Case of surgical tools.'

'Very valuable, too,' Lavenza said. 'Isn't that right, Hans?'

'The microscope, a Hartnack and Prazmowski. I believe I have made testimony to all this. And the knives—fine steel, each blade monogrammed. They would be easily identified, should they ever come to light.'

'Cunning folk,' Lavenza said. 'I doubt they'll stay round here. I've made a study of these types, sir. They move from city to city, fleeing the law. It's their nature, sir.'

The old man, who had so singularly failed to retain consciousness while I reported my misfortune, now seemed roused somewhat. His little eyes flicked back and forth between Lavenza and myself.

'The woman,' he announced, 'was on her way here. Well-known to you. To you, and to your inmates.'

Lavenza bristled. 'Impossible. What you're suggesting—impossible. And damned insulting, sir.' He looked around, as if seeking a drink and, finding none, rallied himself. 'No-one—*no-one* had gone out that day. Frau Eva brings our milk, and eggs, and ham, and other goods. She is beloved by all who live here. I do not accept your implications, sir, nor do I—'

I had resolved to stay an onlooker in this. And yet, without considering, I found myself speaking out in Lavenza's defence, and that of the people in his charge. 'Sir, I can vouch for this. I did my rounds on waking yesterday. No-one had left the building. The doors were locked. All residents were quite accounted for. I will write testimony to this effect, if it would help. In the meantime—is there no sign of my property? I am quite lost without it. These are the tools of my trade, and I would offer a reward for their return.'

That seemed to clear the air a little. There was more debate, my own version of yesterday's horrific find, and, as the old man made to go, Lavenza called him back. He rummaged in his bureau, producing a sheaf of bills.

'I know, I know from personal experience, how hard it is to lose a parent, especially in—such a way.' He pressed the money in the old man's hand. 'For the children. Precious little compensation, to be sure, but it may help to ease the burden. If you would . . . ?'

Goodbyes were said, the trio went their way.

I watched Lavenza, weighing him with narrow eyes.

'You know he'll spend it all on grog, don't you?'

'No. He'll spend a part of it on grog. The rest will reach the family. It's a small town. Word gets about. People know each other, and it breeds a . . . kind of honesty.'

'Speaking of honesty. There are no bandits.'

He reached for the bottle, but I stopped him.

'No bandits,' I repeated.

'I have an enemy. My concern, not theirs. For now, I'll say no more.'

'Some rival, then? Someone you wronged?'

'No, no. Nothing like that. But—thank you, Hans. For your intervention. Thank you.'

I had made him trust me—a little, anyway. Which would make my task a good deal lighter in the months to come.

Chapter Seventeen

'What's this?'

'What it appears to be. A severed arm. Oh,' he reassured me, 'not from yesterday's most awful tragedy. This, I've had for some time.'

'It is also plainly male. Unless the women of the district are as hirsute as I fear.'

'Well spotted, sir. Well spotted.'

It occurred to me to ask him where such specimens might be obtained, so far from any university; then it occurred to me I might not wish to know.

'Take hold,' he urged. 'Go on. Take its hand.'

I was hardly willing. While not unduly squeamish, I had never greatly relished my role in anatomy or surgery classes. Lavenza, nonetheless, lifted the limb out of its tray and held it out to me, as if it were some great prize. From the stump—just below the shoulder—extended wires and rubber tubing. He pushed the thing towards me, saying, 'Go on, go on.' With reluctance, I reached out, touched the soft skin. It was chilly, and a little moist; not unpleasant, like a delicate, expensive leather.

'Hold it. Shake hands with it. Here.'

I pulled a face, wrapping my fingers round the lifeless palm.

'Now,' he said. His free hand spun a dial upon a box nearby.

The hand clasped mine!

I almost leapt out of my skin!

'Great God, sir! What on Earth—'

Lavenza—he grinned, he shook. I believe that he was laughing. 'A mere extension of Galvani's principles. Nothing to fret about.

Relax. Pretend you're shaking hands with a bishop.' There was a certain cruelty in his look, an air of gloating. 'Or a wrestler,' he said then.

A further turn of the dial; the hand's grip tightened, crushing my knuckles. I cried out. Lavenza let me feel the pain for rather longer than was strictly necessary, I thought. The arm meanwhile twisted in his grip like some gigantic, pallid snake. Then, as he flicked the dial back, it relaxed, grew limp. I snatched my hand away.

'Is that it?' I said. 'Such tricks were done a century ago.'

'With frog's legs. The hand held yours. A precise action. Can you appreciate just how precise? Can you?'

I put my hand under my armpit and squeezed, as if to mould it back into its proper shape. The dead hand had indeed gripped mine, much as a living hand might; yes, I could appreciate precision. Indeed, I could still feel it.

'When the grip was tightened,' he explained, 'I simply increased the frequency of impulses along the nerves, throwing the muscles into tetanus. Strong, I think?'

Back in its tray, the fist continued to open and close, growing slowly weaker each time.

'Residual movement. It will pass.' He paced the floor, his back to me. 'We live now at the start of the machine age. This is my belief. Machines for this, machines for that. No surprise, perhaps, that we have come to see ourselves, too, as machines. Clever little mechanisms, you and I. Feed us the proper fuel, we walk and talk and go about our business, cunning toys, like Mälzel's trumpeter. Look at us! Independent of external mechanisms, we can be shuffled off to any corner of the exhibition hall! Put a trumpet to our lips, we play like the band of the French Imperial Guard! That's us!'

I said, 'You play, sir?'

He looked around.

I put my hands up to my mouth in mime. 'The trumpet. The trumpet is your instrument, perhaps? Or do you have a corpse to play it for you?'

He looked at me a moment. Then, dismissively, 'Ah. Humour.'

'Humour perhaps. But listen: I at one time had instruction in the cello. I, too, am a clever mechanism—so my tutors told me. And I should welcome very much the privilege of learning from you.'

When negotiating out of weakness, flattery is frequently one's greatest tool; sometimes one's only tool. Self-absorbed and isolative he might be, but I'd little doubt that it would work upon Lavenza as on others; better, maybe.

So I began the second segment of my plans for him.

I offered him temptation.

⁂

'But your work would go so much more easily elsewhere. No more scrimping and scraping. No more having to divide your time between your projects and these lunatics for whom you care. You could have funding, sir. I know people. I would be able to raise money. In Vienna, say, or Paris. . . .'

I knew nobody, of course, but it was not a lie; more like an anticipation.

Lavenza, though, was steadfast. 'I need solitude to work.'

'And more,' I said. 'Much more! I could arrange protection for you. You have an enemy, you said yourself. He can be brought to justice. You will be free of him, my friend. How's that?'

'He cannot be brought to justice. And besides, I'm in no danger yet, I think. Not for a while.'

'No danger! The man's a killer! And a brutal one. Clearly deranged. He killed the peasant woman, purely, it would seem, for her association with you! This is danger, my friend, whether you call it that or not.'

Lavenza sighed. 'Yes. She was killed for her association with me. Poor soul. Her death served as a message—a reminder, if you like. I am, I repeat, in no danger at present. My associates, on the other hand. . . .'

He looked at me. As the meaning of his look came home, I felt a sudden chill sweep through the room, and moved myself a little closer to the fire.

❦

'The nerves,' I said. 'How does it sense the changes in the floor? Is it able to deduce, or to predict its passage? In short, is there some kind of reason in it? How, for example, would it cope with a small stair, or an obstacle of some kind?'

I had inspected what he would show me of his work. I was baffled; not by the principles, which were ready enough, but by the sheer complexity of it. Magnifying glasses of many sizes, some mounted on stands, were a major part of his equipment.

'It can adapt to changes in the angle of the floor, just as we can. It has feet, Herr Schneider. Feet have nerves, and nerves do what they should. But put a step before it, it will surely trip. For it does not have *eyes*. You follow me?'

'But if one could combine . . . ? If it were possible . . . ?'

'Indeed. If it were possible.'

There was a head, which I was told was that of some convicted felon, mounted on a wooden frame and stinking of preservative; an ugly, grey-green colour, a flabby-cheeked grotesque; yet, manipulated by Lavenza's skilled machinery, and a sequence of electric charges that pumped the air through the respiratory tract, then manipulated the buccal cavity, could recite the vowels as often as you liked. A bizarre experience: watching the mouth change shape, hearing that hissing, like a leaky bladder: 'Ae—ee—aye—oh—you.' But it thrilled me to experience it. I nodded, my whole body rocking with excitement. I asked if he could make it utter words, even sentences. Recite a line of Goethe, say?

'It cannot be taught. Only manipulated.'

'Yes, yes, but—oh. Something from Genesis. God made man out of the clay, something like that?'

'I am not a showman, Herr Schneider. Though it seems that you would turn me into one.'

I told him this was nonsense. I scorned the whole idea, upbraided him for thinking me so low, so mercenary and devoid of principles.

It was, of course, exactly what I'd had in mind.

Chapter Eighteen

This matter of the 'enemy' was troubling me. Several times I tried to probe him on it, but Lavenza would say nothing; indeed, the slightest mention seemed to make him physically uncomfortable, and I deduced it was against my interests to pursue the issue further. No danger to him now, perhaps; but there was danger in the offing, I was sure, and so was he—his very manner indicated it.

The murder was the doing of a madman. There was no doubt in my mind. Yet equally, I held Lavenza's judgement on those folk within our walls. Troubled they may be; some—Herr Vogelsang, for one—had lurid and disgusting pasts. But I walked among them daily without fear. No: this enemy was someone else, a person dwelling in the woods, living as a vagabond, an animal. I recalled the shadow I had seen the day that I arrived. How close, I wondered, had I come to death myself, that day? This was a big man, of extraordinary strength. Not a rival, not a fellow scientist. I theorised he might once have been an inmate here, used in some treatment of Lavenza's. Lavenza had, indeed, spoken of 'evidence' for certain of his wilder claims. In this case, though, his work had surely failed. Its subject had escaped, or been turned out into the wild, and bore a grudge. A grudge which he was clearly big enough, and strong enough, to act upon.

Sleepless in the small hours, I pieced the whole tale together. It was a jigsaw puzzle; the fragments came before my mind as if laid out upon a tabletop. Even the mystery of why one should perform work on so large and dangerous a person became clear to me. Brain operations were invariably long and complex. One's subject must be large and strong enough to survive. Whether we in turn would then survive his vengeance was a moot point.

And in the days that followed? When he allowed, I would devote myself to studying Lavenza's work. At the same time, I would try to plant ideas in his head, as best I could. 'There is some study of this nature taking place in Paris, I believe,' I might remark, or, 'This reminds me of a paper by a doctor in Vienna . . .'

It was unfortunate the aspects of his work which most intrigued me, Lavenza seemed to count as trifles. I had no doubt of his genius; but, as often with such folk, he disregarded triumphs and looked forward to some future labour, of which he would speak little. I often had to pester him into explaining things. When he did, I found that I could grasp the great part of his argument thus far, and then, so many times, he lost me; as if his methods took some sudden leap away from orthodoxy, at the very second when my thoughts were elsewhere; as if I'd blinked and in that moment lost the thread of reasoning. It was tricky, asking him to go back and explain again, without losing his patience. Nonetheless—I was entirely captivated. At Heidelberg, my studies merely bored me; a second, dreary string to my more sociable activities. Here, I could not find sufficiency. Everything he said would come to me in riddles, fractions. Every fact had to be excavated bit by bit. I went at it like a badger, sometimes almost fighting him for answers.

Habitually I spent my early evenings in his quarters. He was looser-tongued when in his cups than in his workshop; and it must be said, such moments of conviviality also gave me access to his liquor supply, which was extensive. (It occurred to me that it must surely be replenished frequently; offering a further possible exit, should I decide to leave. At present, though, departure was the last thing on my mind.)

Then came an evening when, as before, my approach to his chambers was met by voices. One voice, to begin with; his own, impassioned, almost shouting. I stopped outside his door and listened, hesitant to knock. Was he drunk already? He railed, like one of the chronics in the lower cells; he seemed unable to contain himself.

'No no no no! It's blasphemy! You cannot threaten me. You cannot harm me any more. Kill me, if you must, but know that you will never—I am not—you are right, sir, you are right. I am not up to it. You have the wrong man, sir. That's all I'll say. No more discussion, no more—why not? Why?' There was a pause, in which I caught no sound; then, Lavenza's voice again, more quietly now, and shaking, as in tears, 'Can you not call this off? Resign yourself? As I have done? Will you not leave, be decent, as a Christian man? Will you not—oh, for God's love—'

A pause again, but longer now, and this time, it seemed I heard a sound. It may have been the wind, or voices from another wing of the asylum, yet it seemed to me a murmur, a resonance in some way forming words; though their precise meaning I could not grasp.

Lavenza's voice erupted. 'You have no right! None at all! You know the Commandments! Do they not apply? Not to kill, for one! *Not* to kill! Can I teach you nothing?'

'Do no murder,' said the other voice, this time quite clearly. I wondered if Lavenza might be playing both roles, like an actor; we had had no visitors, of that I was quite sure, and this second voice was quite unlike that of our residents—indeed, of anyone that I had ever heard.

Lavenza once more, but now low, and sorrowful: 'So we're at this again, are we?'

A word, a whisper; perhaps a cough.

'Blackmail.' Lavenza's voice. 'That's all it is. Take no high tone with me. You have no right to it.' A pause, then sharp, 'I say you have no right!' And again, resigned, 'We spoke of this before. Yes, yes. It will take time. A journey. But I believe to follow through would be—'

I could contain myself no more. I rapped upon the wood. There was a sudden hush within. Footsteps. Sounds of a key being turned.

Lavenza opened the door, barely an inch or two, blocking the gap with his body. His hair was dishevelled, face pale.

'Schneider, Schneider. . . .' He cast a glance behind him. 'This is a bad night for me. Very bad. Perhaps you should return to your room. . . .'

But I pushed past him. 'A bad night is made good with company.'

The room was empty. The cognac bottle was out, I noticed, and a half-full glass upon the sideboard. Several books had been disturbed from the bookcase. The fire was blazing, but the window gaping wide. The room was like one of those Swedish bath houses in which one may be simultaneously chilled and scalded in the name of health.

'God, man. You'll catch your death.'

I moved to shut the window, but he tugged my arm. 'A glass,' he said. 'Here. Wait.'

I watched him pour.

'I heard you from the corridor,' I ventured. 'You sounded . . . well. A touch distressed.'

'Wrestling with a problem. I like to talk out loud.'

'Ah. So be it, then. . . .'

I took the glass, sipped, and set it down. The fire toasted my front, the wind roared at my back. Nothing for it: that window would be closed.

'Fresh air,' I remarked, 'is a fine thing, though better in the summer months, I think. I knew a chap in Heidelberg believed in sleeping on his balcony. He thought it helped his constitution. By his third term, his coughing and his wheezing were so bad that he was banned from lectures. Fresh air, I do believe, is a most overrated medium, and while I'd scarcely advocate avoiding it, it seems to me that, that, that . . .'

In leaning out to take the window, I had chanced to look down. And there I stuck, frozen: not from cold, but from a kind of failure of volition, for I could make no sense of what I saw.

Frankenstein's Prescription

We were three floors high above the ground. Yet in the glow that radiated out, I saw, scarcely an arm's length below, a kind of face. I say 'a kind of', for it was half in shadow, and seemed in some manner distorted, pressing to the wall, its dark eyes looking up at mine. I was distinctly startled for a moment, before the spark of rationality prevailed, and I dismissed my first thought—that there was someone crouching on a ledge beneath me—and reasoned this was certainly a gargoyle, with its cold, unblinking stare, warped brow and brutish features. Yet I had never seen such decoration angled upwards, so as to face the building's denizens. Perhaps it had been meant as a reminder, a token of philosophy, like a *memento mori*. . . .

I turned back to Lavenza. He was watching me, likewise unmoving. I looked down again.

The face sank slowly in the shadows.

I saw it go, just as a drowning man sinks down beneath the waves; the darkness seemed to creep across and swallow it. There was a rustle, perhaps a hiss of breath; no sound beyond. I blinked. I stared. I leaned out, straining my eyes into the gloom. Saw nothing. I looked to right and left, and up. Above me were the stars, spread out across the sky, and they too, it seemed, were surely eyes, regarding me, eyes in the darkness—had I hallucinated? Was it mere imagination?

'Shut the window,' said Lavenza.

He had slumped into a chair, the bottle in his fist.

'Shut,' he said again, and this time I obeyed.

'Hans,' he said, 'I am in a dilemma. A most terrible dilemma. I fear there may be more deaths soon, unless I act. There have been many in the past—a great, great many. I may need—I may need some assistance. . . .'

'A face. I saw—'

'Yes, yes. My problem—you might say I have been given a commission. It will perhaps involve some hardship. I have no right to ask, of course, but if you . . . ?'

I nodded my encouragement.

'I must make a journey. It will not be easy, but I know a hunger burns within your veins. You, too, desire wisdom. You are, like me, a seeker after truth.'

'Truth.' I echoed him moronically.

'This journey, I must say, may make you wiser than you ever wished to be.'

'Wiser. Um . . . of course.' But I rallied somewhat, falling back on one of my persistent themes. 'If one wishes to be wise, and at the forefront of the present scientific thought, then there is only one place, as I have said to you before. Paris, at least, may prove a little brighter than this godforsaken hole.'

'Paris? Who spoke of Paris?'

'Surely the place to be, sir, for endeavours such as ours . . . ?'

'Not Paris, Schneider. Italy. As I explained. We must away to Italy, at the first chance, before worse befalls.'

I did not see how worse could possibly befall, here in this world of threats and murder and uncertainty. My notions of catastrophe were limited back then.

I much regret that they have expanded since.

Chapter Nineteen

Next day, accordingly, was all bustle, rush and preparation. I rose early—so I thought, having had little enough sleep—only to find Lavenza already wide awake and busy. It was something I would learn about him, though too late, and to my cost: that when he set his mind to an activity, he thought of nothing else. At other times he might seem indolent, or crazed, or merely drunk. Engaged in work, then he was driven. One could speak of it no other way.

Of course, it was impossible to simply shut down the asylum. Lavenza wrote to the establishment's governors—they were based, so I believe, in Heilbron or some other similarly far-off place—protesting urgent family business, which indeed it was, placing the brightest of his orderlies in temporary charge. Thus he might ensure continuance of supplies, even if his name would not, for now, appear upon the dockets. His own quarters he locked, the inner and the outer doors. What lay within would have to wait for his return. (His, I thought; not necessarily ours. Frustrated by his failure to accede to my private plans, I had begun to wonder whether, once his secrets had been learned, I might in some form strike out on my own.)

A second orderly conveyed the letter to the railway station, riding the asylum's decrepit old nag. Yet a third was despatched to the village, returning with a coach and pair—hired, I believe, from Lavenza's own pocket. I noticed that he never blinked at spending money. I wondered what his means were, and how easily this reservoir of cash might stretch to two.

Yet, as I made my plans, both secret and overt, once more our partnership hit stormy waters.

'The railway, sir,' I cried. 'Surely we go by rail?'
He would have none of it.
'I need my privacy. My independence.'
'But—in this weather—'
'I believe that Italy is fairly warm.'

I had not slept long or well enough. I still could barely grasp why we were on our way to Italy, not Paris.

'They're peasants!' I complained, jumping from argument to argument. 'It's centuries since science was a force in Italy. The priests keep their whole nation ignorant. We ought to go to Paris, or to London, or—any of a dozen cities! Not to Italy.'

'I have business there,' he said, as he had said before. 'And that's an end to it.'

And so it was.

Karl drove. There was, as may well be supposed, but little dignity about the journey. I myself looked like a large balloon, bundled in my finery and wrapped in blankets. At our feet, and behind our heads, and, indeed, all round, were items of Lavenza's medical equipment, and volumes from his library. I had, of course, made efforts to bring my full wardrobe, but Lavenza countered me; the excess was now stored within his quarters, awaiting my return—if ever. Our travelling arrangements seemed eccentric, antiquated, but Lavenza remained adamant. 'If Hannibal can do it on an elephant, we can do it in a coach and pair. Why, sir—are you in a hurry?'

Stowed under the seat were a few choicer items from Lavenza's cellars. Purely, he said, to keep us warm in alpine climes.

We had gone scarcely three or four miles before I found myself shivering uncontrollably and begged him for a small advance upon this medicine.

Not surprisingly, he chose to join me.

Only Karl seemed truly happy. It took a while for him to realise he had permission to depart from his accustomed route, but once he did, he hunched over the reins, he cooed and chirruped at the horses, and we managed a substantial pace. I wondered whether, in some deep chamber of Lavenza's heart, he had not engineered the situation solely for Karl's benefit.

Under the influence of alcohol, and with the dark forests passing either side, Lavenza grew confiding, and the story that he told was singularly strange.

⁂

'When you were young,' he said, 'and would not sleep or eat your greens, or be nice to your baby brother—were you threatened with the bogeyman?'

The movement of the coach was practically mesmeric, and the flicker of the passing trees, the same.

'Hm?' I said.

'The bogeyman.'

I could remember—it seemed centuries ago—the horrors of Herr Wolf, and his friend, Herr Teufel, who would whisk me down to hell, I had been told. (For not eating my sauerkraut? A petty sin, it seemed to me.)

Flick, flick, flick, the trees went by.

'The bogeyman? Oh yes. Daresay.'

'Yes. Most children know them. They come in two kinds, I think. One, imposed from without, by parents, nurses, governesses, as a method of control. Be quiet, or the bogeyman will get you. The other is comprised of all those fears we store up for ourselves, the night terrors, the ugly dreams—mm-hm?'

'Undoubtedly.'

I had made a pipe for myself, and was having a devil of a job getting it lit.

'My case was rather different,' he said, 'although in other ways, not too dissimilar. My family, like others, had its bogeyman. I know this very well.'

'Ah-ha.' I sucked the sweet tobacco-smoke into my lungs, exhaling slowly, with the pleasing satisfaction of a task complete.

'When I was six years old,' Lavenza said, 'I saw the bogeyman.'

'Alright.'

'I watched him eat my father.'

I almost swallowed my pipe. I laughed and laughed. Even Karl glanced round to check the cause of the disturbance.

Lavenza, though, showed no trace of amusement.

'I remember it quite clearly, though memory is fickle in so many ways—I remember neither the events which led to it, nor those that followed. Still. We sat together at the kitchen table, the bogeyman and I, across from one another. He was very large, as I recall, so large it did not strike me as unreasonable that he should eat my father. It was a natural thing in the succession of the food chain, as a bird eats a worm and a cat eats a bird.

'The light was poor, but when he turned to me, just so, I could make out his face. It had been very badly scarred, perhaps by fire. The skin at his temple had a curious, rubbery look to it, and the hair on that side of his head grew patchily, where on the other it was long and luxuriant, almost like a woman's. His mouth was twisted, as if he had endured some kind of stroke. But what I most recall about him were the eyes. Set beneath a crag of forehead, they lay so deep they seemed at first mere hollows, black holes, empty of sight. Then he would glance up, meet my gaze, and light would flash there, deep, deep down—like looking at a bullet down the barrel of a gun. You understand? Their sudden, fierce intelligence. It struck me. There was a mind behind those eyes, a mind of such form, such nature, it was beyond all human skill to fathom it.

'My father lay between us on the table. He had been neatly gutted and jointed. His left hand lay close to me, and I was tempted for a moment to reach out and touch it, purely so that I could say I had. But I held back. I knew his hand. There was no question. I knew it by the thick black hairs upon its back, the gold ring on its finger. The forearms, too, I recognised, with their dark hairs that would tickle when he held me, and which I sometimes rubbed my cheeks against. . . . The forearm ended at the elbow with a bloody knob, the kind familiar from the butcher's stall. The upper arm, I think, was some way distant—it was a big table—and here, removed from its conventional links to the shoulder, seemed curiously ineffectual and lacking shape. It could, to tell the truth, have belonged to almost anyone.

'His rib cage was picked partly bare. I remember noting the structure of the ribs and being very much intrigued by this; we were, after all, a family of doctors. The entrails were arranged within a zinc bowl placed approximately where the abdomen would have been. There was probably a smell to them. If so, I have forgotten it. Strange, when you think of the power of smell to evoke memory. Perhaps the numerous dissections I have performed since then have overlaid this and eclipsed its usual mnemonic power.

'Towards the far end of the table, on my left hand side, there lay my father's legs, and his feet, which seemed abnormally large; for, while the rest of him had been flayed of its clothes, his shoes were still in place. Shoes, which we might take for granted in our daily lives, can look . . . very peculiar in such a state, I may assure you.

'The bogeyman spent some time gnawing on my father's arm— the other arm, that furthest from my place. Yet he kept his eye on me. I dared not move. I watched him as he sucked the fingers, stripping the flesh off them. The mechanisms of his teeth and jaws were certainly unusual, more akin to those of some carnivorous animal—a tiger, or perhaps a crocodile—than any man. Immediate hunger sated, he took a knife and began to strip the muscles from the thighs in long, plum-coloured stripes. There was no blood from this. It seemed my father had been drained elsewhere. I rather suspect his blood must have been drunk.

'I watched the creature make a parcel of my father's meat, wrapping it in what was once his Sunday shirt. Then he looked at me directly, and he said a strange thing.

'His voice was hoarse and whispering, an oddly gentle thing, to issue from so barbarous a throat.

'He said,

' "How long, O Lord? Wilt thou forget me forever? How long wilt thou hide thy face from me?"

'It was odd, because my father's face was there, at the top of the table, and I had the feeling he was somehow addressing it, although his gaze was turned away.

'He stood. He had to stoop under our kitchen ceiling. He collected up my father's meat and placed it in a knapsack which had stood beside him all the while. He put this on. His shoulders seemed as wide as our kitchen fireplace. He appeared, at that moment, to fill the world; there had been nothing before him, there could be nothing after. Had he killed me—he could have done it with a quick brush of his hand—I would surely have accepted it entirely as my lot, inevitable, even deserved.

'Yet he ignored me. As he left, his voice came once again, now sad and wistful, "But I have trusted in thy steadfast love. I will sing to the Lord. I will sing. . . ."

'He walked out of my family home. I was orphaned, in a single night. I found . . . I must confess, I found the whole experience . . . exhilarating.'

'Really?'

'I suppose that I was found by somebody. Eventually. I don't recall. At any rate, I was dispatched to live with distant relatives, a great-aunt, who would have no truck with my father's work, or with family history. I spoke about the ogre. I was not believed. A man was arrested for the murder, a tramp, a half-wit. He could not defend himself, he was tried and executed. I was just a child. No-one believed me....'

'Psalms,' I said.

'Psalms? Ah yes. Very good. I am certainly impressed, Herr Schneider. Psalm Thirteen, to be precise. The first verse, and a portion of the fifth. He is very learned, in his own way. There is a missing line, "My heart shall rejoice in thy salvation." Do you think there is a reason why that line is missing?'

I shrugged.

'I've wondered many times. Salvation? Does he want a priest? Does he desire to confess? And who is the Lord he calls upon? The same Lord you and I might call upon, or someone else? Or else my father, as it struck me at the time?'

'But this,' I said, 'Surely this is just—'

'A dream? Delusion?'

'To be honest—' I stopped. He watched me with a look of absolute intensity. As if, despite my disbelief, he thought I might provide an answer.

I struggled to be diplomatic. 'It's well known,' I said, 'someone who's undergone a trauma, especially in childhood—memory plays tricks. As you yourself said. It's possible that, when your father died—a terribly upsetting thing, of course—sometimes the brain creates a metaphor, or mixes up reality and dream, or—there is a school of thinking in Vienna, by which—'

He listened as I stumblingly attempted to explain his life to him, and then he shook his head. 'I meant it all quite literally,' he said. 'It happened just as I described. What's more, you've seen the fellow's handiwork yourself. You of all people should have no doubts.'

'Ah.'

'You have seen the butcher's shop he made of that poor peasant woman, bringing us our milk. By such means he reminds me of his presence. It's his way. Nor was my father the first of my family to die at his hands. I am aware that, unless things go much differently,

Frankenstein's Prescription

my own demise is writ in stone already; I too will die. But I do not intend to stay dead, my dear Hans. Oh, certainly not!'

I merely stared at him. There was no trace of laughter, no irony. And I had seen too much over the last few weeks to scorn his claims.

He said, 'This goes back many years, you know. Many generations.'

Still I said nothing.

'You are familiar, perhaps, with the family Lavenza?'

'Never, sir, till I met you.'

My pipe was out. I sucked on it, tasting the foul cold ash.

'Good. That's as it should be. Lavenza was the name of my many-times great grandmother. Her son was brought up with her maiden name. We have continued with the coinage ever since.'

'Well,' I said, 'family trees are seldom straightforward. Half the royal families of Europe, I am told, are a tangle of incest and illegitimacy. . . .'

'No doubt. But to test your knowledge further. What of the family Frankenstein? Is that name more familiar to you?'

'Ha! Many's the lecture enlivened with a Frankenstein joke, sir. Do you know the one where he combines a cow, a dog, and a Bavarian? First the cow says—'

'Frankenstein,' intoned Lavenza, 'is my true name.'

It was a cause for laughter, beyond doubt; and yet I found I could not laugh.

Chapter Twenty

We were in the mountains, and had stopped to overnight at a small inn; but our discussion was of such a nature that we stepped outside for privacy. Private, indeed, we were; I could see no reason for any decent soul to be abroad on such a night. I puffed my pipe for warmth. Below, some large lake—I knew not which—lay gleaming in the moonlight.

And I scoffed, not for the first time.

'Frankenstein,' I said to him; also, not for the first time.

'Hush. More quietly.'

'Why? You think the peasants will come after us, waving their pitchforks, crying blasphemy?'

'It happened to my grandfather,' he said, in a voice without a hint of jest.

'Still, sir! Nevertheless!' I gestured with my pipe. 'Frankenstein—it's what we mutter to ourselves over a botched operation, a bit of cobbled stitching, or to criticise a colleague's poor technique. It's—a myth, a legend. Folklore. You must have heard the term at Ingolstadt, during your years there, just as I, at Heidelberg.'

'Oh, indeed. And I was greatly irritated by it, too. Although I kept my peace.'

'You tell me you are Frankenstein. This bumbler, this idiot of legend—'

'No idiot. My ancestor, Dr Viktor Frankenstein, was one of the most eminent men in medicine, and would be seen as such, had his tale been properly recorded. Had he lived, indeed, to tell it for himself.'

I did not comment.

He said, 'This is plain, straight truth now. If I stumble in the telling, then my hesitation comes from years of having to disguise myself, my nature and the nature of my family. Come now! Come! You strike me as a man who does not always tell the truth yourself.'

'Do you insult me?'

'Not at all. Merely entreat you to acknowledge common ground. And now,' he turned to me, full on, 'I have let you brood on this all day. I will tell you plain: Viktor Frankenstein is dead, but his creation walks, for it was never alive in the way of you or I. You caught a glimpse of it, I think, from my window, did you not?'

'Preposterous.'

But the image of that strange, distorted face was still too fresh within my mind. I said, 'But—if this is true, then that was a century or more ago! No creature could survive so long. It isn't feasible—'

'Not such a long time, Herr Schneider.'

I tried to reason with him. I sought other explanations. I entreated him to follow scientific reasoning, and so divine the truth. 'This fellow that you fear—some impostor, surely? Preying on your nervousness? Some criminal, some con-artist?'

'I repeat. You yourself saw what he made of poor Frau Eva. That's his calling card. Across the centuries, his little reminders of his presence. . . .'

'Then notify the police! Let him be dealt with properly! Have the fellow brought to justice, and let that be an end to him! No surprise your nerves are shot to shreds! For your peace of mind, your health! For the sake of your work, you must resolve this matter at the soonest chance, or—'

'For the sake of your investment, Herr Schneider. Is that not what you mean?'

'Sir, I do not—I cannot—your words mean nothing to me, sir, less than nothing—'

'Really, Hans. Do you believe yourself so subtle I would fail to grasp your motives? These hints at Paris and Vienna. It was all quite obvious, right from the start. And yet you've got a good heart, I perceive; and, despite it all, a genuine desire to learn, at least given sufficient motivation. You are one of very, very few willing to breach the boundaries of accepted knowledge. Thus, you are here, with me.'

I made to protest, insisting that, while my initial motives had been, possibly, a little mercenary, I had since grown to respect his work entirely for its own sake, to see its purpose, its wisdom, and . . . He held his hand up, silenced me.

'Schneider. I'm not interested. You understand? I don't care what you think, you or any other soul on Earth. I only worry that my fate will duplicate my father's, and my grandfather's, and so forth. The creature wants a gift, a sop to appease it. I am not, as yet, able to give that gift. It wants a mate.'

'A mate?' I stared at him. 'But. . . .'

'Oh, not me, you fool. It wants a female of its kind. A creature such as there has never been in all Creation. It seems my ancestor once promised such a thing. An Eve for Adam.'

We were silent for a time. Below, the lake shore glittered in the dark.

I said, 'You can do this? You believe that you can make, can make . . .'

My voice trailed off.

He shook his head. 'Not yet. Victor's prescription—his notes, his diaries, the traditions handed down within our family—they're incomplete. That's the problem. That's why we die young. He grows . . . impatient with us.'

'You do speak plainly,' I said presently. 'More so than previous, at least.'

'Indeed. Because I must. Because I trust you, I think. Is my trust well-founded?'

I cast about me, hopelessly. 'I . . . I just can't say.'

'Good. And besides: if you should speak to anybody else about the matter—do you think you'll be believed?'

Frankenstein's Prescription

I had imagined it was I who was in charge; I who, with guile and cunning, had manipulated him, steered him where I would, in hope of gain. Whereas, in fact, the situation had been quite reversed, and poor, unworldly Lavenza, the master of the game.

I conceded all of this with good grace, and, indeed, a smattering of admiration. Belief, though, in his wild tale, for the moment still eluded me.

Italy

Chapter Twenty-one

I disliked Italy, for it confirmed my expectations. There were too many Italians. I saw them everywhere. I met them at the inns, and the apothecaries' shops, and at the roadside selling everything from grapes to farmers' tools. I could hardly move for them. It was as if they owned the place! And while the young girls were indeed quite comely, even the most innocent approach produced a scolding from some ghastly black-clad matron, or a narrowing of eyes from young men round about. They did not, I think, fight duels here, but as a people they were known to carry knives, and I did not care to feel the sting of an Italian knife.

There is a kind of northerner who gravitates towards the south like piss running downhill. He thinks, for some unfathomable reason, he has been born at the wrong latitude; he returns after some three or four months and forever afterwards remarks, at every opportunity, 'Of course, Verona is my real home'—or Pisa, or Firenza, wheresoever he fetched up upon his tour. I would have none of this. I hated the unblemished sky, the dusty fields, the miserable bright sun that forced its way beneath my eyelids every morning. An apparent sensuality, the richness of the food and drink, the comeliness, as previously mentioned, of the younger women here—all these were fettered in the black chains of the church and manacles of a persistent, prudish, paternalistic peasant culture. For all Italians are peasants. This is not debatable. Dress them in gold, they are still peasants in their hearts. Ah well. Lavenza had announced that we must come to Italy, and so we had. I planned to make the best of it. At least, I could console myself, we were away from M——.

Karl drove. Under a blazing sun, he huddled in his greatcoat and his woollens, as if we were still high up in the bright Swiss chill. Driving at speed, his smell would waft across us like the odour of an over-ripened cheese.

Lavenza urged us on. He had a map. He had a pencil illustration, a little landscape with his father's name signed in the corner. And, at last, somewhere beyond Sienna, he cried out, 'There! There! There!' rousing me out of a fitful, drunken doze, and pointing to a far hill, its summit toothed with little buildings, its lower slopes half vanished in the haze. And thus, after too many, many days, we reached our destination.

I believed that I would bear the imprint of that wooden seat upon my arse for life, and I was not far wrong.

Chapter Twenty-two

Soft singing wafted through the halls and cloisters, out into the gardens, which looked upon the golden plains of Italy, so picturesque, so sweaty and malarial. Male voices, simple harmonies that shifted back and forth, forever changing, forever new; a constant music, heard yet seldom actually attended to, as if one bathed in it, or breathed it with the air. Its work on me was near-Mesmeric. I found myself both lively and relaxed, sombre and yet joyful; though it must be said that several days stuck in a jolting carriage likewise has a marked effect upon the body and the mind, and the relief from this induced a potent lightening of spirits. The night just gone, I took my first rest in a bed—albeit a narrowly monastic one—and awoke with the sense that life had once again begun. So while Lavenza sought the wisdom of his father, and ploughed the dusty stacks of the monastic library, I betook myself of equally paternal company, and found it pleasantly hospitable—somewhat, in truth, to my surprise.

Father Giovanni was a swarthy, amiable man, muscled like a stevedore. Age had contrived to spread his tonsure wide, and make a cushion of his belly; but it had little touched the power in his neck and arms, nor the breadth of his shoulders. He gave me tea, then glasses of the local liquor, for which I was most grateful. His German was good, if of the Swiss form. Still: one cannot overestimate the need for foreigners to learn a decent language.

'Scared of his shadow.' The Abbot's voice was deep and resonant. 'I haven't thought of him for years, I must admit.'

'Ah-ha,' I said. 'Ah-ha.'

We watched the fields of Italy dissolving in the after-dinner sun.

'I wasn't Abbot then, mind you. Anything but. My mentor had his doubts that I would even make a monk. This must be thirty—oh my. Thirty-five years gone. A terrible long time.'

I agreed it was—longer than my life.

'Herr Lavenza—*il Dottore*, we called him—I remember clearly. His very novelty made him stand out, although he was a solitary chap. I might even say secretive. No-one seemed to know why he was here. He had, I believe, some friendship with the then Abbot, a scholarly Frenchman. For the rest of us. . . . Well, we took him for a lunatic, come for sanctuary. May I ask—you are close to his son, Herr Schneider? Good friends?'

'We have a small . . . business arrangement. And I admire his intellect.'

'Quite so. But where the father was as flighty and as nervous as a virgin—excuse my terms—the son is more a coiled spring, I think, wound tight enough to snap. Does he relax at all?'

'He drinks. Is that relaxing?'

The Abbot smiled. 'For some, perhaps,' and he refilled my glass.

'Tell me. His father . . . ?'

'Stayed for quite some months—perhaps a year. I'm not sure. He was interested in our work, and in our libraries, and—oh, all sorts of things. One came upon him in unlikely places. . . . Once I caught him clattering the spoons in the kitchen, knocking one against another, just to hear them ring. He was interested in our choir. Not in their music, but their physiognomy. He measured their mouths. He peered down their throats, and up their nostrils. Recorded the dimensions of their crania. He was obsessive. At times his interests would be architectural, measuring the chapel and the vestry and wherever, at others anatomical, or metaphysical. . . . And I may say, he performed for us a great many small services, for he was skilled in medicine and the use of herbs.

He earned his keep, and was a welcome guest. But he was here for reasons of his own, which he would not divulge.'

'You guessed . . . ?'

'No.'

'You were curious?'

He made a Latin gesture. 'A lunatic, my dear friend, as I say. Besides, I was a novice. I had more pressing matters to attend to.'

And he topped my glass again.

'We are a singing order, Herr Schneider. You'll have noticed this?'

I nodded.

'Other orders sing, of course. But with us, singing is the *essence* of our worship. Not a part of it, at mass or matins, but its very heart. During your stay here, has a single moment passed when you could not hear music?'

I admitted that none had. He said, 'I think that this is what intrigued Papa Lavenza. He liked the science of acoustics. How sound is made, and how it works, and why one sound may be pleasant and another ugly. He pursued his work with diligence, but he was on his own, would not seek help. . . . And thus, I am afraid, his studies took a very great amount of time.'

'Not the area I understood to be his interest.'

'No? I can think of nothing more important in the world, myself.'

'You read his manuscript?'

'I've looked at it. Figures and equations, diagrams, statistics—it means nothing to me, I'm afraid. Perhaps your friend will make more sense of it. Unless his interest is mere sentiment . . . ?'

I shrugged. I had expected revelations; our miserable journey should have ended with enlightenment of some sort. But there was none in sight. 'I don't think he knows what he's looking for,' I said.

'Well then. In that case, I expect he'll find it.'

There was a wart under the Abbot's right eye; when he smiled, it made him squint.

'You admire his intellect,' he went on. 'And yet, unless I misread, your concerns are far from altruistic. Don't bother to protest.' He held a hand to silence me. 'Before I was a monk, I was a great number of other things. I know the world. I make no judgement. But let me warn you: sometimes, the possession of a gift is less a blessing than a curse. The gifted do not always rise in life, my friend.'

'Father—'

'You know how I became the Abbot here? Was it my gifts, my skills, my great prowess?'

I told him I was certain he possessed exceptional character, and that this had clearly been acknowledged and rewarded. But he laughed.

'Listen,' he said, cocking his head to one side. 'Those are our gifted men, those whose voices bless us day and night. But someone had to be the Abbot, and perform the dreary duties of administration, supervise the brethren and present us to the outside world,' his smile grew sly, 'even to welcome and play host to our few guests. These jobs, which you may deem prestigious, and I deem for the most part dreary beyond measure, have all fallen to me. For one reason. One, and one alone. I have the voice of a crow.'

We talked on, and drank; but presently, I excused myself, walking a little way into the garden, admiring both its colours and its scents, the way that even humble vegetables had been laid out with some eye for their pattern and design. I had found myself a genius; I had grasped onto his coattails with a mercenary greed. But, as the Abbot had reminded me, turning a profit out of genius is no straightforward thing. So far, I had been told a tale to frighten children, heard a name from folklore and from medic's humour, and now seemed faced with a bizarre study of choristers' anatomy. Though then again . . . I had also seen Lavenza's laboratory, where he might gift the dead with a new semblance of life.

And the face at the window, less than a week before.

And the murder.

I turned back to the Abbot, and, for politeness' sake, urged him to speak on. He told me of the history of his order, of Saint This and Abbot That, and I smiled and paid it all but scant attention, until he came back to the matter of the singing, and said something which retrieved my interest with a vengeance.

'In the beginning was the Word,' he said. 'But how was it uttered? The great Word, which gave birth to all things?'

I shrugged, my thoughts still wandering elsewhere.

He told me, 'It was sung, my friend! Such is our belief. Not spoken, not whispered or shouted—the world was *sung* into existence, and we with it! Is that not truly the most glorious idea?'

Chapter Twenty-three

And so, more travelling.

Cortona was a hill town of the sort which travellers call 'delightful'. I often wonder what delights them so. It had its bows to culture, its theatre and its church, its charming views; it had its crumbling and unsanitary buildings, its streets of wearisome, exasperating steepness, its black-clad crones sat like inquisitors in every shadow. Though then again, it also had its tavern, and a local wine which proved both cheap and drinkable.

I had been drinking it for quite some time, while Lavenza was away to ask about a priest. Not any priest, I understood; some fellow said to have worked miracles in times gone by. I confess Lavenza's interest struck me as absurd, unsuitable for any man of science. But it offered me the chance to sit and drink. When troubled by the world, I find this is the best recourse. Either one solves one's problems, or one just ceases to care; *ergo*, this way or that, one's problems disappear. But with the third bottle, the problems were still running through my mind, a farrago of science and philosophy, of genius, blood and scattered entrails. In which my future was now augured, if I read them right.

Across from me sat Karl. His hair had grown since leaving M——; a brush of grey down now offset his skull-like face. He refused to eat, but matched me drink for drink, and in his own fashion, grew talkative, though it was not your usual beer-hall chat.

'I fell asleep three hundred years. Know how I know? Know how? Know how?' He patted at the aforementioned scalp. 'I woke up and my hair was grey. I saw myself—there was a mirror—and my hair was grey.'

He sank a glassful at a single gulp.

'Know how I know we're dead?'

'Don't you have any drinking songs? A few good choruses, perhaps?'

'I was on my coach. This was a long, long time ago. . . . I drove by the morticians. Outside it, on the pavement, lay a turd. And what's the last thing that you do before you die? What's the last thing?'

I thought of Socrates, his disquisition on the final breath. Oh, how sedate it seemed, how pure!

'You shit yourself,' said Karl, predictably. 'That's right, Master? You shit yourself. That's right.'

'Any songs at all,' I said. 'A few good rounds of "Augustine", perhaps?'

'Know how I know the world'll end? I look up at the sky, and—'

'I could teach you if you like. It goes like this—'

But after a few lines, I petered out. The world may have been sung into existence, but song did nothing for our poor mad coachman. I downed my wine. The locals stayed away from us, I noticed, though they took my lira readily enough. I picked at a few olives, ate a little cheese and bread. It was not, perhaps, a bad life, all things considered. I loaded up my pipe while Karl commenced his own life story, or what passed for such within his mind, a tale to rival Munchausen's, though rather less enjoyable. Meanwhile, I thought of other things.

I thought of Frankenstein.

The name Lavenza had invoked, some days before. He had not spoken of it since, and when I broached the subject, he had merely shied away, retreating into old habits of secrecy. So did he really claim descent from that great rogue, that genius, that legend or impostor, that nincompoop, whatever the man was?

As students, of course, we never heard the name in lectures, but it was common enough in the anatomy rooms, as our knives exposed the workings of the flesh; and it was never used in praise. On the other hand, I did recall the jest of certain of my fellows, that they might join together this girl's face and that one's cunny, this one's tits and that one's legs. . . .

'God gets it wrong so many times. It's up to us to get it right.'

❦

The afternoon was half way gone before Lavenza strode in. He clapped his hands, urging us up. I will confess that we were slow to rise, and none too steady.

'Come, come! The fellow's close! They say he's at the lake!'

He gave Karl a none-too-gentle shake; the poor madman was asleep on his feet.

'Ready the coach! We must be off!'

'Hm? Hm? The last trump . . . ?'

'I'll give you *last trump!* Now move!'

I retrieved my pipe from where it had fallen in the creases of my waistcoat; regrettably, the cloth was slightly singed. I wanted to go back to our rooms and change it, but Lavenza would brook no delay.

'I've found him,' he said. 'If we hurry—'

'Priest . . . ?' I said.

'His name is Father Vincini. He is preaching by Lake Trasimeno. I gather he's looked on by the church as something of a rebel. Very popular, though. Very popular.'

'No doubt there's a connection.'

●

With a little effort, and assistance from Lavenza and myself, Karl had our transport up and running within fifteen minutes, though he slouched in the driver's seat, occasionally shivering with giggles.

Frankenstein's Prescription

A fierce light burned down on us. I pulled my coat over my head like an Arab. Enormous sunflowers watched us from the roadside.

'If he can really do it,' said Lavenza, bubbling with excitement, 'this is everything I need. Even just to know it's possible! Then, if I can isolate the mechanism . . . if he'll let me question him, perform some tests. . . .'

'Lavenza,' I admonished him, 'They're peasants. They'll believe in anything.'

'What they believe is not important. What proves true—is everything.'

❦

'It's my conviction,' said Lavenza, 'that in certain individuals, the energies may be unusually strong. Electric and magnetic fields, such as we each possess. Under the right conditions, such force might be transfused from one man to another. It accounts for cases of miraculous healing, the laying on of hands—even, perhaps, as here, a literal raising of the dead.'

'Well,' I said. 'At least you haven't told me that the Blessed Virgin did it.'

'My knowledge to this point dictates an explanation in accordance with my own research. However, I'm of open mind. Give me the proof, the unequivocal verification she's involved, and she'll immediately become a factor in my work. For that, friend Schneider, is true science.'

'You know, I sometimes think you've got a sense of humour after all.'

My remark caused him to frown, and check himself. 'I don't think so, no. No, I was speaking in all earnest. We must be free of prejudice—no matter how sincerely held.'

'You just did it again. What you said sounded exactly like a joke.'

'This fellow has raised two men from the dead. There are testimonies, sworn statements. Of course, we can't yet know the truth. The fellows may have been unconscious, their witnesses deceived or else mistaken. Only in controlled conditions . . . if he'll permit me. I have certain equipment, at the asylum, if he'll travel with us, so please—assume an air of piety, will you? We may have to dissemble if we want the truth.'

Chapter Twenty-four

Lake Trasimeno was a silver shimmer in the lazy southern light. I looked round for a tavern, or anywhere that might sell drink, but Lavenza was more interested in a crowd down at the water's edge. Soon we were bouncing along the littoral in a manner fit to shake our bones apart. I yelled for Karl to slow but Lavenza urged him to go faster. Irrelevant, really, for Karl himself was scarcely in control. As it was, we hurtled in amongst this crowd of peasants like a wolf into a flock of lambs. They scattered, all directions; and Karl tore on, unheeding. Only with a deal of shouting from Lavenza and myself was he persuaded to slow down.

Reluctantly, he turned and brought us back around. Lavenza and I dismounted. There were hostile stares; I did my best to apologise, but my Italian was poor, limited mostly to wines and foodstuffs, and my humble '*Scusi, scusi,*' was not held to be wholly adequate. I helped an old man to his feet, and got no thanks. I heard mutterings among the mob; '*Tedesco*', which I knew meant 'German', and '*cazzo*', which did not seem terribly polite.

Lavenza, though, was quite oblivious to this. Single-mindedly, he barged into the throng, blind and determined as a bloodhound on the trail.

No coincidence we found ourselves beside a lake. Father Giuseppe Vincini, like John the Baptist of old, was fond of immersing his followers in water, no matter how often they might have been baptised before. If nothing more, it gave them some relief from the Italian sun.

I forced my way among the ranks of the infirm, the aged and the merely curious. To my left, a chap laid on a palanquette cried out in supplication. To my right, a one-legged man hobbled on crutches, and a woman, though with no obvious debility, squatted in a puddle, moaning softly. Lavenza made straight for our quarry. The chap stood to his waist in the lake, his black robes floating round him, holding his hands out as if beckoning us on, the pale palms uppermost. A long grey beard trailed down his chest. His age was scarcely guessable. His skin was mottled by the sun, wrinkled like an old glove; thin white hair fluttered feather-like upon the breeze.

Lavenza strode into the water, ignoring all around him.

'Father! Father Vincini! I must talk to you! We have to speak together—with the utmost urgency—'

It was like watching as a very old machine clicks slowly into life; the long delay while cogs recall their former moves, while levers twitch and pistons shudder back to motion. The old man's hand rose jerkily in blessing. His lips began to move; no sound came out, but I could almost read the muted Latin that they formed.

Lavenza caught him by the shoulders, fervently imploring.

'Father Vincini. They say you raised the dead. You brought them back to life. Is this true, or fiction? Father. Talk to me. Father. Father!'

Vincini's hand traced shaky figures in the air. His lips made half-remembered words. The same words, the words of blessing, over and over.

I found myself suddenly longing for the robust health and worldly manner of the Abbot Giovanni. Did priests have no retirement age? Were they simply left to roam around, into their dotage?

'You raised the dead!'

Lavenza was desperate. I had only barely registered the depth of his obsession; and now, to see it so absurdly thwarted, frenzy rose in him. He begged, he cried out. His hands were on the old priest's shoulders. He shook him. Shook him, shouted at him.

He wasn't really rough. Enthusiastic, yes. Not rough.
What happened might have happened any time.
Given the old man's age. His frailty.
Given all that.

'*Can you raise the dead? For God's sake, man! Can you or can you not?*'

At which point, Father Vincini's eyes appeared to fix on him at last, as if in recognition, and a peculiar sound came from his throat; a sound of hawking phlegm, and then a little pop, like the release of a champagne cork. The priest seemed suddenly to crumble and fall back. Lavenza caught him, cradling him above the water. I saw the moment of confusion on his face, the panic as he realised what was wrong. Vincini, of course, said nothing. Lavenza pressed two fingers to his neck, checking the pulse. He put his ear close to Vincini's mouth. But Plato's final breath had gone.

Around me, silence started to give way to muttering. A woman wailed. As Lavenza dragged the old priest's body to shore, I gestured Karl back to the carriage, and took a step or two in that direction likewise.

The sodden priest, now tangled in his robes, lay on the grass. His legs stuck out like two peeled sticks.

Someone said, 'Murder!'

There were others of Lavenza's family said to have perished at the hands of rampaging mobs, as if it were some kind of an hereditary disposition.

If so, this seemed a bad moment for history to repeat itself.

'Lavenza!' said I. 'Come on!'

Indolent he may have been; but he grasped the situation fast enough, covering the distance to the carriage like a champion sprinter.

'Miracles,' I sniffed, and 'Miracles!'

But only after we were safe away.

Chapter Twenty-five

And so to Rome. Inevitably, it may be.

'More priests?' I said. 'More wild geese to follow?'

'There are important matters. . . .'

I was firm with him. 'Which are taking us no nearer to our goal. You have your father's papers. Let us set to work. Let us find you sponsorship, a worthy place to work. All you deserve.'

'Which are taking us,' he said, 'a very great deal nearer. Yes.'

And on that, the conversation ceased.

I believe that I have spoken of my dislike for the south. In Rome, women and cats both hissed at me from side streets. Both looked uninviting. Men in comic-opera uniforms paraded through the streets. I forced myself to view the sights: the Coliseum, the baths, the temples like old rotten teeth. Young men lounged at roadside cafés, weighing one another up. The women, barring these sorry, backstreet types, were all but inaccessible. It was not a city that I took to, not at all.

Lavenza got us entry to St Peter's. Here he wandered, pausing now and then to clap his hands, cocking his head to catch the resonance. 'Mark the echo there,' he might say, or, 'Hear that, now,' and clap again, for me to hear.

To me, it was the sound of clapping hands in an enclosed space. No more, no less. I grew impatient.

'Suppose,' he lectured me, 'just for a moment, all life is but an echo, a vibration in the cosmos—an echo, let us say for argument, of the voice of God. I use the term for want of anything more . . . scientific. Now suppose, in certain places, that echo were to be preserved, were made to last forever, endlessly rebounding from the walls . . . what then?'

'A fine theory,' I said. 'The practicality?'

'The practicality . . . eludes me. But I'll come to it, I'll come to it.'

He clapped again, exciting disapproval from a pair of passing priests.

'There *is* an echo. Who's to say it's not the one I've sought?'

In the Sistine Chapel, he again grew philosophical.

You know the scene: an older man reaches his hand towards a young ephebe, who rises languidly to meet him; both of them muscled like hod-carriers, despite the wrinkled face and white beard of the first. But where I could see the wet-dreams of an aging nancy-boy, he saw something altogether different.

'They're clearly the same person,' he pronounced. 'See how he reaches out—offering his energy, his soul, if you will. Adam seems freshly woken. Jehovah, tired yet determined. There is an ancient science here—the old restores himself to youth, abandoning his grey hairs for the young man's curling locks. This is—'

'An old queen and a bit of what he fancies.'

But Lavenza held his finger up for peace.

He clapped his hands.

We listened to the throb in the air. One could almost gauge the Chapel's depth by sound alone. Lavenza clapped again, again.

'Is this it? The vibration which brings life? Is this the secret which the painter tried to tell us, all those years ago?'

He went on clapping, listening, moving a pace or two, clapping again.

Soon after, we were asked to leave.

Disturbing news awaited us at *poste restante*.

Frankenstein's Prescription

After three years of benign neglect, the asylum governors had sent a representative to check up on Lavenza's work, and ensure smooth running in his absence. This was unexpected. It seemed news of the killing had already reached them; they naturally assumed one of the inmates responsible. In their eyes, this suggested laxness on Lavenza's part, and they had sent their operative to clear the air with the local authorities.

The letter was from Lavenza's chief orderly, who also worked as chef. The handwriting was large and slanted. I read over his shoulder.

> '. . . in the chapel sir they fown things not to ther likin sir and yor sperments they were not to be kept out sir and much was sed not to yor good gras tho I argu menny times and sa watever you mite do sir you ar a fine man, but then they bring out bodys and the peces of bodys and I don no what to sa Now they do not want you to be hed here no mor but hav put this new blok in and will be sendin sumone els in sumer they say sir plus there is polis all round du to the murder of the missus bringin milk to us. I am sory to rite as you wer only ever good to al of us, but they are takin thins out yor rooms and yor kwipmen an thins an ther is nothin mor that I can do sir. But on a briter note, I rit to you that Frau Flicher has gone home, which we is all very pleas by, an she ask to be remember to you, sir.'

He sat down. He slumped into a chair. All the energy he had displayed during our travels vanished, draining from him like a liquid.

'Equipment . . . ?'

I seized the letter, read it through. Could there be some mistake? The orderly was hardly smart, and barely literate, but his meaning was quite plain enough. At first I, too, was shocked and downcast. Then it struck me: this was perfect. It was my chance to prise Lavenza from his shell, just like an oyster. True, I regretted the loss, the workshop and achievements so roughly snatched away, but it meant that I would never more be forced to see that dreadful place. While the doctor slouched, face frozen with despair, I felt a grin spread on my lips.

'But this is wonderful!' I clapped him on the shoulder. 'You can build it all again! Bigger—better—more astounding! And this time,' I said, choosing my words with care, 'in a place where it will gain you proper recognition, where you will get what you deserve, and be acknowledged as the genius you are. Away from all those stupid, ignorant fools—'

'I want no recognition.'

'Don't be silly! Everyone wants recognition!'

But I looked at him, his head down, his shoulders forward, like a tortoise hunched into its shell, and it struck me that his motives were, indeed, unlike my own, or those of anybody I had previously known.

'Well then,' I said. I sat beside him. 'You need money for your work.'

He nodded, vaguely.

'We should go somewhere you can find your sponsors. Wealthy, forward-looking men, willing to invest in your ideas. Hm?'

He said nothing.

'It may take time to build our contacts, to make the right connections. But when we do . . . there will be no more menial jobs, no more taking work below your stature, just to pay the bills. From here on, you'll have anything you want. You'll have engineers to build your mechanisms, surgeons all on hand to slice your corpses. While you devote yourself to higher things. Think of it,' and I tried to fill my voice with awe, 'not as a loss, but as a gain. Not a set back, but as being—set free!'

He said nothing.

'We might go to London—Paris—even to the New World. There is nothing we might not accomplish, you and I! Our lives are our own, our fortune waits us, if we have but the courage to reach out and grasp—'

And in the smallest voice, he said, 'Frau Fleischer has gone home.' And he smiled, and nodded to himself, and then began to cry.

⁂

I worked quickly.

In his distress, Lavenza was unable to deter me. I sold our coach and pair—well, technically, I realise, it was hardly *ours*, but we were in no position to return it to the owner. With the proceeds I bought railway tickets. And I set about recalling names of prominent persons, those with whom I might claim some relation, never mind how tenuous—or, indeed, how spurious. Heidelberg had been a hive of gossip, coming in from all quarters of Europe. I knew the lives of prominent men, men I had never met, men who, had they known me for a meagre, disgraced student, would have passed me on the street without a glance. But desperation spurs one's creativity. A plan formed in my head, as plans were wont to do in those days; a plan for great accomplishment at small outgoing effort. Which was, in such matters, the manner of equation I preferred.

Within three or four months, as I reckoned it, all Paris would be mine.

And so it was.

France

Chapter Twenty-six

They spoke about the Paris Ripper. There had been a girl in Pigalle, another in the Bois; and with the second death, the scandal sheets already had their nickname. They hinted portions of the bodies had been cut away, as if by surgery. I read the story, at first thinking but little of it. I read it at the home of one of my new clients. She told me that the paper had been left there at her bedside by a servant, as an oversight, she carefully explained, though it was clearly she who had been reading it. I touched my stethoscope against her upper chest. She sighed, her bosom (no small item, this) commenced to heave.

'You have a strong, majestic heart,' I announced. 'A queen's heart. A . . . if I may say—a *passionate* heart.'

The mounds of freckled, powdered flesh rose up towards me. I requested that she cough. It was a gentle, lady's cough, more like a hiccup, but I praised her as one would a child.

I tapped upon her sternum with the quiet dignity of the professional.

She was mine for the taking. I knew that. But in this case, I was playing a long game, not to be squandered for a few minutes of fun. Moreover, I was more than adequately cared for elsewhere, when it came to such endeavours. Thus it was mere diplomacy (and business sense) to let my gaze linger a bit too long on hers, to pause as if about to voice some tender, unprofessional emotion; then seem to gather myself up, straighten my collar, and retreat into the cool, safe language of my work.

'Two tablets, twice a day, after breakfast and the evening meal.' I smiled then, all hearty cheer. 'We'll have you right in no time.'

We'll have you right, I thought, because there's nothing wrong with you to start with.

Which in my mind, makes an ideal patient.

※

'Lavenza,' I called out. 'Lavenza!'

I had spent a little of my fee at a bar in St Germaine, a little more with ladies met there, and enjoyed a simple meal of meat and bread and wine. I was feeling in superb mind as I breezed into our rented house. This was the life I had been born for! I clapped my hands, called out, 'Let's have some wine! And fine cigars!'

Lavenza merely looked at me. His face was bloodless, hands clasped round his knees. I placed a drink before him, and he gulped it eagerly; then I sat back, lit up, and recounted my adventures of the day, sparing no detail, no matter how salacious, or how comical.

He stared across the room, as if his gaze were focused on some distant and imaginary point.

I don't believe he said a word all night.

※

There is a maxim for practitioners of medicine, and it's a simple one: *do no harm*. I was careful, and I did no harm, except to cuckold a few husbands, most of whom had long since given up the marriage bed in any case. It may be that I even did some good, for many of my patients needed no more than a sympathetic ear, an hour's company, a little entertainment. . . . How intimate an entertainment might be open to debate. Meanwhile I plied them with placebos. No-one died. Many found their spirits lifted and their health, thereby, improved. It astonished me to think I had been willing to spend years in study, attend Herr Müller's dreadful lectures (no worse, it must be said, than those of his colleagues), sit my exams, and generally suffer the most awful tedium, when all I really had to do was call myself *le docteur Schneider*, print up some calling cards, talk knowingly and nicely, meanwhile rogering a dozen wealthy women behind (as it were) their husband's backs. I had quickly built up quite a roster of such patients, generally on personal recommendation, keen to see the famous German doctor with his boyish looks and suave, Teutonic charm. (Naturally, I falsified my age, presenting testimonials which were, I must admit, not totally authentic; though I felt that, had those people actually known me, they might indeed have viewed me in such generous light. I was, when all was said and done, a fine fellow, if not a very honest one.)

The strategy was simple and direct. Rewards were almost instantaneous. I ate steak now on a daily basis (a necessity, given the athletic aspect of my calling), drank the finest wines, procured cocaine and ether for the further pleasure of my senses. I have already registered my scorn against those of my countrymen enraptured by more sunny climes. Yet, if we each possess two homes, the one where we were born, the one where we belong, I readily admit I had now reached the latter, content and certain it was where I ought to be.

Our house was in a small street off the Rue Faubourg de Montmartre. It was modest enough. At my suggestion, Lavenza, too, had sought to take a public role for himself; as we were sharing quarters, it seemed wise to ensure he, too, possessed a ready income. He became an alienist; his chief client was an elderly transvestite with a taste for stern women. He would send for poor Lavenza at all hours of the day and night, his carriage drawing up outside, filled with the need to bemoan or boast his latest bout of 'sinning'. To this choice of profession I attributed my colleague's melancholy and withdrawal. I had often tried to rouse him from his rooms—the city of Paris lay about us, nothing less!—but he pored over his medical texts, he scribbled in his notebooks. . . . His face was pale as the corpses he once worked with.

'Come on, man! Take a night off! Enjoy yourself!'

He merely shook his head, and went back to his task.

From this, I learned the difference between ambition and obsession. Ambition—which I possessed in plenty—must be geared towards an end, an achievement which in practice may have nought to do with any means by which it is obtained. A fine life, a good circle of friends, the little luxuries that make our time on Earth worth living . . . does it matter if we gain our goals by working as a banker, or a bishop, or a statesman? Or even as a doctor?

Obsession, on the other hand, is an end within itself, looking inwards by its own light. It is the sort of thing, it seemed to me, that leaves one, ultimately, not the director of the asylum, but its inmate.

Could I make this clear to him? Of course not.

'My childhood,' he sputtered, feebly. 'You must understand that it was . . . haunted, every day . . . knowing that *thing* was out there, that it would come for me, as it had come for my father, making its threats and its demands. . . . And if I would not, or more likely could not meet its needs, knowing what vengeance it would take. . . .'

'That "thing",' I said, 'is many miles from here, and hardly likely to pursue us to our present home.'

But he gave me such a bleak look, I half expected him to drop down dead upon the spot.

'Everything I've done,' he said, 'everything I will do—is governed by that knowledge. Does that earn me forgiveness? These crimes. These sins. . . .'

'What crimes?' I laughed out loud. But his demeanour was so sorrowful, I asked, 'Is this some morbid guilt about your miracle priest? Is that it?'

He said nothing, which I took to be a *yes*.

'Let me explain to you.' I drew myself up, folded my arms, a true man of the world. 'I know a little of such guilt myself, and I will tell you: I have found the cure.' I let him wait, then said: 'It is easy, sir. Good food, good drink, a little cognac and a pinch or two of snow; good company and willing women. And time, sir. Time. These things will do it, no mistake. You see me? I scarcely even think of guilt!'

And with that, I bade him a good night.

For the moment, then, we went our separate ways, pursuing our own ends—and in my case, I may say, with fair success.

Chapter Twenty-seven

But I have mentioned corpses once again, a mere few paragraphs above. They scatter through the narrative with an alarming frequency. Indeed, while Paris raced into the bright new century, several of her citizens advanced with equally precocious haste towards an early grave. Corpses were much in vogue, and what began as mere sensation in the cheaper journals quickly gained the status of a major story. Before long, I could hardly read a newspaper or hold a conversation without mention of the Ripper, often thrown with precious little relevance into our talk. A girl here and a woman there. . . . I had had far too much of murder in my last few months, and scorned all such remarks. Yet it was not so much the stories that annoyed me, as the willingness of otherwise sophisticated souls to sink into their foul embrace, as if they truly wanted a small spot of darkness in their lives—a little thrill, just to remind them how unconscionably lucky they most truly were.

'You people,' I announced, 'see patterns everywhere.' (I was dining at my club, an establishment I had seen fit to join for business reasons. On this occasion, I had consumed a fair amount of wine, and bought drinks all round; I had my audience.) 'There is a murder, let us say. And then another murder, somewhat like the first. Are they linked? Perhaps. I have some knowledge of the criminally insane, and their habits are, indeed, repetitive. And it is true that, every now and then, a figure will emerge—some beast born into human form, some monster with a taste for killing, who relishes each chopping of the knife, each bludgeon blow. . . . Oh yes.' I let myself survey the crowd; fine fellows all, dressed in their best, replete with food and drink. 'And yet, how much more often does a man kill for a purpose? For money, say, or for revenge? Or else to free himself of burdens he believes intolerable? These, my friends, are not the motives of a madman, but of some common, ordinary fellow, propelled to desperation. True enough, the act which they inspire may be despicable, but it is not, I hold, the work of monsters.'

I produced my cigarette case, and called to Madeleine, the serving girl, to bring a light.

'Are you suggesting, sir,' a gentleman inquired from the tables, 'that the Ripper is a myth? That Paris and its womenfolk are safe, despite the crying of the scandal-rags?'

I laughed. I had been practising my public laugh, and had become quite good at it. 'Oh no, sir. Quite the opposite.' I paused, allowing Madeleine to light my cigarillo. Her hair had come a little loose, the fine blond strands straying from beneath her bonnet. 'Womenfolk of Paris,' and I gestured knowingly to her departing rear, 'are in the gravest danger—not from any monster, but from each and every one of you.' This caused some mirth among the crowd. I held my hand for peace. 'For which among you,' I gazed about the room, 'has not at some time dreamt of murdering his wife?' This, too, inaugurated some good-natured chuckles, so I commenced my second charge. 'Or if not his wife—perhaps his mistress?'

There was a scatter of applause. A large fellow, who sat before me, tweaking his moustaches, cried out, 'You have us to a man, sir. But tell me—do you imply that one of us might be the Ripper? Is that the main thrust of your speech?'

'Not at all.'

'Well! I daresay we are all relieved at that!'

'I imply that *all* of you might be the Ripper. Is that much clearer now?'

'Sir?'

I had their interest, and I basked in it.

'Hear me out.' I puffed upon my cigarillo, blowing smoke into the air. 'A dreadful murder is committed, then a second, bearing all the hallmarks of the first. The papers tell us that a killer is abroad, roaming the streets and murdering at will. You see the possibilities which open up? The opportunities—for each and every one of you?

'Suppose a man has some long-standing grievance with his wife. She's a spendthrift, an adulterer, whatever it might be. They fight. In normal times, fear of the law might hold him back. But now, the whole world knows—we have a killer on the loose! Should her body turn up in an alley, minus its vital organs—this, our killer's trademark, you recall—will the husband take the blame? Of course not! He need only feign his grief, and let her death be added to the others in police files. Or else that former paramour, a casual, mistaken dalliance, who's now making your life such misery? Who's threatening to tell your wife and children? Who demands you keep her in her luxury apartment, draining your money while she runs around with other men? Oh, the sheer convenience! The blissful ease!'

This drew some sly, conspiratorial male laughter. I let it run a while, then held my hand for peace. 'In short, my friends, what I propose is this. There is no Ripper. More to the point, we have a multitude of Rippers, each hiding carefully behind the mask of he whom the police and papers both mistakenly pursue. For all I know, every man among you has already seized his chance to rid himself of some small irritation, under cover of the Ripper's name. Is that not so?'

'Sir, you are correct.' The mustachio'd man stood up, and he raised his glass. 'Summon *les flics!* I do confess! In truth, we *all* confess!' He pulled a convict's face. 'But before they come to clap us all in irons, may I propose a toast to you, my friend, our newest colleague—surely the Sherlock Holmes of Paris!'

There was applause and cheering. I lowered my head, most modestly, and toasted them in turn. There was warmth between us, and, although I scarcely knew these fellows, it seemed to me there was an accord here I had scarcely felt since Heidelberg. I was among my own sort once again, where I was meant to be.

Only one small incident tarnished an otherwise delightful evening.

Returning from a call of nature, I happened upon Madeleine; she was ferrying a stack of dirty plates towards the kitchen. I stopped before her, caught her eye, privately wondering (not for the first time) how far her duties as a serving maid might go. I was about to speak when she spoke first, taking me rather by surprise.

'I heard your words.'

I smiled, and nodded. 'Words grown prettier in pretty ears,' I said.

'And do you honestly believe that men hold women in such odium?' she asked. 'In such contempt?'

'I—from my experience—'

'For if you do, sir, you are no better than a selfish child, and I can see no hope for you. Or for your friends.' And in the manner of the French she spat upon the floor, a habit both repulsive and, according to all medical authority, decidedly unsanitary.

She was gone before I had the chance to point this out.

Chapter Twenty-eight

Lavenza seemed sunk lower now than ever. I offered him a little cocaine, which he took, although I warned him not to overdo it; it is a drug which may turn upon its master, more so even than the drink. I intended to devote a few days to his welfare, but found myself too caught up in the whirl of Paris life. Besides my medical practice, I was now receiving invitations to a number of quite prominent salons. When I returned home I was often too exhausted to do more than strip my clothes and tumble (usually alone) into my bed.

Another problem, though, began to bother me about the house.

It had begun to smell.

It was hard to be specific, but something—a sour odour—seemed to hit me as I opened the front door. Once inside, it quickly faded, but the sense of something somehow subtly amiss would not depart. I took to opening the windows wide whenever I was home. Even the air of Paris seemed more palatable than the atmosphere within the house.

I naturally suspected Karl. He was officially our manservant, but spent the best part of his time curled up in bed. He was like a cat, it seemed to me; brief moments of activity punctuating day-long naps. We had installed him in a room to the rear of the house, out of sight of visitors. With this he seemed content. It was not a place I chose to frequent, but, at last, I felt it had to be investigated. Steeling myself, I pushed open the door.

Karl lay upon his bed, fully dressed, snoring away. I shook him awake. There was indeed an odour, though the familiar one of unwashed bodies; a smell which I associated now with nothing more than the asylum, as if he had in some way brought a piece of it away with him. I insisted that he draw himself a bath. This seemed a novelty to him, but one which he was willing to pursue.

In his absence, I searched his room, a process much like archaeology. There was debris, and then layers of debris—surely Schliemann had no more profound a task when excavating Troy. My findings were, in general, unsavoury. Clothes do not grow clean, piled in a corner, nor mud and soot spontaneously vacate a carpet. While even the finest French cuisine would grow unsavoury, left for a week or two beneath the bed. . . .

Yet here and there, amid the rubbish and the rotting meals, I noticed other items, little treasures tucked away, which I was sure had not come with us to this spot. Under the pillow—filthy, greying thing—a finger-ring of golden metal, topped by what might have been a diamond—no mean stone, at that. Elsewhere, a brooch, holding a pressed flower; a little porcelain statuette, a nymph against a tree; a set of cheap bangles, of the kind a gypsy-girl might wear; a lovely little fairy-chain, again, in metal that might well have been the gold that it appeared.

I arranged them on his mantelpiece and, spreading a newspaper upon the bed to seat myself, I waited his return.

'And where are these from?'

He was vague, evasive. With his wet hair plastered to his skull, his face an unaccustomed pink in preference to its usual grey, he looked quickly left and right, perhaps hoping an answer might emerge out of the wall.

'Well?'

'Well. . . .' He brightened suddenly. 'Don't know, Master.'

His lips cracked in a nervous and ingratiating smile.

'They just appeared, did they?' I took the ring. 'Let's start with this, shall we? Exactly where did this *appear* from? And how did it end up with you?'

'I—'

'No. Not "I don't know." Try again.'

'I . . . found it, Master?'
'Lying in the gutter, I suppose. Where you'll end up.'
'No, Master! No! It was—it was in a place.'
'Clue, please?'
'Master?'
'Clue. This place. It has a name, I'd guess.'
'Yes, Master.' He looked down at the floor.
'A street? Address?'
Mumble.
'Excuse me? Pardon?'
'Someone . . . people . . .'
'Yes?'
'People give me things.'
His voice was very small.
'You go thieving?'
'No sir! No, I, I, I . . . people are very good to me. People care for me, just like you and the other Master, sir. Everybody's . . . very good here. Very good.'

He nodded firmly, then glanced at me to see if I believed him.

I could torment him no further. Yet I was far from happy with his answers, and had no great desire to feel the wrath of the gendarmerie descend upon our house. I had lost paradise already in my banishment from Heidelberg; I would not lose Paris the same way. So I resolved to keep an eye on Karl, an appendage who, most useful previously, might now have overstayed his worth. I had made a few small contacts in the Paris medical fraternity. I wondered if there might be anyone prepared to take him on, perhaps as a servant, or a mere curiosity. I confess I had somewhat embellished his life's history, making him the elder son of Austrian nobility, disinherited for his idiocy, cruelly dealt with in a home for the inbred, under delusions he had once been coachman to the great-great-grandson of the legendary Dr Frankenstein. . . .

A catch for any well-heeled medical man, I would have thought?

Chapter Twenty-nine

Madame Pluviers lived in the first arrondissement, a little distance from the Place Vendôme. I had at times provided escort for her to the Louvre, or the Tuileries; for sensual pleasure has its higher, as well as lower forms.

Today, though, we would have the lower.

I appreciate directness in a woman. It saves time. And Mme Pluviers was all directness. I had been recommended, she explained, by a certain friend of hers (she was discreet enough to hold back on the name). She explained her husband was a fellow in the oil business, and his work took him away for long months, often to Africa or the Middle East. During his absence she would suffer, she explained, from fits of melancholy, and a pent-up tension which could find no exit in the course of daily life. Those lady-like activities, fit to her station, no longer pleased her. She was restless, disconsolate, her sleeping was disturbed. In short, I hardly had to show my stethoscope to gain an entry to her boudoir, and rather more besides.

Yet ours was not, as I have hinted at above, a purely physical relationship. Mme Pluviers—Rebecca—was a woman of refinement and intelligence. She had an eye for paintings and a taste for the theatre. Moreover, there was much that had been hidden in her life. I was her doctor, and a doctor is a kind of confessor; even to say 'I have a pain in this organ, or that' counts as a revelation of the personal, the troubling—confession of a flaw, a sin of the body no less wicked than those sins of the soul. I soon learned things about her life of which I doubt even the family priest would be aware. For this, I dubbed her, in my own mind, Madame le Plus-vraîs, and it was not always a compliment.

She had been born Jewish, she explained, and married 'out', a matter of great sorrow to her family, whom she had scarcely seen in well over a decade. Her father had disowned her, the Rabbi had attempted to dissuade her from her union. 'I was young and headstrong,' she explained. The matter troubled her to this day. She retained a clandestine contact with her mother, and they wrote letters to each other now and then. Meanwhile, in her married life, her husband passed her off to his associates as having Spanish blood (which was no lie) in order to explain her dark complexion and her curly, jet-black hair. She had never formally converted to the Catholic faith. Her husband had instructed her in all its rituals and formalities. She wondered if she had betrayed herself in this. Not overly concerned about religion in her youth, as she grew older she became less certain of herself and her beliefs. She felt like an impostor. Her small son had a saint's name. He was taught by nuns. Should she tell him of her past? When should she admit to him that history was not as he imagined it? His own, personal history?

She was the woman destined to tell all. In endless detail.

And even she could not escape the fascination with the Ripper.

'He has abandoned streetwalkers. They say he hunts the daughters of the gentry now.'

'Then his motives are quite clear.'

I was a man of Science, after all; she looked to me for explanations.

'He is a creature of the lower caste,' I said. 'A fact which he resents. He aspires to higher station, but unlike you or I, he has no means to grasp what he desires. We may work and strive for what we want. He cannot, or perhaps he will not, take the steps to raise himself. He is frustrated with his lot in life, angry against those he sees as luckier than himself. He covets their wealth. He covets, in particular, their womenfolk. This is a frequent and well-known phenomenon. We find it often in the treatment of mental delusion. A man wants one thing, he cannot have it; he attacks it, or destroys something which in his eyes must represent that tantalising object. As an aside, I believe the preachers one encounters on the street corner, with their fire and brimstone, sin and damnation, are often of this type.'

'Hans!' She wriggled in the bed, just as if she had been tickled. 'So who is the Ripper? Who should the police be looking for?'

'Oh—let me see. They say he has some knowledge of anatomy. A porter at a hospital, perhaps? No. More likely, some crude fellow with a knowledge of the innards of mere beasts. It seems to me that if the police want their man, they could do worse than run a check on everybody at Les Halles. . . .'

'Oh! But that's terrible!' Her body shivered, and her fingers traced their way across my belly. But to tell the truth, I was no more convinced by my own arguments than anybody else's. Quite the opposite, in fact.

'Still,' she said, 'if he resents the upper class, then why . . . ?'

'Did he begin with whores?'

'Yes.'

'Ah. Sweet, innocent Rebecca. That, at least, is plain.' She pressed herself against me, as if the Ripper himself lurked just beyond the quilt, already waiting for her. 'The whores,' I say, 'were practice.'

Was her love-making a little fiercer for our talk? As if to fuck the force of Death into submission?

I quite believe it was.

Chapter Thirty

I began to search Karl's rooms now on a daily basis. Not that I suspected, so much as that I feared, and wanted to alleviate my fear. So I sent him out on errands, meanwhile hunting through his private things. For a man who, not long back, had owned nothing more than he stood up in, his room had become cluttered. A few items were hidden, under the pillow, or tucked beneath the bed—those things that took his fancy, I suppose, for few of them were of much value—but a great deal, equally, was on display. There was jewellery here. Rings and necklaces and earrings, and a ladies' choker, studded with semi-precious stones. I found a pair of long silk gloves. If Karl had taken to the pleasures of women, these did not seem like the kind of gloves such women might have worn.

More disturbing still were items of feminine underclothing. I could well imagine what he used them for, and as a student of medicine, could not condemn the practice; we are born to the flesh, after all, and the flesh has needs and requirements familiar to us all. Yet certain of these items looked to be of silk or satin, and of quality I could not imagine he might actually purchase. Was he stealing? Thieving from laundries? Or was something else involved?

I left his room, strode into the lounge, flung open the window for some fresh air.

'Really,' I said, 'I think it's time we set our goals a little higher, eh?'

Lavenza was in such a brown study he scarcely noticed me. He sprawled upon the sofa, one leg propped up on the armrest. His eyelids flickered. It was the fiercest animation he could muster.

'You should be opening a clinic. Never mind the odd few patients here and there. A clinic is a steady income. Not an asylum. Only the desperate need an asylum. But a clinic—a fashionable clinic. I know a little of society, sir. The world is full of rich neurotics, for only the rich have time and leisure to support neurosis. They beg, sir, they beg to be divided from their wealth! And then, remember your research! Why are you not assailing the peaks of your profession, man? Why are you not lecturing at the Sorbonne? Mounting an exhibition of your work?' I eyed him steadily. 'If you cannot duplicate your innovation, then it's a poor show indeed. But if you can—and I believe you can, sir!—then I can think of any number of potential backers. We'd raise the money for the thing in no time. Damn it, man! Remember your research!'

'Research?' he said. And nothing more.

What was wrong with him? It was like talking to a block of wood.

'Another matter. Our fellow, Karl. Has he been abroad much recently? Especially at night? I'm here so seldom now I find it hard to keep a track of things.'

Lavenza looked at me. His lips opened as if he were about to speak, then thought better of it.

I walked around the room, deliberately exaggerating my footfalls in the hope of catching his attention. Soon I was almost stamping.

'Karl,' I said again. 'He worries me.'

This time he did speak. 'Karl?' he said. 'What's happened to him? Is he alright?'

'Oh, he's alright. I was just curious. His activities. At night . . . ?'

'He goes out at night?'

'I don't know.'

'Ah.'

Lavenza seemed to draw back inside himself. I continued with more forceful tones.

'He has some items in his possession. Items of feminine apparel. He says somebody gave them to him.'

Lavenza scarcely changed position, yet I felt him stiffen all at once. Then he looked at me directly, and his tone was irritable.

'If he says somebody gave them to him, then they did. Whatever else he may be he is not a liar.' He looked up at the ceiling, as if in imprecation. 'Now for God's sake, leave me, will you? Can't you see I'm trying to think?'

Chapter Thirty-one

'The Ripper, dear Paulette, is nothing but a fiction, an invention of the newspapers, too silly for your wise and very pretty little head. You should pay no heed to such horrors. I was suggesting you stay home at night merely to . . . avoid the general unpleasantness of city life.'

I ran my tongue over her lower lip, tasting its saltiness. My medical examination was proceeding at its usual pace; I had quickly learned her preferences, filing them away in that part of the brain reserved for such. (Pleasing a woman is a vital art—it's the only way to get invited back.)

'There is always some hysteria that accompanies these panics. Best to stay away until it's done. Promise me that, hm? You promise me?'

She purred. I moved a little lower, pressed my lips against her throat. My fingers traced the folds between her legs, light as a feather. She wriggled under me.

'Journalists need to sell papers, police need to solve crimes—or appear to solve them, anyway.' I caught her nipple gently in my teeth, then let it go. 'Their salary, their offices, their jobs—'

'Don't stop,' she said.

'This Ripper,' I went on, 'is altogether too convenient, and when things are too convenient, they're seldom true. Do you know anyone—anyone at all—who's fallen victim to him? Personally? Anyone who even knows anyone? Of course not! And for good reason, as well.'

'Go on, go on,' she said.

Frankenstein's Prescription

'What we have here is rumour. Chinese whispers. A good, dark, scary story. The police won't catch the Ripper—they may claim to, of course, but that's another matter. There is no threat to the womanhood of Paris. There is no—'

'Hans,' she said, 'when I asked you to go on, I didn't mean for you to waste your breath in talk. Now will you please shut up and do what you came here to do?'

So my examination went ahead, and very sweet it was. She quickly caught the rhythm, bucked and thrust against me. Her breath was thrilling in my ear. All went well, in fact, until, seeing the time was going on, I began to move towards my own climax. I drove and pumped for all that I was worth. The sweat came dripping from my brow. And then, just as it seemed I was about to spend, something stopped me, and I froze in place.

It seemed an age before I heard her voice again.

'Hans . . . ?'

I stared around the room. But we were quite alone.

'Hans? Is something wrong?'

I rolled off her. I lay upon my back, staring at the ceiling. My heart thumped, but no more with passion; now with something far, far less congenial.

I muttered my excuses, reached out for my clothes, dressed hurriedly. She could do no more than follow my example, dressing likewise, following me helplessly towards the door. As I was about to leave, she whispered to me urgently.

'What is it? Don't I please you any more? Are you bored with me?'

I shook my head, I mumbled more apologies. My hat was in my hand. I fought the impulse to turn tail and run.

She straightened my lapels, brushed some flecks of dirt away. 'I can do anything you want. Would you like me to dress up in some way? Or have one of the servants join us? Would you like that?'

I was unable to reply.

'We could—we could—' She used words she was clearly unaccustomed to pronouncing. Her lovely cheeks pinked as she uttered them. On other days, I might have been delighted by the sentiments, but now, I hardly heard. I did my best to reassure her. But I could never tell the truth: that for a fraction of a second, as my balls prepared to empty, I had observed a figure standing at the bedside, its face contorted in a look that might have been contempt or hatred, or even some sardonic pleasure; and a dark patch on his shirt that might, it seemed to me, have been spilled blood.

That figure had been known to me.

Its name was Grundig.

Chapter Thirty-two

Perhaps it was the drink. Or the cocaine. Or the ether in which I occasionally indulged. Was I hallucinating? I had kept a hectic pace over the last few weeks—more so here than at Heidelberg, for now I was a respected doctor, and had to live the part. Moreover, I had money to indulge myself. And opportunity, oh yes.

On my way home, I called in at a bar to calm my nerves. I told myself that I could not, truly, have seen him. To think otherwise would be irrational, unscientific. Was it, then, merely a pang of conscience, or some freak firing of nerves inside the brain, caused by the rigours of Paulette's athletic love-making?

Behind the bar there was a mirror. I leaned upon the countertop, watching the people come and go, until, despite my better judgement, I became convinced that Grundig was about to walk into the room. The idea, the very picture of it, grew in my head, became obsessive, all-consuming. Any moment now he would appear. And I'd give him a piece of my mind. I'd ask him what the hell—yes, what the *hell*—he was doing, bothering me, when he should be quietly tucked up in his native soil, dead and gone, like any normal corpse. I planned my speech in detail, I murmured it under my breath (attracting not a little interest from the barman and the other patrons). Only when I caught sight of my own face, watching from the far side of the glass, did I realise how absurd the whole thing was.

I stood up, swayed a little, threw some coins upon the bar, and made a hasty exit. Once out, I glanced back, to check the place's name. Here was one Parisian drinking hole I should be careful to avoid in future.

Chapter Thirty-three

Karl had given me no notice he was going out. I had specifically requested that he do so; but he had not. Only the soft click of the door alerted me. So I rose also, silent as a hunter, and I followed.

A hint of fog clung round the gas lamps. I hugged the shadows, stepping quickly, one to the next. I was still fit, athletic; the drink and the cocaine might tell upon my mind, but not, as yet, my body. I was not afraid. I felt myself a match for any ruffian I might meet on the Paris streets—and certainly for little Karl. But was he armed? The papers spoke of lacerations, amputations, which must mean a blade. I had never known him use a knife, or even carry one. And yet with Karl, what could one guarantee? Like Lavenza, he was death-obsessed. Who could guess what he was up to?

I tracked him, it seemed, half way across the city. Karl, Karl, where are you going? More than once, I was tempted to give up; the lights and laughter from a bar or restaurant, the scent of meats and savouries . . . lures which I for once resisted. Briefly I lost him, his little, rat-like form scuttling ahead of me; but then I saw him once again, and still he had not thought to look back and catch sight of me.

So we came, at last, to possibly the last place I might have expected.

It was a church. One of those thin, stern, backstreet churches, a church as narrow and forbidding as a black-clad priest. And as I watched, he tugged open the door, and slipped inside.

I hesitated for a moment. Waited in a doorway, listening. And then I followed.

Frankenstein's Prescription

A soft light filtered through the windows. For a moment, I was blind; and then I saw him, squatting like a crab there in the aisle. He pulled out something from his pockets, but it was not a knife. I watched. I saw the way he crept up to the walls, then stretched his arms out—

It was string he held. Nothing but string. It seemed that he was measuring the floor—laying a length, swinging it round, moving a few more yards. . . .

I stepped out of the darkness.

'Hello, Karl,' I said.

He showed no surprise. Perhaps, when you believe that you have slept for centuries and everyone you meet is dead, it may be that the world has lost its power to shock. At any rate, he simply glanced up, his face a smudge upon the dark, and nodded. 'Master,' he acknowledged, and continued with his work.

'Most people,' I remarked, 'would come to church to pray. You seem to have a different aim.'

He said nothing.

'This is some mission of Lavenza's, I presume? His new interest in resonance and sound, that kind of thing?'

Karl still said nothing.

'Is this why you go out at night, Karl?'

'Sometimes, Master.'

'No other reason?'

He said nothing.

'I'm interested. Those items in your room. Do you find those at night, as well?'

Silence. He hunched over his labours.

There was a large, heavy-looking candlestick within an alcove near the door. I took a step towards it, let my right hand fall, as if by chance, upon its base.

'Karl,' I said, 'have you ever killed anyone?'

He looked up then. He put his head on one side. 'Killed, Master?'

'Killed. You know. Murdered. Butchered. Strangled, possibly. Burnt. Knifed. Bludgeoned. Shot. All that sort of thing.'

'Don't think so, Master.'

'Even by accident?'

He shook his head. It seemed to wobble, as if loose upon his shoulders.

'Would it worry you, do you think? If you had?'

'Don't know, Master.'

He bent to his work, crawling down the paving slabs, his legs splayed out, a frog, a spider in the dark.

I said, 'It worries me.'

He had finished his first set of measurements. He scuttled round to measure width-wise, too.

I said, 'I thought that nothing bothered me. Nothing except ugliness and poverty, and lack of opportunity. But now that I am freed of such encumbrance, it seems that something does concern me, after all.' I looked around; the dim shapes in the windows, the statues on the walls. 'I'm not a saint, Karl. I've no wish to be a saint. I don't want to repent and live a godly life. But then again . . . let's say I have regrets. Regrets, that's all.'

He cast me a glance. He looked puzzled, from what I could make out, and put his head down, as if my words embarrassed him.

'It's for Lavenza that you're doing this?'

'Yes, yes. The Master. And the other Master, too.'

'The other Master?'

'Yes. The big Master.'

The big Master? Did he mean God?

'You measure churches . . . ?'

'It's the sound. It's like you say.' He paused, looked up, bright now, pleased that he had something to explain to me. 'He wants a sound. It's in the measurements, in the . . .' He fumbled for the word.

'Acoustics?'

He nodded. I said, 'And this is what the big Master wants, too?'

'I—I think so. Mustn't talk. No. Mustn't talk.'

'Karl. You must talk. I'm your Master also, you recall? So you must talk to me. Tell me. Tell me about the big Master.'

I had it clear inside my mind: the pieces fell in place with a dramatic suddenness. I knew that some of the insane suffered from voices in the head; sometimes mere commentary, sometimes great commands that seemed to have the force of God behind them. Such voices had told Joan of Arc to drive the English out of France. What then had they told Karl?

He put his head down, almost shyly.

'Come, Karl. You can talk to me.'

'He . . . he brings me things.'

'What kind of things?'

He turned his back, pretending still to work, although he wasn't.

'Those things in your room?'

He grunted.

'Women's things,' I said. With one hand, I clasped the stem of the candlestick. 'Karl. Look at me now, Karl.'

Reluctantly, he turned.

'Stay where you are.' The metal was cold in my grip. The touch of it seemed to anchor me, and gave me the illusion of control. 'I must ask you something, Karl, and I want you to answer truthfully. Alright?'

'I think so, Master.'

'Good. Now, Karl. Listen carefully.' I took a breath. 'Are you the Ripper?'

He said nothing. I said, 'Do you understand the question?'

'Yes, Master.'

'Alright. Now, once and for all: are you the Ripper?'

'Oh, Master—'

'Have you been killing women?'

'No! No *no* no, Master!'

'Did you kill those women, Karl?'

'No Master, no! I wouldn't, I couldn't, it's not me, it's not, I can't—'

'I think you did.'

'I love women. I love them just as you do, Master, though—at greater distance. I could never, never—'

'Those items in your room.'

Silence.

'How did you come by them?'

He put his head down.

'The truth, this time.'

'Gifts. . . .'

'From whom?'

Nothing.

'From whom? A name, anything, tell me, for Christ's own sake. Come on!'

'Big Master,' he whispered. It was barely audible. 'Big Master.'

'You're telling me you didn't kill the women. I must assume you know who did.'

Chapter Thirty-Four

I was a fool. I might have cursed myself, had I cared to take the blame for anything, which in those days I did not. For while I drank, dined and caroused, and made what seemed to me most vital inroads in Parisian life; while I imagined that Lavenza languished, and Karl followed an even more unsavoury pursuit—rather, they conspired. They worked. They sought to make Lavenza's masterpiece. And they said nothing to me. Nothing.

I confronted them now, these conspirators, here, in the lounge of our home, this house which was still paid for in the greater part by my own labours.

'Am I not trusted? Am I not, then, your companion? Your partner? Your friend?'

They glanced at one another. Then, a little warily, towards the fourth man in the room, who lay there, sprawled across the couch, and who had uttered, so far, not one single word.

The silence wrapped around us like a tourniquet.

*

'The papers are still proffering their lurid tales,' I had remarked, but days ago. 'Some poor girl trips and bumps her head—and lo! The Ripper strikes again! Can we give credit to such nonsense? Can we begin to think of it, without a laugh?'

*

It was not a person.

This fourth man in the room with us.

Oh, it moved like a person. Spoke like a person. Even looked like one, after a fashion, though a person of a strange and frightening demeanour. Yet every sense I had, every instinct told me it was something else, that neither thought nor felt nor functioned as did I or any other member of the human race.

Simply to look at it appalled me, though I could scarcely stop myself.

Most of all, I dreaded that it might look back.

◆

'This Ripper, gentleman—this fine, fine nonsense. A stew of lies and rumours, served up for the evening edition. I ask you: how can we, sophisticated fellows that we are, believe such idiotic maunderings? Are we not men of the world? Are we not, indeed, the cream of Paris?'

A good natured chuckle ran around the club, and a little scatter of self-satisfied applause.

I had done it. I had made my speeches. I had sought to reassure, divert attention, knowing that the impact might be tiny, almost ineffectual; but knowing, too, that I was being loyal, striving to deflect an anger that I feared might be directed against Karl—whom I, too, half-way suspected as the killer. The whole thing was so jumbled in my head. Was it sane, this way of thinking? To elevate companionship so highly over justice?

Yet it was virtue of a kind. It was loyalty, and hope that I could somehow find a way out of the maze for both myself and my companions. A virtue, yes. Or close as I could get to one.

But Karl was not the killer. That fact had now made itself quite clear to me, and with a visceral intensity Lavenza's grisly tales could never have prepared me for.

He was big, most certainly. I had been told that he was big. (I use the convention of the male pronoun, for the creature was distinctly male, though I was disinclined to dignify it with a term so human—so *humane*, perhaps.) Yet he was no larger, on the whole, than the biggest of the porters at Les Halles. What distinguished him—I thought about this often in the coming weeks—was a kind of density, a solidity, as if he had been carved of stone rather than flesh. He wore an outsize coat of military cut, like an army greatcoat, with brass buttons and shoulder-straps; beneath it, a blouse of dark material. He wore coarse, peasants' trousers, patched with leather at the knees. His hands were placed upon his thighs, palms upwards, in a curiously formal pose, like a statue of the Buddha. The hands were disproportionately large, the nails long and horny. The middle finger of the left hand was half gone, a wagging stump.

Beside him on the sofa was a battered, khaki-coloured knapsack.

It was easier to watch his clothes, his hands, his baggage, than to look him in the face.

He was aware. He said little, but he was aware of us, aware with an appalling intimacy, so it seemed to me. As if nothing could be hidden. He saw the way Lavenza twitched and shuffled, and Karl crouched in the corner, hoping to be overlooked. While as for me—I was too near to him. My friends, perhaps unconsciously, had left me nearest him. I felt like the protagonist in a Roman arena; and even though a heavy oak table lay between us, I was sure that if he chose he might just reach across and seize me in one single, giant hand.

'Ah yes,' Lavenza said, steepling his fingers nervously. 'Yes, ah . . . um.'

'Yes? Yes what?'

I faced him, deeming him the easier to challenge.

'I—we would have told you. You were busy. And, um, not....' His face made queer shapes, as if he wanted to communicate without the creature knowing. 'Please, Hans. You were so supportive. Just bear with me. Until . . . ah.' His eyes flicked back and forth. 'Until we . . . have more time to talk.'

I was so desperate now to hide the fear I felt that it burst forth as anger, indignation—hurt.

'I wasn't worthy to be told? I, who pay your bills, who offer funds, who—I, who have worked so hard to make a place for us within society?'

'Hans, please—'

The figure on the couch remained there, but it cocked its massive head, attentive to the change in tone.

'Or is the great seeker of knowledge, Herr Doctor Lavenza, no longer so indifferent to the calls of glory? A glory he declines to share?'

Lavenza made small, fluttering gestures with his hands, trying to shut me up.

'So much for high intentions,' I mocked. 'So much for—'

There came a sound like a gunshot. I ducked. I spun around, half terrified.

The creature on the couch had clapped his hands.

He brought his arms down slowly, placed his huge fists on his knees. It was the first time I had brought myself to look directly at him for any period, and I recalled Lavenza's tale: the bogeyman, he'd called him. This was no bogeyman, no child's dream. The head was like the head of some enormous heathen idol, a great, misshapen mass; it bulged out in great lobes of bone, covered by a thinning fuzz of darkish hair. On one side of the face was scarring, and I think the cheekbone had been partially exposed; the flesh was puckered here and rubbery to look upon. The brow, as I recall, was marked by heavy creases, as if his skin no longer fitted him.

As he raised his head, I saw the muscles shift within his face, and his gaze went from Lavenza to myself, and back again.

'Their eyes were opened, and they knew that they were naked.'

The thin lips barely moved. The voice was low, surprisingly soft. I held my breath. I felt as you might feel in the presence of a rabid dog, that even the most gentle movement might enrage it, provoke it to rip out your throat.

Instead, the creature tugged open its knapsack, pulled out a parcel wrapped in brocade cloth, and placed it, with extraordinary tenderness, upon the tabletop.

'Here,' he said, fixing Lavenza. 'This is my choice.' He rose to his feet—there was a strange grace to him, a fluidity at odds with both his size and brutish looks. Lavenza and I quickly shuffled backwards as he strode towards the door. But he paid us no more heed. He was gone into the hall; a blast of cold air swept around us as the front door opened, then shut, almost silently. I moved to the window, saw his shadow pass—and he was gone.

Lavenza fretted. He moved first for the brandy, then restrained himself. His chest lifted and fell as if upon the verge of panic. He was muttering under his breath. I had never taken him for a religious man; remarkably, it seemed to me he was reciting prayers.

He unwrapped the creature's parcel. In the square of brocade, its edge ripped through by some inhuman strength, lay two small, delicate items, so pale as to be almost white.

I have always loved a woman's hands—they speak almost as eloquently as her face, and, notwithstanding all the nonsense of the fortune tellers, I believe that in the hands you can read character, just as in the eyes. And these were lovely specimens, the fingers long and slim, the nails filed to exquisite almond-shapes and painted to the colour of pearls; each knuckle with its delicate, delightful whorl of skin, the faint hint of veins, the knob of wristbone. . . .

There was no more. Only a slicing through the meat, a severing of the arm's twin bones.

Frankenstein's Prescription

While watching surgery, I have faced many dreadful things and never flinched. But now my stomach rose up in rebellion, as if trying to deny the vision of my eyes, and I ran out of the room, scattering my half-digested dinner as I went.

Chapter Thirty-five

I did not sleep.

I lay upon my bed, my thoughts caught in a whirligig of motion; yet they offered me no sense, no purpose, no course of action I might sensibly pursue. Night thoughts are seldom valid in the morning, and I knew this, yet possessed no means with which to shut them out.

In time the dawn rose, bleak and grey, and I rose with it. Some panic made me leave my bed and dress, as if I might at any moment have to flee the house, the city. Yet, having got so far, and having made myself a pipe in hope of calming my too-agitated nerves, I found that I did nothing, merely sat, and brooded.

Once more, it seemed that death had come intruding in my life, upsetting my arrangements, making misery where I believed I had acquired a paradise.

This, I resented. This, I would have fought, had I known how.

Mid-morning, a boy called with a letter for me. I opened it mechanically. The letter was from Mme Pluviers, demanding to know where I was, why I had missed our early-morning consultation (I had noticed she was always hungriest for sex during the first hours of the day; some matter of the hormone cycle, possibly?). She begged me to send word, if I could not send myself. If I were ill, she said, she might spare a servant to look after me.

Ill I might have been, but with a sickness that no servant could alleviate—nor even the charms of Mme Pluviers herself.

I tipped the boy, bade him inform her that I suffered from a mild distemper, nothing that required her intervention; but that I would not have her catch an illness from her doctor, of all people!

I would be in touch soon, I said, and greatly regretted missing our appointment.

The boy turned, but I called him back, tipped him a few more centimes.

'Tell her,' I said, 'if you would—tell her I looked ill.'

'Wouldn't be a lie,' the boy said, cheerily. 'You look like death warmed up, sir.'

'Thanks.'

I shut the door. Lavenza had come down the stairs and he was watching me.

'Hans,' he said.

'Hans? Not *Schneider*, now, then?'

'We should speak.'

'It seems to me we should have spoken some time previously, before all this began. Before you made me party to this—this massacre.'

'None of it was my choice. God knows, I wouldn't . . . but you've seen him now! You've seen what he's like. What he's done—it means nothing to him. *We* mean nothing to him, none of us, except in how he plans to use us. That's how he is. My family has been in thrall to him for more than a century. This is our life, for God's sake—born into servitude to, to *that*—'

His hand fell on my shoulder, but I shook him off.

'Enough.'

'If you'd but listen to me, give me the option to explain.'

'He's killing women.'

'Well. Yes. But in his view, that's merely a . . . by-product of what he really wants to do. It's a side-effect. Unfortunate, perhaps, but . . . it means no more to him than you shooting a wood pigeon. I have reason to believe, good reason, if I can do the things he asks, he may leave us alone. He says he'll go away somewhere. To some Pacific island, possibly. . . . My family will be free of him. The world will be free. I can go on to lead a normal life, to further my research or—better yet. To give it up, get married, live as you do, or as any normal man. You can't begin to grasp what all this means. You can't imagine—'

'And what it means to those who die for him? To their families, their mothers and their fathers, their husbands?' I turned from him, I raised my fists as if in invocation. 'And to think, I actually suspected Karl! In all this sorry business, I thought—'

'Karl wouldn't harm a fly.'

'No.'

'You had me worried for a time. I feared you might report him, yet you didn't. Why?'

'Why do we speak of Karl? He's not the guilty one.'

'Yet you believed he was. And you did nothing.'

'Untrue! I searched his room, I followed him, I was making an investigation of his movements—'

'You suspected, but you had to find the truth out for yourself, to deal with matters on your own, without access to the law. In other words, you had to save his life. Yes?'

I remembered he had once used practically the same words of his patient, the so-called Beast of Bremen. I wondered then what such a life was worth, coming with so high a price. But I hid my doubt in a display of indignation.

'You suggest that I would stand by, doing nothing, while helpless womenfolk are massacred and chopped like butcher's meat? You think I would allow—'

'I think you are a man of science.'

I shook my head. 'Oh no. Oh no no no.'

'I think you are. You are also a man who has, I believe—and like myself—known little in the way of friendship. Oh, companionship, most certainly—we're different fellows there, alright. But friendship, that's a rarer thing. And I believe, because you know its rarity, you are a man who values loyalty in friends. And gives it in return.'

Loyalty! That tainted word!

'I know no loyalty. I don't want loyalty. I want to be away from here, from this house, from this stink, from—'

'Listen. Listen. Hear me out.'

He sat down, beckoned me to sit across from him. Reluctantly, I did.

'This creature—I have grown to know him somewhat, through the years. In his own view he is not immoral. Far from it. He was born into a world never intended to receive him. His own creator —my ancestor—fled from him, repenting his creation. I spoke of loyalty. This creature has no loyalty to us; it shares our flesh, our form, but it no more resembles us than does a lion or a tiger. It feels no sympathy. We are the dust from which it was first made, and nothing more. I've spoken to him. He doesn't question things as we do, doesn't feel as we do. There are certain ways in which he's like a child, whole areas of sensibility of which he has no slightest comprehension, not even an awareness, while in others, his perceptions are acute. The miracle—the real, true miracle—is that we've kept the murders to so few. He does not kill for sport, at any rate.'

'The woman at the asylum.'

'Yes. As I said: not for sport, but as a message to me. A reminder.'

'Is it only women that he kills? Is there resentment? Some fixation?'

'No. He kills whomsoever he likes. I know that all too well. And yet . . . the women. My ancestor, you see—he promised him a mate. Promised him, and then denied him. Cut him off from Eden. He came to me. We made . . . a bargain.'

'When was this?'

'Soon after we arrived. He has a way of . . . tracking people. Perhaps by smell. I don't know.'

'And you—' But I turned away. 'Oh, this is hideous! That package last night! And all of this, all of this—'

'He insisted on fresh organs. He insisted he would pick them for himself. I didn't tell you, Hans, because I knew—well, I had a feeling you'd react this way.'

'And so I have! Is it any wonder! This is horrible, this is—unbearable. I can't stomach it.'

'Ah.' He fidgeted. He turned his toes in. 'Well . . . there's rather more to it, as well. As things turn out, in fact.'

I looked at him.

'Monsieur Baldin—the patient you so kindly arranged for me. You know his tastes.'

Baldin—the cross-dressing old masochist. What part had he in this?

Lavenza picked his nails while he spoke, and looked uncomfortable.

'He has, as a result of his, um, interests, come into association with the local gendarmerie. I believe he funds their bicycle racing team or something of that kind. In return, they overlook a few . . . matters of possible embarrassment to him. Well, it seems. . . .'

'Must I wait all day for this?'

'It seems he has made friends among their ranks, as a result. What you need to know, Hans . . . ah. Think back, now. Think back to the day we met. What a day it was! Frau Fleischer, perhaps one of my greatest triumphs—I like to do good when I can. When my nemesis permits. And you remember your trunks? And how distressed you were?'

'How could I not?'

'Yes. The creature has been excising the organs of his victims. He has been using medical equipment—a fact quite readily ascertained from the nature of the incisions. A good set of knives, a bone saw . . . Your knives, in fact. Your saw. Do you see the implications here . . . ?'

I thought for a moment. My head was in a whirl, and still immune to logic.

'That can't be proved. And it means nothing, either way. What are you trying to do? What are you suggesting?'

'Surgical blades are delicate, and must be used with care, as you well know. It seems that one broke off, snapped against the ribs. Think for a moment, please.'

I did. They were fine quality blades—the very best. Only the most amateurish, brutish use might cause them to give way like that. I had bought them in the week that I arrived in Heidelberg, determined everything about my life should speak of excellence, whether my clothes, my manner, or my tools. Other students sought to purchase instruments at second hand, or used inferior makes, assuming they would pick up something better as they climbed in their profession. But I knew the importance of a first impression, and my instruments were of the best, and on each one my initials were engraved, making them personal, making them—

'No need to worry. Or not yet, at least.' Lavenza raised a calming hand. 'We have time. Plenty of time. The police,' and for a man without a sense of humour, he seemed dangerously close to laughing then, 'the police believe this is the work of an English seaman, perhaps a ship's surgeon, newly arrived. Hence the sudden spate of such unprecedented killings. Plus, they have the evidence of the blade. With its initials, I believe, quite beautifully engraved.'

Initials. I cast about a moment, helpless, only convinced I would be framed for murder, for the acts of this inhuman creature. Then it dawned on me.

Hans Mitton Schneider.

Had the tale been about anybody other than myself, I too might have laughed.

Chapter Thirty-six

And so we went down to the cellar, and I viewed his work. This dreadful blasphemy. This horror. No longer did I gasp with awe over Lavenza's gifts, his mechanisms and discoveries; rather, something twisted in my guts, to think of them. The desecration of corpses was a minor matter, after all; the slaughtering of women, quite different.

Yet I felt better once I saw the specimen—the body, to speak plain. It may sound strange, but this was science, and Lavenza had been right—I *was* a man of science; and in science, I still felt at home. Once more, and almost instantly, I found myself enclosed within the cold and distant world of surgery. Nothing was personal. This object—not a living, thinking human being, but mere parts, wires and levers, tubes and pumps, glands and bones and soft tissues. I even found a thrill begin to well in me again, much as it had when I surveyed Lavenza's workshop back at M——. Here, then, was the great adventure. The great voyage of discovery to which all human history—my history, at any rate—had led.

Still Grundig hovered at my shoulder, watching me. Once or twice I glanced around, trying to catch him, but he always seemed to move beyond my sight; a flicker or a shadow in the corner of the eye. After a time, I made excuses, went upstairs and took a small pinch of cocaine, which seemed to banish him efficiently. Then I went back to the cellar.

'No-one dies,' Lavenza said. 'I know this now. Nothing is lost, only changed. Life is a vibration, a pulsing in the ether. These women will all live again, no doubt of that.'

I sniffed excitedly. In this state, I came close to believing him.

'This is a problem to be solved, Hans, not a crime. Not—what did you call it? Not a massacre. More the reverse. Indeed, an anti-massacre.'

'Like on a chair,' said Karl.

'This is my goal for all mankind: to reverse the cruelties inflicted by blind fate, and an uncaring God! Whatever sins, whatever wars and terrors and brutalities, the day will come when, with a turn of a dial, a flick of a switch, all sickness will be healed, all losses won; when mourning will be just a prelude before birth. I can feel it, Hans! I can almost—here, here. See her. The first. The new Eve. See.'

Skin soft as dust, its tones as varied as the music of an orchestra. The shoulders lightly freckled, breasts and hands together of an equal whiteness; the belly darker; legs long and golden, feet almost Nubian in shade.

No head. No head, but from the neck bristled a hundred tiny tubes, a forest made of straws, breathing the chilly air. . . . A metal muscle pumping slowly on the chest, opening, closing the ribs. A whiff of vapour every time, as if she were a factory, a chimney letting loose the by-products of some mysterious, unfathomable industry. . . .

'This is—' I said.

'I don't like how it's come about,' Lavenza said, glancing round as if he feared spies in every corner. 'I'll tell you now—it was hardly short of blackmail. I was forced. Yes—forced. Yet the result—this is the thing we dreamed about—the thing I've dreamed of all my life. I believe that even now, I stand upon the very threshold of my dream, the brink of an unprecedented triumph—'

'This,' I said. My heart was pounding in my ears, it almost deafened me.

Lavenza beamed. His eyes glittered and shone.

'Is,' I said.

'The Abbot's papers helped. Nobody dies, Hans. No-one dies. I am the resurrection. I am the resurrection and the life.'

'This is.'

I toppled sideways. Karl moved to catch me and I crumpled onto him, and the two of us dropped in a heap. The room seemed to be very far away. Lavenza running, only backwards, and without moving his limbs. Perhaps he wasn't wired up properly. I shouted to him, but already, he was too far off to hear. The walls were moving with him. Likewise Karl, at an extraordinary distance, yet he managed to stretch out to me. His face became unreasonably large. He was closer now, and closer. His mouth fell open and I noticed each one of his brown, eroded teeth, looking like rows of withered capstans on the Hamburg docks. I grew convinced that he was trying to bite me. I put my hand up, flapped my fingers at him. 'No, no,' I said. He was like a large dog, worrying at my face. He barked. He drooled. He filled my vision. . . .

His hands were round my throat. I wriggled, trying to shake him off. He ripped away my collar.

His mouth came open, dark and stinking.

And swallowed me down whole.

Chapter Thirty-seven

I was in my bed. I did not recall retiring there. I still had on my underwear, and my waistcoat. Also my shoes. This seemed odd: surely it was easier to take my shoes off first, before my trousers? There was some appointment that I had to keep. I called out, 'Karl! Karl!' but my voice made scarcely any sound. I struggled to get up; no sooner had I done so than I sensed the room extinguishing itself, like a gas flame being turned down.

I had the good sense to fall backwards, onto the bed, or else I might have brained myself.

⁂

'Now look,' said Grundig. 'Hear me out. You are entirely typical of your class and kind. Bourgeois intelligentsia, so-called. Better known as parasites. Jews, free-thinkers, internationalists. Parasites all.'

He strutted back and forth about the room. His arms went up and down, a rapid, jerky motion like a child's wind-up toy. He didn't look at me.

'I'm not—' I said.

'Your kind—privileged, of course. You think the world owes you a living. And what was your grandfather? Your great-grandfather?'

'I—'

'Some tinker, mending pots for pfennigs, I'll be bound. Toiling on another's land. Some peasant, some lout, some unwashed dunghill of a man—'

As he spoke, his hands flashed back and forth across his face, like something in a kinematograph. His movements and his talk seemed quite at odds. And he did not regard me; his blue eyes seemed quite absent, focused elsewhere.

Then I remembered he was dead. So this was how the dead were, I thought, suddenly curious; the mismatch between sound and image made a certain kind of sense, a logic, like the separation of the soul and body. I wanted to ask questions, but of course, he was too bound up in his own affairs to hear.

'The blood of warriors flows in my veins,' he said. 'The blood of Prussian fighting men. We shall raise our country up again. We shall throw out the despoilers, restore our land to honour and to greatness, a place where men can once more hold their heads up high, where women—'

'Ah. I thought we'd get to that.'

He showed no sign of hearing me.

'—women will be freed of their defilers, those Lucifers who ride upon their backs—'

'If you believe that's what we do,' I said, 'You should have paid attention in Anatomy.'

Only now he turned to me. His arms ceased movement; still a little, intermittent tremor in the shoulders shook him.

'You exploited her.' His voice was low and hard. 'You used her for her money. You took her gifts. You wooed her, only to extort her riches, and, when they were gone, encouraged her to steal from her father, from her siblings, all to provide you with the cash you spent on drink and women of the street.'

'Well, put like that, it sounds excessive, I agree, but it must be said, the family had plenty. And she was well rewarded. No question there.'

'You ruined her! You damned her, you scarred her reputation to the point where—'

'No, it would have all been well if she'd just kept her peace. Instead of boasting of it every chance she got. Those little girl-girl talks, those little confidences. That's where her reputation went.'

'No boast, you blackguard, but a cry for help.'

'Ha!' I laughed. 'This thing between my legs was once the most desired instrument in all of Heidelberg. Among the womenfolk at least. They longed for it, more than they longed for ballgowns, milliners' confections, fine silk gloves. . . .'

I put my hand upon my crotch, aiming to display the implement in all its glory, but it was gone! My groin was smooth as a doll's! I felt about the sheets, as if I had mislaid the thing. Grundig watched me with a sneaking pleasure.

'Dear, dear! The soldier is without his sword! Where I, you see, am fully armed! Look at me! Look at me now!'

But already, his voice had dropped an octave, and slowed down to a creeping growl; and when I looked at him, he was no longer Grundig, but the monster of last night, the bogeyman sprung from Lavenza's childhood, with his blunt, misshapen head, a dark coat folded round his massive form.

'Understand,' he said, 'the dead are always stronger. We cannot be fought. Our ranks grow every day. You cannot conquer us. Your science and your mumbo-jumbo are as nothing; the mere progression of the hours brings every one of you nearer to joining us, with every beating of your flimsy, fragile hearts. You will become as we are. You will swell our numbers. You will look upon the living with contempt, with greed—with envy. Come that day, you will—'

I screamed. An awful, strangled scream. My voice had been returned to me, but twisted, broken. There were footsteps on the stairs. The door swung wide. I was in bed, and thin light filtered through the heavy curtains. Karl and Lavenza hunched above me. Lavenza touched my brow; he pulled my eyelid down, clicking his tongue. He looked into my mouth. He took my pulse.

'Dear chap,' he said. 'You have been overdoing it a bit, now haven't you?'

Chapter Thirty-eight

Lost. No other word for it. Lost. My father urged me to attend a church. But did he love me? Did he care for me? Would he know me on the street, if we should pass each other, years from now?

Lavenza hunched up at my bedside, spooning soup into my mouth. It was awful, greasy stuff. It dribbled down my chin. I tried to push him off. He made me take another sip, and then another. 'Swallow,' he insisted, and, 'Very good,' as if I were a child. Yet had my father sat like this, tending my needs through childhood illness? Had he too fed me soup that likewise dribbled down my chin?

It was a year since I had last set eyes on him, yet still he towered over me, a force I fled in vain; the rebuker of my sins, bestower of both cash and judgements, always busy, always strong; and when I pictured him, I saw him with his back half-turned, a scowl on his half-hidden face. My father. . . .

Rich man, church man, landowner, industrialist.

My father. . . .

Never loved me.

Oh, he clothed me, gave me shelter, sent me to the finest schools. . . . But love? Love? Not as I wanted to be loved, not as a father ought to love. I saw it now, and saw it with the black-pit misery of illness; saw too, the way my whole life since had been a bid to gain approval, if no longer from him, from others of a very different stamp: my friends, my women, any casual acquaintance who for some reason or other took my fancy; when all I really wanted, all I would have asked, was just a simple smile from dear old Dad. . . .

Frankenstein's Prescription

The tears began to trickle down my face. Lavenza dabbed at them. He clucked and muttered, flustered with embarrassment; and presently, the meal complete, he made some vague, kindly remarks, and left me to my gloom.

My father was a distant, lonely man. Today, he would be seen as hurt, emotionally injured in some way; there are whole schools of medicine devoted to such ills, as if they were mere broken bones or 'flu symptoms. And yet to me, he was a tyrant, whose demands I neither met nor understood. I was a late child, hailed as one to brighten up his middle age. But nothing I could do would please him. We were different creatures, different species, almost. He thought in numbers: balance sheets and units of production, scores and tallies, scripture to extol the righteousness of honest toil. I was my mother's child. Her little pleasures—the silks and velvets that she wore, her love of perfume and exotic foods—were remnants of a buried sensuality, crushed out of her by circumstance and by convention. Yet blocked in her, it had emerged in me with fullest vigour. I was naturally indolent and pleasure-seeking; though driven, too, by father's dictum that a man must make a name, and win respect in life. To my eldest brother Max would go the bulk of the estates, and Edvard would pursue some lesser role, while I—I would become a doctor, perhaps a surgeon or consultant, as I boasted. My father remained unimpressed, and only grudgingly agreed to let me study. He held the purse: I could not run no matter how I tried.

All through that afternoon my fevered thoughts dragged on. At times it seemed I wrote to him, a long and heartfelt letter, setting out my quarrel in the plainest terms. I would say the very things that I had never dared to tell him face to face: 'I ask you how I might have ended other than I have? How not become the person that I am, given the person that you are?' I wanted him to understand, accept his guilt, to clasp me to him and embrace me. 'I am what you have made me, Papa, dearest Papa, I am your own true son. . . .'

But I became confused. My mind slipped in and out of dreams. There came a time I seemed to hear a voice calling my name, not my father's but a woman's, shrilling *Hans! Hans! Hans!*

He should have bailed me out of this, I thought, he should have sent me money as I asked. . . . He should have saved my life. Had he but given me a loving word, a kindly glance—above all else, a few more marks—then all my troubles would be gone. . . .

'Hans! Hans!'

The face of Mme Pluviers danced before my eyes, but as I reached for it, floated away as if it were a mask cast in a river.

Later I slept, and Grundig came before me once more, holding his palms out like a martyr in an Italian fresco; his kinetic frenzy was all gone, but he tipped his head to one side in what seemed to me a terrible display of sentimental pleading.

'It's all about you, isn't it?' I lambasted him, though I was not sure why. 'Seldom have I met a man so utterly self-centred, so incapable of sympathy for others. You disgust me! Just because you're dead, you think we ought to all kow-tow and say how sorry we are, don't you? You think we ought to rush around—'

He struck a pose, Pietà Jesu, one hand on his breast, his eyes raised up to Heaven.

'It's not so bad, in any case,' I said. 'You've got it easy now. It's the rest of us, stuck here, trying to cope. It's not as much fun as it looks, I'm telling you.'

A silver teardrop dribbled from the corner of his eye. He was mocking me.

'We struggle. We get old. We get ill. We have all sorts of things to deal with in the meantime. It's a nightmare. Honestly. A bloody nightmare.'

'Oh, don't worry,' said he. 'You'll wake up.'

'I might. I might or I might not. What business is it of yours, if I wake up or not? What right have you to say such things?'

I woke up.

Really woke up. My head was clearer than it had been now in days—perhaps in weeks. The room was cold. Cold, and silent. The fire had gone out. Where was Karl? Was I abandoned here, left on my sickbed like an old man? I rolled over in bed and swung my legs out. I felt my leg-hairs prickle in the chill. I took my robe from the nearby chair, wrapping it around me. When I stood, my head swam for a moment; bright silver points went floating through my eyes. I was still weak. I called for Karl, and for Lavenza. No response. And so I dressed, and headed for the cellar. But the cellar, bar a few old benches and some lengths of lumber, was quite empty. The great work—Lavenza's masterpiece, the monster's sop—was gone, and he with it.

Chapter Thirty-nine

There came a moment then—brief, yet undeniable—in which I felt the most extraordinary lightness of soul. It was as if a burden had been set down, a great responsibility renounced. No longer need I care what happened to Lavenza, or his work, or little Karl—or the monster. I was free. I could continue my Parisian career, go on till I grew rich and fat and gouty. . . . Yet, even while a part of me rejoiced, other emotions rose within, not least of which was anger. Few feelings are more powerful, in my own experience, and even lust may quail before the power of wrath.

Lavenza's secrecy, his creeping about and lack of trust, now irked me well enough to send me back upstairs and to his room, which I proposed to search as I had once searched Karl's. If he could not include me in his plans, I saw no further cause to treat him as a gentleman. He had not behaved like one. *Ergo*, I proposed—while having no exact plans of my own—to help myself to anything of value left behind, whereupon I, too, would vacate the premises. The room was untidy, indeed; the bedding flung back, clothing scattered on the floor. It was not even clean. But a quick glance, and a rummage through the drawers, suggested this was not a man who had fled, intending never to return. His possessions were still here. I thumbed a stack of papers. I searched vaguely for a strong box, or a bank roll. And then, from the hall, I heard the front door close.

I was out the room in seconds, red-faced and guilty-looking. Yet peering down the stairwell, I discovered not Lavenza, as I had supposed, but Karl, his quizzical, marmoset face peering back at me as if we had last spoken not ten minutes earlier.

At once regaining my composure, I trotted down the stairs to meet him.

'Where is he, then? Where has he gone? Where's the equipment?'

'Who, Master?'

'Lavenza. The *other* Master, damn it! Don't try to hide him from me. Where is he, then?'

'Busy, Master. He wants the copper wire.'

'Busy where?'

Karl attempted to dodge round me. I caught him by the coat collar.

'Ow! In church, Master. He's gone to church.'

※

Karl had commandeered a small cart, of the kind street-sellers use. Together we loaded the drum of wire onto its platform, and I rode with it while Karl, fitted between the shafts, propelled us at considerable speed along the Paris streets. I tried to question him as to Lavenza's actions, but he was either too shy or too breathless to respond. He spoke once of 'the big Master', which I did not like. I attempted to ply him with a cigarette, but this was hardly the moment for it.

'The church,' I said. 'This is the business with acoustics, isn't it?'

'Don't know, sir. Don't know Master's business.'

'You moved the body, didn't you?'

He swung us about, negotiating an especially tight corner. I clung to the sides of the cart.

'And the batteries. The capacitors. And all the rest.'

'Sir, we had to. The Master said. The other Master. And the big Master. He wanted it. He helped.'

'No doubt, no doubt.' It had occurred to me that only superhuman strength could have removed Lavenza's paraphernalia so swiftly and so secretly.

Another thought came to my mind.

'You don't much like the big Master though, do you, Karl?'

'He . . . makes me fearful, sir. That's all.'

'Perhaps he threatens you? Perhaps you want defending from the big Master? I can help, you know, Karl. I can help.'

In the pockets of my coat, before leaving the house, I had secreted my pistols. After all, if one has a talent, one should be willing to use it, should one not?

But Karl twisted around to face me, even as he pulled us down the street.

'No-one protects from big Master, sir. Do what he says. Big Master speaks, wants something—don't matter what we want, sir. Not me, nor you, nor first Master neither. Do what big Master says. That's how it is.'

Is it? I thought, and I touched the smooth gun metal in my pocket, thinking, this time, perhaps someone should show a little spine, and tell the big Master just where he got off.

It was, I must confess, an easy thought to think, with the wind in my hair, my guns to hand, and the big Master nowhere in sight.

Chapter Forty

It was the same church. Some ecclesiastical wrangle had kept it out of use for months, and its dimensions fitted well Lavenza *père*'s prescription. In short, it could hardly have been more convenient for our unholy purpose. I let Karl enter first, rolling the drum of wire before him. The interior was gloomy, lit by candles; the windows had been masked where possible with dustsheets, lending a necessary privacy. The 'big Master', I was relieved to note, was nowhere to be seen, though evidence of his handiwork was all around; the place had been transformed, a tribute to his strength and stamina. Not seeing him, I felt myself relax. If it came to a fight, then let the fight come on another day, for preference far in the future. There was much to occupy me now.

Before the altar, propped on saw horses, there stood the catafalque on which his Eve was laid. The body, wrapped in bandages to shield the soft tissue, lay half-submerged within a bath of fluid. Lavenza bent across her, adjusting wires that protruded in what seemed to me a very dangerous, haphazard manner. Such was his concentration he ignored our presence utterly.

'What's this?' I said. 'Trying to wake her with a kiss?'

'Hans—my dear, dear Hans.' He still did not look up. 'Come to help, I see.'

Job done, he checked his fingers, wiped them on his surgeon's coat, and carefully arranged a smile upon his face; then grasped my hand and shook it with a fierce intensity.

'Schneider,' he addressed me, man to man. 'Schneider. So good to see you in fine health once more.'

He kept shaking my hand. I think he saw the anger in my eyes; he was afraid, perhaps, that if he let me go, I'd hit him.

I said, 'You would have left me on my sickbed.'

'Oh, I don't think so. No, no—surely not. . . .'

'You can release my hand.'

'Of course.' But he kept shaking it. 'Matters have proceeded—faster than we planned. There was an incident—a matter—distressing, but we must move on. As it is, I can predict with near one hundred per cent confidence, this whole business will soon be done. Oh yes. The curse of Frankenstein will end tonight!'

'You mean to give him what he wants?'

'Best way, hm? I thought that we'd decided that. Best way. I think this place will do. I've made a few modifications. I think this ought to work . . . and if not—well. We'll see.'

He stopped pumping my hand, clinging to it a few moments more, eyeing my face.

'You've come to help us, though. Isn't that right? To help, yes? Are you strong enough? Do you feel up to it?' He at last released me, clapped me on the shoulders, and at the same time called to Karl, giving instructions like a drill sergeant, 'Bind the wire round tightly, but evenly! Evenly! You know what that means?'

Karl stooped to his work. Lavenza drew me on one side. He must have reasoned he was safe with me. He confided, 'I am much afraid, as I say, that there has been an incident—a conspiracy of circumstances, really, making action our immediate recourse. I had hoped for your recovery, so we might both, as it were, venture out into this new and thrilling realm together. But unfortunately. . . .'

'What?'

'Monsieur Baldin. He sent for me. I assumed it was another fit of guilt following his little escapades—I believe he has a new whore. She lets him wear her basque and soiled knickers (he laid great emphasis upon the soiling, I recall) while she lays about him with a hair brush. Such a strange man. But . . . ah. Yes. He sent for me to warn me. It appears that the police have grown suspicious of us. We're foreigners, when all is said and done, arrived in town not long before these dreadful killings. . . .' He tutted, shook his head, like any bourgeois with a newspaper. 'And—well. I understand that you have made yourself something of an apologist for this Ripper which the papers have dreamed up. Would that be right?'

'I have done no such thing!'

'In prominent company, furthermore. Such matters do get noticed. And the matter of the blade. Your—ah—initials. I had hoped we'd get away with that, but . . . clearly not.'

My mind was slow. I said, 'You mean they take me for the murderer?'

'I wouldn't go that far. But they do make a connection, yes.'

And then the next thought struck home. 'You planned to leave me for them.'

'Oh, not at all! But—as I say. I needed to act quickly. You were in no state to assist. And then, this other incident—we have acquired a head, you see. A very fine specimen. I insisted that he harvest at a distance from the house, and from ourselves. But he doesn't listen. And I'm afraid all this made it seem . . . wise that we abandon ship, as it were. Temporarily.'

'You were going to leave me there! You were leaving me for the police!'

'Oh, not at all. Besides, you would have told them everything—about me—and him—and about my work. What good would it have done?'

'I would have gone down as a liar or a madman, and you know it! While you would have escaped scot free!'

I stood there, fuming. Lavenza, smiling nervously, said, 'Come on—let's have a drink. I've put it off till now—clear head and such—but let's take a swift cognac together, eh? No hard feelings?'

'No hard feelings?'

'It's almost over. Do you know how much that means to me? This—this hunting I've endured. This nightmare that has been my life, my family's lives, knowing that we must be cut down any time. . . . It's almost done. In just a few hours, I will walk away a free man. Can you imagine how that feels? As if you were condemned to the scaffold, and then at once, the verdict has been overturned. As if—' He caught himself. 'I'm sorry. That wasn't perhaps the wisest image. But you do see, don't you? Tell me that you do?'

He was almost jumping up and down in his excitement.

I took the bottle that he offered, and, all at once, the strain of the experience began to tell. My legs grew weak. My head swam. I dropped onto the nearest pew.

I took the bottle, though I hardly had the strength to drink.

Chapter Forty-one

The life of the fruit fly, *Drosophila*, is made shorter by the efforts of copulation and egg-laying; this is proven fact. Virgin *Drosophila* are, bar accident, much longer livers than their more sexually fulfilled kin. And not merely the fruit fly suffers thus. Honoré de Balzac claimed to lose a novel each time he made love. (A curious statistic, given that he published more than forty of them; was he either super-humanly prolific, or else far less libidinous than he portrayed himself?) Catholic priests insist that they derive a certain sanctity from staying celibate, at least if they can keep their hands off the choirboys. And there's a man named Brown-Séquard who thinks that extracts from the testicles will help preserve our youth. (Why extracts, I wonder, when I already have two healthy testicles attached?)

Whatever the truth, there is no doubt that sex and death, death and sex are hopelessly entangled in our minds, if not our lives. Sprawling on that church pew, delirium still chewing at the edges of my mind, it struck me that Grundig and his ghost were, in fact, quite wrong. Between the two great matters of our lives, the twin poles of our fate, the paramount, o'er-leaping force (if I may put it so) was surely sex, not death. Even this creature of Lavenza's wanted sex, and to such end, the man had turned this church, this place of funerals and marriages and christenings, into a kind of temple to the act, a palace in which even the great vaulted ceiling took on a curiously female aspect to me, the lips of its arches enfolding, fit to draw me in; and I confess that seeing this I felt that I was not in my right mind at all. Yet the argument (I present here only a schematic, the rest long lost to memory) absorbed me so much that I lost track of Lavenza as he marched about, fussily adjusting this and that. I think he must have called my name a half a dozen times before I answered.

'Sir . . . ?'

'Here, here. Check the temperature. It should be blood-heat, no more, no less. There may well be a surge after the first shock of electric power; if need be, cool by adding fresh liquid from here.' He indicated a large pewter jug placed on a balustrade. 'Use sparingly, mind you. If the temperature falls, this switch will heat the coils under the catafalque. You can stir with your hand—it's quite safe. Until I say "shock". Then it might hurt.'

The body lay immersed in fluid, face and form entirely bandaged. Only the nose and mouth emerged into the air. A length of tar-black hair coiled out between the wraps, wafted by the slow, small currents of the tank into ever-changing curlicues and arabesques. I felt a strange and almost overpowering tenderness on seeing it; an urge to reach down, stroke it, tuck it back in place. I shook my head to brush away such thoughts. I sought to bring the scientist in me to bear, and not the sentimentalist.

I said, 'You've discontinued respiration.'

'Not necessary. That was simply to preserve the tissues during preparation. Homoeostasis will maintain for long enough to suit our purposes. In a short while, believe me—she'll be breathing for herself.'

'Brain death?'

'Occurred at about 19.20 yesterday, Herr Schneider, so it's a little late to worry about that. The procedures by-pass all such niceties. I'm not *reviving* her; you know that. This is quite different. Furthermore, I think that brain-death is essential: it wipes all pre-learned patterns of behaviour. Like dusting off a slate so we can write anew. She will awake, *tabula rasa*.' He twisted two bare wires together. 'Incidentally, I caught your reference when you arrived. A fairy tale, yes? Awakened with a kiss? The kiss from my batteries, no less!' He gripped my arm. 'This time—this time, I surely do believe I will succeed. I've come so far, I've lost so much—it has to happen. Yes.'

The strand of hair stirred gently in the current. It captured my attention; it coiled, it twisted, serpentine.

'19.20,' I repeated.

'Hm.'

'Very precise.'

'Yes. The little . . . difficulty I referred to earlier. He killed someone, two streets away. I'd always said he should be careful, but. . . .' He looked round warily, and his voice dropped to a whisper. 'He's impulsive. You can't talk to him. He's no regard for law or what to us is rational behaviour. He's not a man. You know that, don't you?'

I nodded.

'What he is, I'm still not sure. I don't think even Viktor knew exactly what he'd done in making him. Poor, poor Viktor. I've read his diaries. He was a product of his age, a pure romantic. A little pocket Werther, full of secret sorrows, poetry and lust. Not too much of a scientist at all, I am afraid.' He checked the thermometer, suspended in the tank. He checked the little dials around the sides. 'All my life, you see, the family—at least, so long as they were still around—the family has held him up, revered him. For generations we've been trying to repeat what he achieved. And always with that—that *thing* watching over us. But I wonder now if Viktor wasn't simply lucky. Conditions were just right, everything fell into place . . . and we've spent all these long years since trying to replicate his little accident. Luck, I think, can play a major part in anybody's life. It might be worth making a study of. . . .'

'Bad luck,' I said.

'What? Oh, possibly, possibly. . . . Wait! Here we go! Now, keep an eye on things, and when I shout—don't touch, alright?'

He signalled to Karl. And there, perhaps, the most curious part of the equipment was assembled: on a table by the choristers' stalls, Karl had placed a pair of wind-up gramophones, so incongruous I

Frankenstein's Prescription

had at first ignored them, or presumed they had been here before Lavenza came. And yet, not so. At the sign, Karl dropped the playing arm onto the record. I looked to Lavenza. He was busy checking through his wires and capacitors and what-all else.

And then, the sound of voices filled the hall.

I was listening to Bach—the Mass in B Minor, I think the Sanctus. The acoustics of the place were good; the thinly-reproduced sounds echoed, thrummed upon the walls, upon the vaulted ceiling. I noticed both the gramophones had enlarged horns. As one record drew to an end, Karl, frantically winding the other player, dropped the needle into the groove on that; for a moment weird harmonies enveloped us as both works played together. Then, from underneath a bench, he produced yet a third machine, with a third record upon it.

'I'd like a choir,' Lavenza mused. 'A proper choir, in a real cathedral. Imagine that? And a true ceremony, for the birth of a new, extraordinary creature—'

I leaned over the body. The contours of the face were visible beneath the muslin wraps. A long, straight nose. Large orbits for the eyes. The cheek bones high, the chin perhaps a little weak. . . . I was, when all is said and done, something of an expert on the female form. This was my type, most certainly. The black hair drifted, seemed to shimmer in a rhythm with the music. . . .

'Hands off!' Lavenza yelled, and, 'Shock!'

I jumped back. He pulled the lever; it fell with a crash. The body shuddered in its tank, the liquid splashed and rippled. There was a sound like paper tearing; an ozone smell sharp in the air.

The music stopped.

Lavenza ran across, bent over the body, peering at it anxiously, much as when I first arrived. A tongue of bandage had slipped loose from the face, showing soft, smooth, honey-coloured skin. Lavenza checked the temperature. He checked connections, clicked his tongue.

'Master?' inquired Karl again.

'Yes, yes.' Lavenza didn't look at him.

'You want music, Master?'

'Yes! Music all the time. Like I told you.'

Once more, Karl set about cranking the gramophone handles, two at a time.

'Music, Master! Music!'

'Don't overwind.'

Two more shocks ensued. Through all of this, I did nought but stand and watch; I recall at one point, as he bent over the lifeless figure, checking for pulse and breathing, thinking what a lovely woman she must have been whilst alive—her head, at any rate.

The thought would haunt me through the coming weeks and months; the coming years.

'Louder, Karl, now. Louder, please.'

'Won't go no louder, sir.'

Lavenza quickly moved to check the gramophones, twisted the horns, pointing them towards the ceiling. He was growing anxious; he must have hoped for a result by this time. The music rose, a seething wall of voices, and he yelled again, and flung the switch.

Somebody said, 'Your music's wrong.'

I knew those tones. I had heard them only once before, yet they were cut into my mind as if inscribed in acid.

It was a voice I had prayed very much that I would never hear again.

Chapter Forty-two

How long had he been there? I forced myself about, dreading to see him, hoping that the voice had somehow been an echo, an hallucination—God knows what.

It was as if a piece of masonry detached itself from the wall. A stone on the move. He stepped out of the shadows, into the body of the church, and the music of the Mass rose round him, swelling, roaring; will the reader think me fanciful if I suggest the sound appeared to shatter on his body, like an ocean on a great rock, leaving him untouched, unscathed, the chorus booming and rebounding from him like the waves in a storm?

Lavenza, flustered, made awkward, up-and-down gestures, as if he couldn't work out what his hands were for.

The creature pushed his way between the pews, shoving them aside as if they were mere stage props.

'I remember.'

His eyes set on me, glancingly, and I moved back, away from him.

'I remember being born. I remember how it was. How it sounded. How it felt. I remember my Creation.'

He strode into the aisle.

'The life was shot into my veins. The Lord cried, "*Fiat lux!*" and then the light inside my skull caught fire, so fiercely I could never shut it out again, and even when I sleep, the colours dance upon my eyes and tease me with a mockery of life; and the sounds I heard still thunder in my ears. My thoughts are just their echo. My words only corruptions of those first, divine vibrations, half-remembered, half in dream. I was not born as you are, helpless maggots, squirming through your first few years of life. I was born awake, and I was born full-made. And I remember.'

He turned from us, marching down the church, and I felt the tiled floor shudder at his step.

As he passed, Karl shrank into the choir stalls. But the monster never even looked at him.

'Prepare your lightning! Play your music!' and he vanished through the doorway to the bell tower.

I looked then to Lavenza; but Lavenza looked to Karl.

'You heard him. Play.'

The voices of the Mass cranked up again. They swept around the hall.

And then the bells began.

It felt as if the sound would shake my bones. And it went on and on: relentlessly, tirelessly, unceasingly, until the very air seemed to congeal and ring, and Lavenza, shaken from his stupor, ran to his batteries, checked the dials, called, 'Shock!' and the body—

The muslin wrap slipped from her face. There was an eye, open and limpid brown, though dead and motionless, here the soft curve of a cheek, the jut of nose, a curl of black, black hair gummed to the forehead. I reached out, hesitantly. . . .

'Shock!' Lavenza cried.

I said, 'Rebecca . . . ?'

There was no mistaking it. I knew that face as surely as I knew my own. Some women are forgotten easily, they slip out of the mind with one's post-coital ablutions, but not her—not Madame Pluviers, Madame *le Plus-vrais*, Madame who could talk and talk and tell you intimacies you had neither dreamed nor wanted to imagine. . . .

Lavenza paused, hand on the lever. He called out to me, over the clangour of the bells, 'What's wrong, man? What's the trouble?'

He thought I'd found a problem with his apparatus! He imagined his procedure was amiss!

So solipsistic, he could conceive no other reason for distress. As I tugged and tore Rebecca's wrappings, he ran over, and tried to hold me back. I shook him off. He was yelling, screaming at me: I would ruin everything, I must be careful, what had come over me? Yet I pulled at the bindings, seeking to free her from Lavenza's apparatus, half convinced in some part she was still alive, somehow rendered senseless for this mad charade. I cradled her head. I tugged at the bandages, until I saw what, perhaps, I might have expected to see. It shocked me, nonetheless.

Beneath her chin, running the full length of her jawbone, was a seam. A red welt, stitched with the finest stitching.

The neck beneath was not Rebecca's.

I knew Rebecca's neck. It was, to tell the truth, somewhat broad, with a crease that ran around it like a choker. Where this was long, and smooth, and shapely.

I stepped away, my reason struggling with my heart, trying to force myself to see the truth. Something caught the back of my legs; I fell into a pew. Lavenza, meanwhile, disregarding me, rushed round, tending to his mechanism, racing to undo whatever damage I had done.

And through it all the bells rang on, with no sign of fatigue; an endless, unremitting din. Yet I became aware, too, of another sound, as if an echo, though much lower down the scale: a booming, repeated at intervals, a basso counterpoint, perhaps, to the music all around.

My mind was reeling too much even to consider this. But I saw Lavenza look up, suddenly worried. He glanced towards the door. Then I looked, too. And at the next boom, I saw the bar that we had put in place shake visibly. I watched for what seemed like an age. And, boom! It shook again.

Someone was trying to break in.

Lavenza raced back to his batteries. He did a final check, he hit the lever—

The body shuddered. Rebecca's deep brown eyes rolled upwards in their sockets, her mouth gaped as to scream, then at once fell slack again. Yet these were not her eyes, her mouth, I told myself. Not any more. True comprehension came to me but slowly. I had believed I heard her voice in my delirium; yet say it had been genuinely her, come visiting (a thing I had forbidden her, for fear that she might meet one of her rivals there)? Her knock going unanswered, she must have called up to the windows, hoping to rouse me. I had not replied. And she, departing—ah, God! Had run into that beast, that creature, that hell-spawn of Lavenza's. Oh, I could scarcely think of it! The bells rang, and the air stank, and the bar across the door gave an almighty crack as one of the restraining brackets shuddered loose. Only moments now and our pursuers would be upon us. Some instinct for self-preservation took me, and, moving like a sleepwalker, I climbed over the bench on which I sat to crouch behind it. And just in time! With a final thud and a wrench, the door came open, though in part restricted by the bar, which was still anchored at the further end. In the doorway there were gendarmes; their silly cloaks and foolish caps struck me as ludicrously funny. I began to laugh. My mind was not quite right. I heard Lavenza shout once more, the lever dropped, there was a stench of smoke upon the air. Something was wrong with his equipment; whether by my doing or some inevitable process of attrition, I could not know. But clearly, now, the game was up.

And the bells stopped.

The sound had gone on for so long it seemed to echo in my ears, as if my own skull had been changed into a bell and rang in sympathy. I peeped over the back of the pew. The crowd was no longer merely at the door. One by one, they pushed their way inside. Four men in uniform—and behind, an untold rabble, drawn by the excitement. I was in trouble. I knew this. I knew, too, that this time I would not escape as lightly as at Heidelberg. I felt the weight of the pistols in my coat. I reached into my pocket, gripped

Frankenstein's Prescription

the stock of the Luger. I drew it, tentatively, cautiously, wondering if I were about to take that fatal step across the boundaries of the law. At such moments, time slows. One has leisure to assess a situation, consider it from every angle. I watched, as the police caught sight of the body. I saw their mouths drop open, and their eyes go wide. Yet already, something else distracted them. One pointed, cried out. The others turned—slowly, it seemed, as if underwater—and they froze.

The beast had come down from the bell tower.

There was no urgency in him. No rush or hurry. Indeed, his steps were smooth, his walk the flowing motion of some great, unholy animal. His face was set, expressionless. His big coat flapped about him. He seemed slow yet covered ground at an extraordinary speed. Before the officers had even drawn their guns he was upon them. He took the first as he was reaching for his weapon; seized his gun arm, snapped the wrist—I heard the bone go—and swung him sideways, straight into his colleagues. He took down their commander almost with a casual gesture, grabbing his coat and flinging him into the air. Then to Lavenza, he yelled, 'Do it! Do it now!'

Lavenza stood, mouth working helplessly, unable to make words.

'Bone of my bone!' screamed the monster. 'Flesh of my flesh!'

The creature seized the balustrade before the altar and, with a few quick twists, he wrenched it free, lashing it about him like a club. The men had fled into the doorway, but were blocked from the retreat by the press of bodies at their back.

They were trapped.

I saw Lavenza turn once more to his machine.

And Karl, recovering from his initial stupor, began to wind the gramophone handles furiously, till the music of Bach once more whirled through the air. It was madness. It was lunacy. I stood up, feeling my coat swing with the weight of my remaining weapon. I was thinking with unusual clarity, as if, the more the chaos round me grew, the calmer I became.

I moved quickly now, bent double. I grasped Karl by the coat and dragged him from his precious toys. He screamed, protested. I pointed to the choristers' door, enshadowed in the corner, and I launched him at it.

Next, Lavenza, absurdly bent over his work.

'This way, you idiot! This way!'

The crowd had for a moment fallen back, but now they forced the door full open, and with that, gathered courage. Two shots were fired in quick succession. I saw the monster jolt back, almost surely with a bullet in his shoulder. It stopped him for a second or two, no longer; yet in that time, two more gendarmes darted sideways, into the body of the church, to flank him. I heard the commander's voice cry *'Tuez! Tuez!'* but the monster, rather than fleeing, leapt at him with a speed that I could barely register, lifting him up and shaking him like a rag doll. He scarcely seemed concerned to do real damage. He was like a cat in a nest of mice. Was it sport, or rage? Or some emotion indefinable in merely human terms?

Lavenza made his final checks. I could have left him. Barely an hour back, I believed he had abandoned me. Should I not then treat him in kind? And was he, too, not some sort of a monster, allowing what had happened to Rebecca—and to all these girls?

I do not know exactly why I acted as I did, putting myself at risk. I had never shied from my own selfishness; it was a part of who I was, and much the greater part. But now, forsaking my own flight, I ran at him. He pulled the lever. I was upon him, and he fought me. He was like a drowning man who strikes out at his rescuer. The harsh, electric tang of smoke began to fill the air. He shouted, 'Look, look!' but I would not look; I shoved him bodily towards the door, and then we ran, to the small dark door at the rear, where Karl stood, waiting humbly, amusing himself by counting on his fingers.

It was over quickly after that, although those next few minutes were among the most anxious of my life. We plunged through a small dressing room, where clerical vestments hung, flapping in our faces as we passed; then into a storeroom, stumbling over boxes, cans and other paraphernalia. From behind there came a thunderous crash, spurring me on. I found the outer door. I struggled with it. It was locked.

'Key!' I shouted. 'Key, key, key!'

Lavenza merely looked at me.

'Why should I have a key?' he asked.

'Look for one, man! Look for one!'

I felt about me in the gloom, I blundered into darkened corners, collided with—of all things—a stack of gardening implements, a rake, a hoe, a spade—and, clutching the last, I hacked at the lock, without doing much more than loosen it. Then I raised my pistol. Two shots followed, and we were out, into a kind of sunken entranceway, as yet overlooked by our assailants. And we ran. Past startled figures in the street, past gas lamps and past darkened windows . . . and when we could not run, we walked. We walked and walked, but not back to the house. For that was lost to us—that, and all else we possessed.

'You—you—' Lavenza wheezed from the exertion. 'You were like a hero from a novel, sir. I was—I am—most grateful, most—impressed. . . .'

I would not look at him. I led them both, him and Karl; Karl, whose church-measuring had gone somewhat to his head, and now counted the cobblestones as he went, only to lose count after a dozen or so, and start again, aloud, '*Ein, zwei, vier, fünf* . . .'

I could not even find the will to tell him to shut up.

Chapter Forty-three

'She sat.'

'She did not.'

'Sir, she did!'

'Hush,' I say. 'Someone will hear.'

'Nonetheless,' he whispered. 'She rose up. She moved. She *sat*.'

6 o'clock, and Gare de Nord already crowded. Our argument was briefly interrupted by a baggage trolley, pushing its way among the early morning throngs; in stepping back, we collided with a well-heeled bourgeois family, en route to God knows where. Apologies were swapped. Then, before they got the chance to strike up conversation, I turned my back, and made Lavenza do the same. Better be thought rude than have our faces stick inside their heads, to be identified if questioned. . . . We had tickets for Dieppe, and planned to cross to England, perhaps lie low a while in some quiet, rural area, then move to London. Meanwhile, time slowed. I stamped my feet as if to hurry it.

Lavenza said, having to speak too loudly in the din, 'Your problem, sir, is that you lack the scientific method. Heidelberg has failed to give you discipline, sir, so you see merely what you wish to see. Where I observe the facts. And I am telling you, before you utter one word more: she moved. Most certainly, she moved.'

'She did not sit up!'

'She stirred, at least. She raised herself upon her elbow. Then . . . fell. Death, once more. . . .'

'No.' I shook my head. 'No, no.'

'I have succeeded. Or I would have done. My triumph snatched away from me, it's true. But having done it once—'

'No more, please. No. No more.'

The Dieppe train was late. I watched a superintendent check the coupling of the carriages across from us, prior to departure. I peered along the line, hoping to see our transport in the distance. . . .

Karl tugged my sleeve.

'Master,' he said.

I tried to shake him off, but he persisted. Then I saw what he was looking at.

Out on the station concourse, something was happening. No great fuss; but I could make out the caps of the gendarmerie, slipping through the crowd, singling out this group and another, questioning, demanding.

I looked to Lavenza. 'This train,' I said.

'Dieppe . . . ?'

'Forget Dieppe. This train is about to leave, and we leave with it.'

'But our baggage—'

'But our lives,' I countered.

Belatedly, I had discovered there were more important things than clothes; thus, with no more than those we wore, I hurried my companions onto the departing train. It steamed away; poor Karl got dragged along the platform till I finally hauled him inside. He showed no disgruntlement. Perhaps, when one has slept for centuries, and died, and all the rest of it, such minor inconvenience no longer matters.

Belgium

Chapter Forty-four

The ocean lay as cold and dreary as a dead fish; my mood, the same.

It was a harbour town. The lank North Sea moaned at its door. Late visitors from Antwerp and Bruxelles roamed on the beach, pretending it was still high season; but when night fell, they bundled off back to their rooms to huddle from the chill, damp air. For entertainment, there was a restaurant or two, a small theatre, and a few bars. We had funds for none of them.

We shared a room. Paid in advance. I discovered that Lavenza snored, at least when he could cease his listless pacing of the floor and sleep a few hours. Karl, meanwhile, slept all the hours he could, curled up like a cat. At intervals he cried out, babbling some nonsense from his madman's dreams. I don't believe he ever woke himself, although he woke me many times. Our life of luxury was long since gone, and what remained appealed to me not in the least.

I sleep-walked through my days. My purpose was to fetch provisions, and contemplate our next move—not that I did. I was in limbo. I could make no decisions. Even Karl seemed better motivated than did I; he measured out our room with his string, informed Lavenza it was much too small, and clearly the wrong shape. Lavenza, meanwhile, was like a man in a trance. At times he took his notebook and began to scribble frantically, only to cease a moment later as if stifled by the sheer futility of his endeavours. Or else he might spend hours simply staring at the wall.

Our house in Paris had been watched. That much was plain. Surveillance had begun, perhaps, mere hours before our attempted apprehension. Surely, they had not seen Lavenza move his workshop across town, into the church. What they had seen, rather (as I reasoned it), was Karl returning for the wire, and then leaving with me—with the man whose scalpel, finely initialled, had been found broken in the body of a victim. No English sailor now, oh no. I had killed before, of course, and been duly punished for it. But would I now be hanged for a deed I had not done?

And Rebecca—ah. They would know me from Rebecca, also; for by now her poor remains would rest in a police morgue, along with the parts of all those other lost, unlucky women. They would know I was her doctor. I forced myself to block out sentiment, close off whatever feelings I might have. My normal instincts must return to me; self-preservation was of paramount importance.

Each day I read the newspapers. At last I saw an item on an inside page, a fanciful tale devoted to the decadence and debauchery of the French capital, where it seems a black mass had been held in an abandoned church—a black mass, and human sacrifice, no less! There were no names, thank God, and some doubt as to numbers. A brawl with the Satanists, it was explained, had left a number of policemen injured. There was talk of 'unspeakable crimes' and 'hideous discoveries', thought to be linked to recent killings in the city. Decency, of course, forbade description, but the paper hinted salaciously that the victims were all beautiful young women, and the church was being used for some kind of infernal, anti-Christian rite. Its author finished with a heartfelt prayer of thanks that staff, proprietor and readers dwelt here, in a decent, God-fearing land, and not among those devilish Parisians. I read the article and flung it to the floor.

'She moved,' Lavenza said. 'I saw her move.'

'Shut up.'

'No use denying it. I saw it.'

'Write to the newspapers. Tell them.'

'I'm not saying she lived. Not more than a few minutes—seconds, even. But she moved. And if the problem's just one of longevity, that's something can be solved, don't you think? Consider, for example—think of the first living things on Earth. Were they slow-livers, eking out existence, sluggish descendants of a single freakish accident? Or little flashes of life, sparked here and there by random processes, over and over, until one . . . stuck, as we might say? If we go back to first principles—'

'Fuck first principles.'

He looked at me, shocked, not, I think, at my anger, but that I should be so disinterested in what, to him, was such an all-engrossing topic.

'Hans. You are a scientist. Surely you're fascinated?'

'Oh yes. Fascinated.'

I put my hat upon my head.

'Hans—'

I did try not to slam the door.

But I didn't try too hard.

※

It was that vague, deceptive evening light, not truly dark as yet, but full of shadows. There were fishermen preparing boats down on the beach, and a small fire burning there; but I wanted nothing of their company. I trudged over the sand, leaving the town behind. The beach went on for miles. A dark, wooded hillside rose up, marked here and there by tiny lights of cottages or farmhouses. I felt that I could walk all night. It might have offered some solution; yet what a dismal one! I saw myself, a homeless vagabond, reduced to farm labour and begging for a living. . . . I clenched my fists. I felt the tears prickle my eyes. I had possessed so much. I had so nearly had a perfect life! In Paris, and before, at Heidelberg—and twice it had been snatched from me. What was my future now? To be reviled and persecuted, like Lavenza's monster—for whose crimes I was now held responsible. Yet I was innocent. (Almost innocent, for Grundig's ghost still sometimes whispered in my ear.) I was gentlemanly, handsome, well-connected. I was a doctor. (Almost a doctor.) I was. . . .

Yet my catalogue of virtues scarcely comforted, only serving to remind me what was gone. I walked on. The sand slid underneath my feet. I wept, I wailed to myself, believing I was quite alone.

A voice said, 'And they heard the sound of the Lord God, walking in the Garden in the cool of the day. And they were much afraid.'

I froze, mid-step. I didn't turn. I didn't speak. I felt the hairs creep on the back of my neck. And I believed, in that moment, my troubles were concluded; for I believed I was about to die.

Chapter Forty-five

'The Madame,' said Lavenza. 'She wants another week of rent. Or notice.'

'You've got money?'

'If we don't eat.'

'Pay her,' I said.

'Did you hear?' he said. 'If we don't—'

'Pay her. We'll eat.'

'You sound sure.'

'I'm sure.'

'Sure, but not happy, I think. Are you contemplating something foolish, possibly? Or have you found another of your wealthy women?'

'Neither,' I muttered, and would say no more.

'It's just,' he said, 'given our circumstances, I'd imagined that the thought of eating would have made you happy. Very, very happy. And yet plainly, it does not.'

I would not answer, pretending to be lost in thought. Rather, I changed the subject. 'You spoke about the family home.'

'What?'

'Castle Frankenstein, is it called? You spoke to me about it, some months back, and have made passing reference since. Where the creature was first born, you said. Where you grew up, I believe you said.'

'The Castle.'

'Yes.'

'You must miss it, I'd have thought. Particularly now.'

'The Castle.'

'As I said.'
'The Castle's where we go to die.'

※

I set off down the beach, much as before, this time with pistols hidden in my coat. They dragged on it, thumping my thighs as I walked. I cannot say I planned to use them, yet they comforted me, at least the first half mile or so. Yet as the town dwindled behind and I moved on into the dark, that comfort became small indeed.

Several times I stopped and looked around. Once I called, 'Hello . . . ?'

Only when I reached the point of giving up and starting back, I grew aware of him. The object I had taken for a boulder or a rocky outcrop, black against the surf, suddenly shook itself and shuddered to its feet.

I saw his arms swing, and his head lift. The fright consumed me; without conscious thought, my feet moved, shuffling me backwards, and I slipped and thudded to the sand.

A heavy burlap sack plumped down beside me.

'There,' he said. 'Food. As you asked.'

He did not approach. I mustered some small semblance of my dignity and thanked him, though polite words seemed incongruous in that bleak, empty place.

'Do you not intend to open it? To check the goods?'

Was he mocking me? I clambered to my knees, and with some struggle pulled open the neck of the sack. A glorious smell rose up. New bread! I felt my stomach stir with longing. I produced a pack of lucifers, better to view the prize. Here was bread alright—the crusty local kind—some apples, and a number of squashy, muslin-wrapped parcels; but my joy was suddenly soured. I was reminded of the story that Lavenza told, that horrid tale about his father's death. I looked towards the great black figure, looming like some heathen idol.

'This, ah, this meat . . . ?'

'Yes.'

'What kind of . . . ? That is, what animal . . . ?'

'It's beef.'

'You're sure?'

He nodded.

'You're certain that it's beef?'

'I slew the beast myself. I broke its neck.'

I contemplated this a moment, wondering what strength it took to kill a cow, then re-fastened the sack, and stumbled to my feet, in the process putting a little surreptitious distance between the monster and myself. Not, I suppose, that it would have truly helped me, had he turned on me; he would have caught me in a second.

'Has he agreed?'

I said, 'I'm . . . negotiating.'

'Negotiating?'

'We're still discussing it.'

A slight change in his posture sent a chill through me, and I said quickly, 'I can do it. He just needs to see the sense. Give me a few more days.'

His silence begged more explanation. I flapped my arms. 'We're not like you,' I said. 'The way you act—as if there's only one thing in the world that matters. We're not like that. We're difficult. We're . . . complicated.'

I picked the bag up, intent on exit. But he told me, 'Stay.'

The guns weighed in my coat. I looked again for comfort there, but it had fled entirely.

'I want what the Creator promised,' he said then. 'I have been cast from Eden, yet the sin was not my own. The sin was His.'

I did not want to anger him. At any cost. I told him my theology was poor, I could not comment on such matters; I was a doctor of medicine—'A student of medicine,' I corrected myself, and not of divinity.

'His sin was my creation,' said my new-appointed tutor. 'That much is clear to me. And yet, did I create myself? Did I ask to be created? How could I? So the sin was His. This, then, is logic; it seems unassailable. And where, then, does it leave Him? By His own rules?'

'I . . . don't know.'

The creature pushed his face towards me, massive shoulders straining at his coat.

I stepped back hastily.

'You don't know,' he mocked. 'You spend your days with Him, and yet you know Him not.'

There was a sneer in his tone, so unexpectedly human, I found myself almost bristling at it.

'He's just a man, you know. Lavenza. Frankenstein. Whatever you call him. He's just a man.'

'And you? Are you a man, as well?'

'Of course. This is ridiculous. Of course I am.'

'But not like Him.'

I hesitated for a moment. A wave crashed down, a sound like thunder, the ocean battering the thin, frail strand on which we stood.

Spray dabbed my cheek.

'Well—not like him, no. Perhaps not. But he isn't God! The way you talk about him—it's as if—as if you—'

'Not your God, no. Mine.'

'But, but. . . .'

'Do you have a different word for him? Another title, that perhaps has slipped my guard? I can remember being born. His face, as He raised my eyelid for the first time, and He looked into my soul. We saw each other. I remember the precise drumming of His words upon my ears, though at the time the words meant nothing. These words are with me now. I heard them on the day the world began.'

It was a strange thing. He was older than I by a century and more; and to be frank, he terrified me. Yet in other aspects, he was still a child, his understanding almost laughably simplistic.

I did not dare to say so. Rather I paced. I swung the sack from hand to hand.

'You've got to think,' I said, 'that in reality—in real terms—'

'In your terms.'

'Well, ah. If you like. But—the man you speak about as the Creator. This man. My friend, Lavenza. He's not who you imagine. He's your Creator's—oh, great-great-grandson, or more. Your real Creator's dead. This is his descendant. Once you grasp that, you can see why—'

'I know how you renew yourselves.'

'How we . . . ?'

Then I realised what he meant.

'It's not exactly . . . not renewal.'

I began to wonder whether to explain the whole process of human reproduction to him, or if I could; why a child might have his father's eyes, his mother's nose, and die of something that had killed his grandparent. But as I contemplated such a possibility, the creature said, with great firmness, 'I too wish to renew myself.'

'Well, yes, that's . . . understandable. Of course it is. But this man is not your Creator. Your Creator died. This is a different person.'

'I wish to renew myself.'

I took a few steps backwards.

'Tell him.'

'I'll ask again.'

'Tell him.'

I nodded; I have always thought that gestures hold a little less commitment than do words. I walked backwards on the sands, still facing him. Then something struck me.

'The first words,' I said.

'Yes?'

'Your Creator's words. You said that you remembered them, though you didn't understand them at the time. What were they?'

He was silent for a moment. His head went down between his shoulders, and in a voice without emotion, mere quotation, he announced:

'The little bugger's worked.'

At which he turned, and strode away into the surf.

Chapter Forty-six

The little bugger's worked!

I had no children then, nor thought of them, but even I knew this was not the way to greet a new life; even a monster might deserve a better welcome to the world than this.

As the Viennese school has it, such snippets of our childhood stamp themselves indelibly upon our souls, and make us who we are. It seems to me a worrying proposal, given the mess which constitutes most people's early lives. And while I might not wish to analyse so strange and dangerous a creature, it occurs to me to wonder if the twisted nature of his entry in the world had not produced some dreadful impact; if things might not, in better circumstances, have gone a little differently.

I said nothing of this to Lavenza, nor of my meetings with the fiend. So far as he knew, I went out to meet a new acquaintance—a woman, I had hinted, when he pressed me—and returned with food, in payment for my services.

I would have welcomed such a life. Oh, would I not!

Instead, with feigning nonchalance, I broached to him the monster's suit.

'But there's equipment in this Castle, surely? You spoke about a workshop, I believe.'

He did not reply.

'We have already lost your two laboratories. But we will not give up! We must fall back on resources we still have. In addition, as I might remind you, we are fugitives. It would do no great harm if we vanished for a time in some remote spot, to rusticate ourselves, indeed, thereby to carry on your work. . . .'

But this, likewise, brought no response.
'Where are your goals?' I asked him. 'Your ambitions?'
'He'll find us there.'
'Maybe. What of it?'
'I failed to make his bride. I came so close. But he will find me now and kill me. Returning to the Schloss would just be further acquiescing in his will. There is a pattern here, you see. . . .'
'But, but—to do it on your own terms, though? Not to acquiesce, but. . . .' I strained for words. 'There may be an alternative.'
'Oh yes,' he said. 'An alternative to life. There may be such a thing, indeed.'

⁂

'There was an angel, brightest of them all, who sat at God's right hand. His name meant "Lightbringer", and for that duty God created him. Yet then, the Lord God cast him down from Heaven, deep into the Pit, where all is pain and tears and suffering. Was this the way things should have been? Was this fair? And was it just?'

'I don't think I can say.'

'But you are all made in His image, are you not? You little folk. Each one a miniature Jehovah. Is that not so?'

'I wouldn't put it . . . quite that way.'

'You wouldn't put it quite that way.'

'Sir, if I had known you back in Heidelberg, I might, with one or two companions, set up a rather jolly erudite debate upon the matter. As for now . . . I don't pretend to know the mind of God.'

'Adam and Eve, his children. Driven from Eden, yet another angel set to guard its gates, wielding a flaming sword. Is this what fathers do, I ask?'

'Some fathers, possibly. Bad fathers. Not all.'

Yet as I spoke, I had a sudden picture of my own Papa, with his lists of rules I had been made to copy out so many times as punishment; the smell of his cologne, the wet woollen odour of his overcoat when he came in from the rain . . . His rage, his laying down the law, his strict and ordered world, hemmed by the church on one hand, the counting house upon the other. And while a small part of me longed for a return there, and to the certainties of infancy, it was a very, very small part. In my heart, I knew why I had left.

'Or Abraham,' rejoined the monster. 'Commanded by his Lord: "Kill me a son." '

'Rescinded,' I said, quickly, 'and a ram sent in the child's place.'

'Oh, as may be. But Abraham was willing. And who's to say what crimes that story hides?'

'You are determined,' I remarked, 'to render all of Scripture to a single theme.'

'Are you religious?'

'Not especially. My family has a religious streak, but no—not I.'

'You should be,' he said. Then, 'I have to be. I have no choice.'

'How so, sir?'

'I saw my God. Beheld Him clearly as I see you now.'

We were both silent for a time. And when he spoke again, he was still set upon his theme, his single-mindedness unsettling and yet wearisome in almost equal measure.

'I hear a father must chastise his son. Is that not so?'

'I—well. Perhaps.'

'And the purpose that it serves?'

'I—' But again my own father appeared before me. I heard his words, so often harsh, dogmatic, the judgements that he passed upon his children, and all others; for years I'd longed to slip the leash, be free of his restraints, his tyranny. Rebellion had been planted in the nursery, a creeping weed forever hiding from his gaze. Later, at Heidelberg, it blossomed, smothering all else. And that rebellion was as much his work as mine. His punishments, his endless rules, his notions of the done and not-done in society. And then, as I became the thing he inadvertently had made me, all at once he stopped my money! And sent me spiralling down, into my present state, here, talking nonsense with a brute who might destroy me with a single blow.

'The purpose that it serves?' I said. 'It gives them power, that's all.'

'Which otherwise they would not have?'

'They do it to direct their children. To make them as they would prefer them, not as they are. To make them little copies of themselves, yet meek, subservient to them. A father's power . . . is absolute.'

'You see? And even your God Yahweh had his own son slaughtered, did he not? Was that a show of power? Chastisement? To keep him as the Lord would have him be?'

I was tired. But some remnant of my childhood lessons still remained. I said, 'No. That was redemption. Salvation. It's theology.'

'I am my own God's son. How might I be redeemed? How saved? Do I die, in order to redeem myself?'

'You are his creation, not his son! Stop asking me these questions. I can't answer you. I don't know! Lavenza is his son—his son's son's son's son. I don't know how long ago. Your God is gone. You know that. Surely you know that.'

'Oh, I do. I killed him. Eat, he said, this is my flesh. Drink, this is my blood. And we became one. He is in me now, a part of me. Is that not right and fitting? Is that not how it ought to be?'

I moved from foot to foot, frightened and shameful of my fear.

His voice was soft, as gentle as a mother's with a child.

'Listen,' he said. 'I'll tell you how the world was made.'

I dared do nothing but remain, and hear him out.

Chapter Forty-seven

'First comes thunder. First the thunder, then I fall . . . I fall, and fall. Black Heaven roars above my head, and I am cast down like the lightning, falling out of Heaven, falling . . . flung into the abyss of the world. This is my start. This is my birth. Many, many leagues from here.'

I felt again the weight of the guns, pulling at my coat; and wondered if a well-aimed shot might yet decide things—through the eye, perhaps, into the brain? Difficult in daylight, though, and near-impossible at night.

'The lightning fills my veins. The thunder booms inside my skull. The light, the sound—they wipe out everything. My memory of Heaven . . . The Lord God breathes His life into my lungs. He puts his lips to mine. He speaks to me, and me alone. . . .'

' "The little bugger's worked",' I said.

'In doing so, he binds me to the Earth.'

'Unfortunate,' I said, unsure how to respond.

I dug my hand into my pocket, producing, not my pistol, but my pipe, which I began to fill. I was cold; I hoped the smoke might warm me somewhat. And maybe ease the terror in my heart.

'You,' he said. 'You people. Are you clay or spirit? How do you define yourselves?'

'Well . . . speaking scientifically, I don't believe the spirit can be properly considered—'

'Some think that Heaven is a paradise. Others, oblivion, the void we secretly desire. Is that what we require? The peace of non-existence?'

'Not for myself, sir. No indeed.'

'No. But you're a man.' There was—not exactly contempt in his tone, but dismissal, as if he'd asked opinions of a child. Which I suppose in years, compared to him, I was.

'Those first days. I remember them. His love for me. His first born. His chosen one. Day and night he fussed over my body, with neither pause nor rest. No bride was ever more attentive to her husband, no mother to her son. And yet already there was laid the germ of enmity. For in his heart, *he knew not what he did.*'

'But surely,' I said, 'to have made a life! Such an achievement—surely, surely—'

'He knew it as a doctor. As a man of science. But He was my father, in the way you speak of fathers, and He had a father's failings. He wanted a machine. He wanted a device that would indulge its Maker's image of Himself, mirror His desire, obey His will before He even thought to give command; that would anticipate His wish, and never stray, nor think much for itself. . . . A creature separate, and yet entirely His, and of Himself, of His intention and His doing. That—and no more. As you yourself described to me. As fathers do. You have confirmed with every word His actions and His thoughts.'

I made to protest, but rather filled my pipe, said nothing.

'At first He kept me strapped upon a slab. It was most cunningly designed. It pivoted; swung this way, that way; with the mere release of clasps and pressure of a finger, it revolved and spun, positioning me vertically, horizontally, or any way inclined. I could not move; my arms and legs were strapped in place. I never questioned this. The slab seemed part of me, a turtle's shell. And all the while, God tended me, examined me, explored my being. *Fiat lux*—He shone His lights into my eyes. I winced with pain, yet saw that He was pleased, and so permitted it. The mere expansion of my pupil was a joy to Him. He held out candles to me—here, and here, and here—then watched me as I traced their movement back and forth, back and forth. . . . The ordinary functions of my body gave Him such delight in those days. My one wish was to please Him. In His pleasure was my own. And this was all I knew.'

The creature put his head down for a moment. His breath steamed in the moonlight. 'My God. My Lord.'

'I too,' I told him, 'had a father much like yours. He loved me in my infancy, I think. But later. . . .'

'For brief times he would release my arms, instructing me, "Hands high!" raising his own arms in the air. Dutifully then, I raised my arms. He grinned, he danced upon the spot, as if I had performed the most delicious trick. "Hands low!" He cried. I put my hands down low. Again, I was rewarded with his praise. He clenched his fists for joy. I clenched my own fists, unaware the game was over. He saw my move and frowned. I also made to frown, but the muscles of my face were less expressive than his own; he did not recognise my efforts, and rapidly re-bound my limbs, for fear that I might struggle to escape.

'Escape was something which, at that time, I could not conceive. Escape to where? His workshop was the world, the universe. I could picture nothing else beyond. When He appeared there in its midst, it was as if He stepped from nowhere. When He left, I mourned, as one might mourn the death of one's most dear and treasured friend. Some three or four exits and entrances took place before I reasoned that His absences were temporary, He was likely to return. Nonetheless, His leaving pained me, and I hoped that, if I pleased Him, He would stay.

'Accordingly, the moment He unbound my arms, I lifted them, without so much as waiting for command.

'It was my great mistake. My sin. I had anticipated His delight, yet the expression on His face. . . . I dropped my arms, as quickly as I could. Too late. The damage was now done. I had moved, and of my own volition, a thing of dreadful consequence to Him. He rapidly and fearfully re-bound me, then, rather than linger as I hoped, He fled the world, leaving me alone, confused, and deeply troubled. This time, had He gone forever? I cried out, using the voice the thunder gave me. I knew blame, I knew despair. But more—I had done a thing which I believed was right, and was required of me. His response was to abandon me. How could this be?

'I waited. It may be several days went by; I owned no sense of time. When He returned, He brought the angel host. Where once had been sweet intimacy, of myself and God, now swarmed these brutish, lesser beings, with their strange smells and their guttural, unpleasant cries. They looked on me with fear. I saw that much. They bound me down with heavy ropes, lest I should burst my straps. And my Creator—He set about instructing me.'

'You spoke together? You had language, then?'

'I had the language of the thunder. He, the tongue we now speak. He taught me A-B-C. He taught me Thou Shalt Not. He taught me one-two-three. He gave me words in the belief that words would limit me and tame me. In the beginning was The Word. But I had language from a deeper time. I had the language of the thunder, drummed into my brain; the language of the lightning, printed on my blood. He had required a puppet. I was a creature of free will. My first free act—my first intended act—was to dissemble, and to feign submission.

'For this, I was rewarded.

'So began my true instruction: not the High German I mastered with such ease, but the pathways of my dealings with the Lord. I saw that, contrary to my initial sense, his interests and mine were now at odds. My ways are not thy ways, saith the Lord. This, while it perturbed me, also gave me some considerable thought.

'A cage was built. Stout beams of wood, nailed with iron. The angels laboured on it, day by day. I watched their work, fascinated as if witnessing true magic. I saw Creation taking place before my eyes. The cage stood eight feet tall, ten feet across. This would be my house, my prison in the Universe. It granted me the liberty of movement, to a point, but also placed restrictions; most of all, a barrier between myself and God. We spoke together, but no longer felt each other's breath. We could no longer touch. He had created distance: length, breadth, depth. He had created distance, and then placed me on the further side.

'Does the Creator love Creation? We assume so, but then "love" means different things, depending on one's viewpoint. Is it love to set free? Or restrain? The parson talks of love, then hammers out his rules, like any tyrant. Love there may be. But a love of laws, restrictions? Is that love?'

I could say nothing. The sea boomed, echoing the thunder of his tale; and he cocked his head, as if to listen to its words. He froze thus for a while, then shook himself, went on.

'The angels of the day were sombre and efficient. They worked beneath His gaze, scrupulously bent to His commands. But in the night, as vision was occluded, so too was reason, logic, order. The Creator seldom came; instead, the night angels had their dominion. Five of them, who sat with candles and with lanterns and played games around a table, shuffling cards and throwing dice. They taught me words the Maker never spoke, and, when I uttered them in daylight, I saw first horror and then rage upon his face. Likewise, they laughed if I should touch myself, and encouraged me to do so; again, an act that drew His censure in the daytime.

'Still, for long hours they ignored me. At night, unlike the day, there was much laughter and much talk. I wanted to take part. I wanted their attention, just as I craved the Maker's; and though in part I loathed them and resented them for coming between Him and me, I was unable to resist their lure. I called to them. I cried out, in sounds not yet quite human speech. They shouted back, urged me to silence. One took a poker, heated in the fire. He jabbed at me between the bars. I had their interest then. They laughed, they roared, watching me cringe and duck away.

'I waited till I knew that all were watching, and then did what seemed the simplest thing: I seized the poker, regardless of the heat, and pulled it to me, so the man's hand came between the bars. With my other hand, I seized his fingers, and I squeezed.

'There was no more laughter that night. The injured man was hurried from my sight, never to return. The angels were more wary after that. I had not won their love, but I had forced them to take note, and to respond to me, with which for now I must make do.

'There was . . . an unsettling incident. It was some time later. The Maker brought a woman in to see me. (I had reasoned, by this time, that a world of some sort must exist beyond the workshop; that the angels and the other creatures who appeared here, and indeed, the Lord himself, did not abruptly spring into existence as they crossed the threshold. Yet the nature of that world was still obscure to me. More haunting was the fact that, when He stepped out of the room, the Maker's life went on, away from me; a notion I found terrible, lonely and isolating in extremes.)

'He brought a woman, as I say. She was tall and slender, delicate as rose petal. He would at times produce for me odd gifts, to see how I reacted; flowers, a book, a magnifying glass. I imagined he had brought her in a similar capacity. I reached out. . . . She stepped back, her hand up to her mouth. She hid her face. He spoke to her, softly, gently, sadly: *This is my sin,* He said. He confessed to her. *This is my sin you had to see.* I cried out. I cried, I am a man, I am a man, I am a man, not a sin! My voice was strangled, hoarse. He took the woman from me. Oh, what beauty she possessed! Her scent was . . . it was something I had never smelled before. When she was gone I strove to conjure it, to summon up the memory . . . I could not.

'Then there were other matters. The night angels grew slowly bold again. One evening they brought in drink, and plied me with it. This, it may be, was their vengeance for the harm that I had done their colleague. I was a toy to them, as I was a toy to my Creator, too. I roared and sang and howled. The world spun. God descended, drawn by the display. He raged as He must once have raged at Lucifer. The night angels were banished. They were not replaced. When darkness fell, the universe would empty, leaving me alone. Was this my punishment? I had no sense of time. The nights rolled on interminably, and I seldom slept.

'Yet I was planning. I had studied the construction of the cage. I had been fascinated by the nails that held it all together; they seemed a weak, ramshackle form of binding. In truth, they proved a little stronger than expected, but I was able with some effort to prise apart the beams, one from another, to wrench and twist them free. And this I did.

'When morning came, I had already left the world. I walked out. I walked out into Eden.'

'Well. I doubt that,' I remarked.

'I was born in thunder. Raised in darkness, in the confines of a prison cell. Why should I not believe I was in Eden, then? Why not?'

Beyond, the surf still beat against the shore.

I lit my pipe.

The smoke brought little comfort. Still I sucked at it, hoping to alleviate my fear.

Chapter Forty-eight

'Picture me then, among the orchards of the castle. Apples everywhere. I eat my fill. Once, I meet a group of gardeners. They flee in panic at the sight of me, abandoning their shears and scythes. I test the blades upon my fingertips; intrigued by both their sting and by the bright red ooze that spills out from my skin. Yet always, always in my mind, I have the thought of my Creator, and a longing for His love.

'I reason that His love can still be won. That I must demonstrate my worthiness and my devotion to Him. So I step out from the trees. I walk across the lawn. I open wide my arms. "Lord, Lord, here am I."

'Sharp pain stabs my shoulder, knocks me to the ground. A moment, and I hear the crack of what I later learn to be a gunshot. A wisp of smoke drifts from a window on the building's second floor.

'God's thunderbolt. Later, I pry it from my flesh, the little metal pellet. I carry it here with me still. A relic.'

My pipe was out again. I knocked it on my heel to empty it.

'Sir, I do not dispute the harshness of your life. Nor the unfairness of it. Even so—'

But he spoke on, ignoring me, like a man held in a trance, obsessed with all the details of his singular existence (even now, I find it hard to call it 'life').

'For days we play the game. I hide. I call to Him. "Dear God, oh God, my Lord." I am the prodigal; the one who fled and wishes to return. If He will only speak to me I feel my life will be made well. If He could see my misery, away from Him, He would relent, and call me back, to sit upon His right hand side. For God is just, but God is merciful. His anger is a moment, and His favour for a lifetime. . . . So the scriptures say. And yet I saw no favour. Neither then, nor now.

'One day He sent His angels, hunting me. They carried guns, and sabres, and pitchforks. Some were upon horseback. But I knew the castle grounds by then, also the woods around, and I evaded them with ease. I had been cunningly constructed, large but also nimble, and when I chose it, silent as a mouse. I let them chase around; I kept them secretly in sight, and when that proved impractical, they gave away their own positions with their hunting horns, their uncouth cries, their clumsiness. At last I chose to show myself. I was at a distance from them, seemingly racing for the woods. But as they set off in pursuit, I dodged and circled round, concealed by outbuildings. I came up from behind, seized three or four, and left them broken on the ground just like the puppets that they were. This was my message to Him. After that, I hid myself a while. I changed my tactics, let Him think that I was gone, vanished from His lands, His presence. In truth, though, I was closer to Him than He could imagine.

'I did not count the passage of the days and nights. I pondered more on distance, while I yet remained in Heaven's bower. The woods, which had initially appeared to ring the world, a wall around it, now revealed themselves a world all of their own, each step opening further visions, undreamt possibilities. Beyond them, I surmised, must lie the countries of the Bible, and of casual conversation; the lands of Hamburg, Stuttgart and Gethsemane. This new knowledge, crowding through my head, still further anchored me within the world of matter and gross things. I struggled to retain that sense which I had had at birth, of something other, of an origin beyond all origins, and yet it faded, and refused to be recalled.

'I let Him think me gone. The angels would patrol, often striking deep into the woodland; but I covered up my tracks with diligence. I was a ghost. I was there and yet invisible to everyone.

'I watched Him bring His bride back to the castle, no doubt considering me safely gone, His realm His own once more.

'The woman fascinated me. Unique in my experience. I could not say why I felt so helplessly compelled by her, so drawn; to the extent that there were moments when I loathed her for the things she made me feel, moments I would happily have torn her limb from limb.

'At night, I climbed the castle walls. I slipped with ease from ledge to ledge, my balance never faltering. I watched as slowly, with surprising clumsiness, he peeled her garments from her. Shy, she turned away, shutting her eyes. And I was there with her; had she but known, she need have taken only one or two small steps, reached out her arms, and she would lay her hands upon me. I hung outside her window, feeling I could hang that way forever; or at least until the show was done.

'Naked, she seemed smaller, and more delicate. An oyster peeled out of its shell. She hid herself behind her hands. She asked that He might douse the candles. He said the dark would hide her beauty. He was on His knees. He seemed to worship her—the Great Almighty God at prayer—but there was also, it appeared, a certain sly delight in her discomfort, a pleasure in her blushes and contortions. When He entered her, she cried out. He did not stop. He did not speak. This was His triumph, eclipsing or erasing any triumph He had gained at my making. And in this, I am astonished. For the crude inherent rhythms of biology meant more to Him than work, than life. . . . More to Him by far than I.

'Watching, and listening, I could feel my own loins stir. I resolved at once to have Him make for me a bride, a creature of my own kind, that I might no longer be lonely. I would confront Him, press my suit. . . .'

The night was now far on till morning. I was cold. I pulled my coat about me. I looked at this poor creature with his ugly, melancholic head, bulging like a sack of rocks, his soft, hoarse voice, reciting as by rote.

I said, 'He made the promise, but then failed to honour it.'

'Quite so. He said He would, but He recanted. So I killed Him.'

'And since?'

'His sons, His daughters. I have laid my contract on them all. All failed.'

'And died.'

He inclined his head a fraction. I thrust the point home. 'While you live. Alone.'

Even in the dark, I saw him tense; his muscles bulk, his shoulders spread, his head go down. I spoke more quickly.

'I am not of your creator's clan. You understand? There's nothing to be gained by harming me. Is that quite clear? And yet it may be I am able to assist you. Do you follow?'

He did not reply. I said, 'Sir, tell me that you understand.'

His voice was hushed. 'I understand your words,' he said.

'Well, good. That's good.'

I drew myself up, ready to speak strongly, then for prudence's sake, took three or four steps back, away from him. 'There is a lesson in this, sir. In all these years of solitude, misery and murder. The lesson is that you have killed a great, great many, and still not gained your wish. For killing is the wrong route, sir.' I took my pipe out from my pocket, but did not refill it. Rather I fidgeted, turning it over in my hand for comfort. 'The answer lies in understanding—the word you used yourself. If you could understand your Lord's work, you too could be as He was. Can you grasp the possibilities of this? Can you?'

I heard the high, feigned optimism of my tone.

I only prayed it sounded more sincere to him than it could ever do to me.

Frankenstein's Prescription

His head went down, his shoulders up; I heard the low, faint hissing of his breath, like the sound of some great steam engine.

'Some nights I dream,' he said.

It was hardly the response I had been looking for.

'The same dream, many, many times. There is a fire . . . I feel the heat of it.' He raised his face, as if to catch some hidden warmth. 'Then, in my dream, I burn. I die.'

I hugged my coat around me, shivered in the damp night air.

'I have seen many deaths. But now I feel it, cell by cell, and nerve by nerve. The slow extinction of all things. Blackness and silence.' He took a long breath. 'Peace.'

'This is . . . this is something you anticipate? Or, or—' A new thought struck me. 'You wish for it?'

He raised his head a little, turned to the side, a move I took to be a shrug.

'The spark of life, once set, clings to the flesh, and will not loose its hold.'

'Not so with us,' I said.

'Some nights, when I dream. Some nights I fail to die.'

'Well,' I said. 'It's just a dream. . . .'

'No. A dream is primal knowledge.'

'But not real . . . ?'

'Before Eden, there were dreams.'

My fingers found the gun-butt in my pocket. There would be no time better, perhaps, while he was so preoccupied, obsessed with his bizarre, meandering confession. 'I bow then, to your primal knowledge.' I clasped the butt, I slipped a finger through the trigger-guard. 'You say you do not die?'

'I melt.'

'Ah-hah.' I still did not remove the safety catch.

'Like candlewax. I flow. I feel myself dissolve and seep into the ground. Each clod of earth, each root, each worm, each insect takes a part of me. I grow up with the grass and with the trees; I am devoured by birds and beasts and cattle, who are themselves devoured by men; and thus, little by little, I become the world. I am its seasons. I am its days and nights, its cycles of consumption, defecation, growth; I am a snake that swallows its own tail. Yet in all, I find no joy. Nothing but longing—longing for cessation. To be free of this. This loneliness. This life whose actions are repeated endlessly, time and again.'

I had seen him as a clever toy, much like Lavenza's flesh automata at M——. A mechanical man. To hear him speak like this disturbed me. For now I glimpsed an inner life, a life of feeling and imagination . . . alien, yet horribly familiar, also; horribly human.

'Sir,' I said, 'you have my sympathy—'

'I do not want your sympathy. I want one thing. One specific thing.'

'A mate, of course. And you must follow my instructions in this. You will become as God, you will become as Viktor Frankenstein once was, if you just sheath your anger for a time, and listen—'

'What I want,' he said, 'is a redeemer.'

'And you shall have her! You shall have the means, and the skills, and all that you require!'

'The Bible speaks of sin,' he said. 'And of repentance. But my first sin lay in being born. Am I to blame for that? For the act that sprang insensate matter into life? Is that my guilt, my shame?'

His voice rose, angrily.

'I want redemption.'

His breath sounded like metal scraped on stone.

'Salvation.'

Perhaps it would be possible to kill him. He was close enough. A well-aimed shot, to whatever vulnerable part he might disclose. Through the eye, into the brain. It might be possible. And then a fire. A pyre. Just like he said. And shovel the remains into the surf, rid the world of him, once and for all.

But he was too close. Too near to me. And I was too afraid.

He rose onto his feet. His form was vast; from where I sat, he seemed to cut the sky in two. It struck me that no gun short of a cannon might destroy him, and in his flesh he could already carry round a pound of pistol-shot, with no more than the mildest of discomforts.

'I am alone,' he said. 'Who can redeem me? There is none like me. Who then? You, sir? You?'

'You are not like us, sir, no,' said I. 'But surely—this enmity you bear our kind. Can you not set it aside? Can you not find it in your heart . . . ?'

'My heart is a dead man's.'

'Then trust me, sir. Let me find some means to rekindle it.'

Chapter Forty-nine

I woke Lavenza. He cried out, and tried to seize me by the throat. He fought with me, convinced I was the monster come to kill him. But I was stronger, and I held him down.

'You have to teach him. It's the only way. Otherwise, he'll never leave you. You, me—even poor Karl. He'll kill us all.'

Lavenza squinted, tried to focus in the dim light. 'I told you that. He'll kill us all, yes. I told you.' His voice was tremulous, but filled with certainty. 'We failed him. So we die.'

'No,' I said. 'I've seen him. We have made a pact. If you too will agree, them it may be we are safe from him. For now, at least.'

⁂

A café terrace, early morning; we sat there in our hats, scarves and overcoats. I smoked my pipe. There was money in my pocket once again. I did not choose to think where it had come from; only to contemplate the breakfast spread before us.

'We go to your castle. Your family home. He follows us. Once there, you will instruct him. You will take him as your pupil. When he has your knowledge, he will have no further use for you. Or me, for that matter. We will be free.'

'He won't see it like that.'

'He has agreed already.'

'His mind is fractured. His reasoning is different from our own. You make a bargain? You understand its terms in one way, he in quite another.'

'He wants the power of God. I say we give it, and have done.'

'If it were ours to give.'

'It was your ancestor's. Tell him what you know. Afterwards, it's up to him.'

'And he's too big. Too clumsy. The surgery is delicate. The machinery. . . .'

'He does not strike me as so clumsy, sir. Big, but also swift, and dangerous. Make him as you would be. Make him as God; leave him nobody to blame except himself.'

'This will go badly. And the castle is . . . it's not a place I wish to see again. . . .'

'He has agreed. And there is something else,' I said, looking Lavenza in the eye. 'It seems to me, once there, in your family home—the place he was created—might there not be some way to destroy him, also? Once and for all?'

It was a wild hope, and yet it won Lavenza to my plan. Such plan as I then had, at any rate.

※

The creature had provided the train fare, and a little more. We made a shabby trio waiting on the platform, Karl, Lavenza and myself; our luggage no more than a few bags stuffed with bread, dried meats and fruit, our clothes now worn and, I regret to say, all somewhat odorous. To think that, just a week ago, I was the toast of Paris salons! I tapped my fingers restlessly. In truth, I had no grand scheme; only a sense that, if I stopped, if I did nothing, I would crumble. I would sink into a despair so terrible that I would never break its bonds, and all the wrath of Heaven would descend on me. My sole objective now was to keep moving, and hope to God—if I might use the name—that matters might in some way be resolved. And I would walk free of the mess, ready and able to resume my life.

But there was much to do before that time. There was the matter of Rebecca to be settled, for a start. Poor Madame Pluviers. It was rarely the case that I regretted my behaviour with the fair sex, and I believe that, even now, it was not so much regret I felt, but an emotion so seldom present in my soul that I could not at first put name to it.

In honourable terms, I might call it the need for justice, for settling scores, restoring harmony.

But in my heart, my thoughts were much less noble. I had been baulked, betrayed, and I could not forgive.

In my heart, I hungered for revenge.

Germany

Chapter Fifty

On horseback now, we rode through orchards, long since overgrown and gone to seed, up stone steps scabbed with moss, into the ruins of a Chinese garden, where the statues leered at us out of the foliage; onto a muddy, pitted drive. . . .

A homecoming of sorts.

No castle, though, this grand Schloss Frankenstein; rather a house of monumental size and stern, block-like design, fortified due to its loneliness and to the bandits which had once—and likely still—roamed hereabouts. The lower floor was all blank stone, broken by a single door and, at the side, great iron gates topped off with barbs. Above, high, narrow windows gleamed like fire under a late-day sun.

At sight of it, Lavenza spurred his horse. He craned up in the saddle, straining for some odour of the place, perhaps. An energy compelled him. I had seen it growing through our journey, watched him re-awaken, scribbling notes for hours on the train, then leafing back to overwrite, cross out, or squeeze new lines between the old, exclaiming, muttering between his teeth, much to the grievance of our fellow passengers. Indeed, at one point he was banished to the corridor, where for all I know he kept on working till the sun came up and breakfast was announced. He spoke of new plans, better plans. They were opaque to me, as mine probably were to him. It had taken all my powers to persuade him here; yet once resigned, the notion seemed to catch him like a flame to paper, creeping stealthily along its edge, blazing at last to fullest flower. The transformation pleased me. It offered, as may be, some hint of hope in what were now the direst circumstances.

The monster would be close, I had no doubt. Behind us, or ahead, but close, for sure. Here was his crucible, his wretched Eden; an appointment he could scarcely fail to keep.

Lavenza clambered from his mount. He gazed about him, put his head back, stared up at the house; he ran his fingers through his hair.

'It's smaller,' he said. 'Smaller than I'd thought.'

'You're larger.'

'Well. Yes. Possibly. . . .'

We worked quickly in the fading light. He had a key which, with some effort, opened the gates into the inner yard. Here were stables, and a well—still functional—and several small, slate-roofed workshops, including what appeared to be a forge. A pile of timber had been stacked under a tarpaulin by the wall, huge lengths, cut from the tallest woodland trees. Across the stone above was daubed a message: 'Shall not the judge of all the Earth deal justly?' It was the red paint used for rust-proofing; the letters slashed and spattered on the wall as in a fury. Lavenza saw it and the colour drained from him.

I took his arm.

'My friend. Let us indoors, shall we? Before we catch our death.'

•

So it was Karl stabled our horses, found our firewood, and drew water. Indeed, he was invaluable; and for a man whose inner life had been so much in turmoil, showed an admirable practicality. It was as if he still performed his chores at the asylum. Nothing worried him. In what had been the drawing room, he set a blaze, boiled water, and made tea. He dusted armchairs and swept debris from the floor. We settled to a strange imposture of domestic life. Red sunset lit the room. From here, we had a view across the lawns—a wild sea of grass—and over to the woods. Were I a general in a war I could have wished no better spot. Even Lavenza seemed to have recovered from his fright outside, and strolled about, examining the furniture, the curtains, bric-a-brac, quietly enthralled by all the flotsam of his infancy.

We ate dried meat, and bread, and Karl, still foraging, found schnapps, with crystal tumblers, pouring drinks for each of us.

'I am amazed,' I said, 'to see so much here still intact.'

Lavenza shrugged. 'The family lived well,' he said. 'Just for a time.'

'Still. The place is not impregnable, and people being what they are. . . .'

'Oh. Well. Let's say it has a . . . slightly suspect reputation roundabouts. Mm-hm?'

'Now I'm surprised.'

'Ah. That's a joke, I take it? I hope it was a good one. Irony, I think?' He gulped his drink. 'And of course, there are the twins,' he said.

'What twins?'

'Nothing to worry about. You'll meet them by and by. Or not, depending how they feel.'

'Another Frankenstein secret. Like the bodies in the cellar. Like the murders.'

'I was not responsible.'

'Relax. Relax. . . .'

But we could not relax. The tensions of the day stayed with us; the talk grew thin, the booze did little to enliven us. Instead we sank, each into his own dark reverie, until at last I made excuses, rose and left the room.

Lavenza scarcely seemed to notice my departure.

⁂

I stopped to fill my pipe, which I can do in the dark, and then stepped out beneath the stars. The air was chill. On three sides, the black walls of the house rose sheer; and on the fourth, a little lower, lay the stables. It felt like standing at the bottom of a pit.

I lit up, sucked the soothing smoke; blew out, and watched it vanish in the gloom.

'Well then?' I said.

A chunk of shade detached itself, off to my right. It moved without a sound, except just now and then the rasp of coarse cloth rubbing, but no more.

'You're here,' I said.

'But I must leave soon. I have other matters to attend to.'

He was not close, but even so, I found his presence overbearing. It was all that I could do to hold my ground.

'What other matters?'

'None of your concern.'

I gestured with my pipe, feigning insouciance I did not feel.

'Oh, well. And when might we expect you back? Within a week? A month, perhaps?'

'I am not bound by roads as you are. Nor by time. I travel where I will. A day, maybe. Or two.' His great head lifted, and he looked about himself. 'The place is familiar. We have met here many times, my Lord and I. He, or his father. Or his father's father. Many, many times.'

He hunched down, squatting on his heels like a farmer.

'You brought him to me.'

'He was keen. He wants to help you if he can.'

'In some beliefs, they say that the Iscariot is sacred, for without him no redemption could begin. His kiss, the first act in Jehovah's plan.'

'No kiss. And I'm no Judas. Bear that in mind. There'll be no dying here, you understand?'

'You wish to bargain, then?'

'I wish what we agreed.'

I puffed my pipe, and with my other hand thrust deep into my pocket, dug the nails into my palm until I bled.

'These matters that you speak of,' I said then. 'Will you confide their nature? Tell me exactly when you will return.'

But he was gone, and I had never heard him leave.

Chapter Fifty-one

'The filth! The dirt!'

He stamped and kicked; the dust blew up in billows, and the morning sun shot through it like the rays of glory in some old religious painting. Rested and refreshed, Lavenza strode about the room wide-eyed, inspecting everything.

'This—I remember—the table that I used to hide under, to watch the grown-ups come and go. But the room seemed so much vaster . . . like a palace. Grand, astonishing. . . .'

'I've told you. You were small. As we grow up, the world diminishes. We find our place in it, and are no longer overwhelmed.'

'Our place?' He looked at me. 'I have no place in it, friend Hans. You know that, surely?'

I was used now to his doom-laden remarks—his Werthers, as I called them—but today, although the words were much the same, he himself seemed almost brimming with good humour. It prompted me to broach a subject then much on my mind.

'Suppose,' I said, 'suppose that you could walk away? Forget your quest?'

He made a face, wrinkled his nose.

I said, 'I'm serious. We might not return to Paris, true. But we could try for London, or Vienna—or the New World. Take new identities. New names. Become mere practising physicians. Could you be satisfied with that? To live the life of normal men, perhaps to moan the fate biology lays out for us, but no longer to question it or try to change it? Not to dream that one might circumvent or triumph over pre-ordained fatality? Accept our lot? Could you do that?'

He hardly stopped to think.

'No, Hans. No.'

'At any cost?'

'At any cost.'

So I had made my offer. And there, with just a few brief words, he sealed his fate; and mine, though I scarce knew it at the time.

Had I planned well? Attended to each detail, all eventualities which might arise? Was I alert to danger, thoroughly prepared, forearmed?

Of course not. Such a route was foreign to my nature. I was a schemer, yes, but my plans were simple fancies, dreamt up to the rhythm of a railway car, or half-asleep in some provincial inn. At Heidelberg, I had relied on charm to see me through, but even charm could not deflect a fatal bullet. I saw things only in the most immediate and personal of terms: I had to free myself from this long duel between Lavenza and his creature, and do so in a way that might ensure my fortune and advantage. There were darker motives, too: anger and pique and bitterness, and maybe guilt, as well, that muttered to me from the shadows of my mind; but these, I did my best to shut away. I held only the vaguest sense of any plan; indeed, at heart, I still hoped some unguessed-at chance might suddenly present itself, solving my problems with but minor effort and—more to the point—minimum risk.

As strategy, this was not really Napoleonic. Yet a fragment of Lavenza's cheery spirits lodged in me, and once more I began to speculate upon my future—even to assume that I might have one. I saw the distant goal, though not the road to it. And for now, that seemed enough.

Frankenstein's Prescription

It might be I should choose a diplomat's career over a doctor's, I considered. Why not? I had been told I had a silver tongue, though in truth, the people who said that were mainly female, and their meaning not, perhaps, one for polite society.

Recalling all the women in my life consoled me somewhat. (Though I stopped short, deliberately, rather than think about Rebecca.) I brushed my clothes down. (I had slept in them; they seemed to stick to me now like a second skin.) I organised Karl in the production of coffee for us all. As I did so, Lavenza wandered away, into the back rooms. I thought nothing of this till the drink was ready. I called to him. Heard no reply. Karl put his head on one side. 'Want me to look for him, Master?'

'You stay. I'll go myself.'

Mild anxiety now pricked at me. There was probably some simple explanation—I myself experienced a strong desire to urinate—but it worried me, nevertheless. I pulled my coat about me, felt in my pocket for tobacco. I'd had little chance to look around the place last night. Now, leaving the main room, I picked my way over the debris, filling my pipe up as I went. I trod lightly. I did not call Lavenza's name again. Not that I feared to warn him of my presence; more, I feared, half-superstitiously, alerting someone else.

I searched, too, for a water closet. I found none, but a broken pane of glass at roughly the right height gave access to the inner yard. I pissed through this, watching the steam billow like bonfire smoke. It was a wonderful, refreshing thing, and I reflected on those daily pleasures of the body, overlooked by both philosophers and sensualists alike. Was it not a marvel, to feel such relief, to void a whole night's water in this way? Had I believed in God, I might have given thanks for such a pleasant mechanism.

Next, I sought to ease another itch, lighting my pipe. It may be pleasure is no more than the relieving of discomfort, like a good scratch. Who knows? I drew the smoke into my lungs, coughed a hearty cough, clearing the chest and head. Then, thus fortified, resumed my search.

There had been long dilapidation here. The moth and rust and rain and wind had done their work. I picked my way across a mass of fallen drapes and rotted cushions, and in one room the remains of a false plaster ceiling that lay scattered on the floor. In just a single spot did I see signs of violent or deliberate destruction; a great display cabinet had been overturned, half-blocking the entrance, and only with some difficulty could I enter. Broken glass and crockery lay everywhere. The cabinet itself was massive—I had to walk over the back of it—and heavy, so that it might have taken three or even four strong men to move. Or one, if he were large enough, and he might still be called a man. . . . A Sherlock Holmes would probably have read the place's history, but I saw merely wreckage, dusty battlefields, and hurried on.

Somewhere a door opened and closed, deep in the building's heart.

I walked faster. Here, a flight of worn stone steps sank down into the gloom. Again, a sound of movement; and, with some reluctance, I started to descend. Almost immediately, I caught Lavenza's voice below.

'Here. Here now.'

Was he addressing me? No. The tone was wrong—soothing, almost cooing.

I had no lantern. I kept one hand on the wall to guide myself. Soon I was in a set of cellar rooms. The darkness was not quite impenetrable; small windows near the ceiling gave a little smoky light. I heard a rushing sound ahead, as of the wind, and, more surprisingly, a chuckle: Lavenza's laughter, which I had hardly ever heard before. I reached a final door, left just ajar, and slipped into a soft, monastic twilight.

I stared about me, all else forgotten. This, surely, had been built as a cathedral. The high, vaulted roof, some three storeys above, windows of tinted glass, their light now half-obscured by moss and dirt. . . . Yet a cathedral for a secular age, with neither icons nor statues, but great towers of machinery, so much vaster than those which filled the workshop back at M——; this, indeed, was certainly the prototype, of which M—— had been mere shadow, like a child's toy by comparison.

Lavenza stood, his back to me, positioned in the very centre of the hall. He was not alone. Yet his companions—if such they were—were as nothing I had ever seen before, not even in my dreams. I watched them from the doorway, struggling to accept the scene, and comprehend exactly what was taking place. Two globes of light were floating in the centre of the room, circling rapidly above Lavenza's head. Each, I think, was about the size of my fist, and their glow was not a constant thing, but wavered intermittently; nor did it light the hall around, but seemed peculiarly focused, twin drops of concentrated energy. I had the oddest recognition that, unlike the works of Mr Edison and friends, these strange globes were in some way *made* of light, just as a man is made of flesh, or a tree of wood; like the ball-lightning which people claim to see in thunder storms. Lavenza's gaze was wholly fixed upon the pair. He raised his arm, he clicked his fingers, made little murmurs as one might do to a child. One globe immediately dropped out of its orbit and commenced to circle dizzyingly round his upraised forearm, followed quickly by the second, until it seemed a ring of solid light encircled the man's wrist. I had seen nothing like this ever in my life, not even from the most acclaimed theatrical illusionist. Lavenza drew his arm back, made a throwing move. The two globes leapt up, almost to the ceiling, hovering for several moments. They bobbed, swayed, buoyant as a ball in water. An energy appeared to crackle through them. It was extraordinary. Lavenza beckoned. He made a hissing sound between his teeth. The two orbs sank towards him, spiralling gently down.

And I stepped forward.

At once, they froze, suspended in mid air. Then, with a sudden rush, they bounced up, hit the wall and ricocheted across the hall, veering at the last moment and disappearing through an open door down at the farther end. I could do nought but stare.

'You startled them,' Lavenza said, himself quite unsurprised to see me there. 'They're very shy, you know.'

'Shy.'

'They don't like sudden movement. Changes in air. Unfamiliar smells. You do smell, by the way.'

'You too.'

'Do I? Ah. Perhaps we can arrange for some hot water. I'm sure that Karl could draw us up a bath.'

'Even at the asylum, you had a certain . . . odour. It seemed impolite to mention.'

'Dear. Dear dear.'

He smiled, and for a second, in the soft light, he was almost boyish, uncombed hair draped in his eyes, a small half-smile on his face.

Then he said, 'Careful where you tread.'

I thought at first that he was issuing some general warning, to beware the house's mysteries; but following his gaze, I saw the floor ahead of me had rotted and gone through, a broken-edged blackness sinking to the depths below.

'There are repairs to do. The place is not the way it was.'

'Still,' I said. 'Good to be home?'

'It's a surprise to me, but—yes. I'm . . . very pleased, I have to say.'

'Your friends?' I gestured to the door.

'Oh—' Lavenza flung his head back. 'I haven't seen them in—it must be twenty years at least. I'm just amazed that they remember me. After so long. Don't you think?'

'These are the twins you spoke about . . . ?'

'Oh, yes! Very good! That's what we'd call them, Papa, Mutti and myself. *Where's the twins*, we'd say, and *Let's go find the twins*. We liked to speak the local dialect. The servants' talk. I didn't see that much of Papa. He was busy, or away from home. . . .

Mutti did her best. I don't believe she understood. I don't imagine he'd explained things to her. You wouldn't, would you? There's a dreadful creature, and it follows me about. . . . He was . . . he was secretive. I only learned his story much, much later. My heritage. . . . He kept his journals, his notebooks, scattered where his travels took him. I had to put it all together. It took years. Our serving girl, Maria, helped me out. She was closer to him than my mother was, I think. In many ways. A gipsy, full of old blood, superstition. Long memories, the travelling folk. Their memory's a home for them, their only stable point. . . .'

'Lavenza,' I said. 'Tell me what they were. Those things? Were they solid? I've never seen such a phenomenon! Like will-o'-the-wisps, yet of such size! Tell me, please?'

'Ah. Hans. You catch me reminiscing. It's becoming something of a weakness here. . . . The old place brings back memories. Not always happy ones, to tell the truth, but—all I have.'

'I understand.'

'No. That you'll never do. And be glad.'

'My own parents—'

He straightened, slapped his thigh and began to strut about the place, talking like a tour guide, keen to show his learning.

'See the shape of it? It's been altered, of course, and may need altering again, to get the proper resonance. And it's too cluttered. It's my memory of this place, obviously, which made me choose the chapel for my workshop, back at the asylum. But I lacked specifications. Now, with father's notes, I may at last see things through to their end.'

'You're pressing on, then.'

'Oh yes. Nothing else for it, I'm afraid. Nothing else.'

'The women—'

'Never fear, dear Hans! Your precious ladies will be safe this time. I give my word on that.'

'So.'

He clapped me on the shoulder. 'Well then, well then! And what do you think of the twins, eh? Aren't they pretty?'

'Truly. But I asked you what they are.'

'Some creatures of my grandfather's. Or great-grandfather's, say. As a boy I'd play with them for hours. Although they're timid, and don't always come when called.'

'Their nature?'

'Oh, some effort to maintain the spirit in a disembodied form. An electro-magnetic field, or some such. Simpler, I suppose, than the corporeal type. None of the mechanics to be bothered with. I don't entirely understand. Fond as I am of them, it never struck me as a worthwhile course. Though now, perhaps . . . well. I may change my mind.'

'They were—incredible.'

'Yes. Dogs, I think, originally. At least, I've always thought of them as dogs. I had names for them when I was small. I've forgotten now. They were . . . oh, this will sound extremely silly. But we were far from anybody else. Other children. So they became my playfellows. I'm glad that they remember me.'

'Karl's making breakfast.'

'Good old Karl. I'm well looked after, aren't I?'

'Your spirits seem considerably improved since we arrived.'

'They do, I know. I just woke up this morning, thinking, here I am again! I put it off so long, when it was clearly something I was meant to do. Should have done it long ago, in fact.'

'Before Paris.'

He shuffled uncomfortably. Then he raised his chin, nodding upwards.

'See the vaulting? I'd wager the proportions here match those in Papa's manuscript. And there—notice the far wall? Rebuilding work. A little crude, it's true—done on the cheap, I'd say—but clearly meant to bring the place in line with his ideas. He was astonishingly clever. Really.'

'No doubt.'

'Do try to sound impressed, old man! This is the goal mankind has sought since first he stepped down from the trees. At last within our grasp! So give a little credit, eh?'

'Your father failed.'

'Now how can you say that? Here we are, right on the brink, and you tell me that he failed?'

'But if he hadn't failed,' I said, 'we wouldn't be here. Would we?'

Chapter Fifty-two

I needed time alone.

I sat a while there in the drawing room, smoking a pipe and contemplating my position. It had occurred to me, and more than once, that I might simply leave; unlike my companion, I should not have come here in the first place. At times the urge became so strong that I would actually rise, start to gather my possessions—but always, then, it passed. And I remained.

The shutters were swung back. The day was fair, the sky a clear, cold blue, the sun pleasant and warming through the glass. The view here was considerable. At its limit were the woods, a wall the creature had once thought of as the boundary to the world. Off to my right, the gardens and the orchards, spilling from their confines, and the lawns, now overgrown, rippling like water in the breeze. Nearby were several large trees, sycamores, and presently I caught sight of a jay, foraging among their branches. It was a restless bird, taking flight from limb to limb, now hidden in the foliage, now out again, a flash of white and beige and black. I watched it, wishing it would halt a moment, let me see it fully, but it did not. Here was a beauty I might once have passed up as irrelevant, but which today delighted me, teasing in its quick, elusive moves, and busy, hurried industry. And it struck me that this bird would still be here tomorrow, with its beauty, and its dashing, flashing purpose; while Lavenza, Karl and I might not.

When finally the bird flew off and failed to return, I put my pipe away, and went down, once more, to the great hall.

At that point, I had little else to do.

'This is not, I think, your former apparatus.'

I chewed dry bread. Of all the things stored in the house, a little food—dry biscuits, ship's rations—would have been more than welcome, and was the one sole item I had not yet found.

Lavenza's face was dirty, grimed with dust. He had remained here through the morning, pottering with these peculiar devices, the use of which I could not even start to guess. 'My father's,' he explained. 'Or possibly my grandfather's. Or great-grandfather's. Again, I am afraid, I'm not entirely clear. . . .' He eyed the dusty plates and broken wiring, flaking paint and rust. 'I'm working on it. Cleaning it up. An interesting principle . . . I think—once Karl has fixed the generator—well. Listen.'

He raised his hands over his head, clapped with cupped palms. The sound snapped, sharp and sudden; seemed to pause a moment, then the echo rolled back and reverberated, harmonics ringing in my ears—a curious, unfathomable quality, gone before the mind could quite lay hold of it.

'I don't say that it's perfect. But it's close.'

'Your Sistine Chapel.'

'A crude attempt to act on principles not fully understood. Where this, I think—'

He clapped his hands.

Again.

Again.

The sound throbbed in the walls, the floor; I felt it through my riding boots.

'Hans,' he said, seizing my arm.

'Lavenza.'

'If things should go amiss.'

'They won't.'

'But if they should. Now, this is most important. Listen. I need your word. Your very solemn promise. Your word as . . . what? A gentleman? A Christian?'

'As a man, Lavenza. And not much of one, I sometimes think.'

'I want your promise. If he does what I think he will, and I do not survive—you will bring me here. You will lay my body here, upon this bench. Precisely here. The generator must be running. These wires—I shall have them clean by then—attach them here, and here.' He touched his head, above the ears. 'You'll need a bandage, or adhesive of some kind . . . I'll see what can be found. This is important. I can't stress that enough.'

'Very well.' I spoke through half-chewed bread.

'I'll leave it all in place. Just bring the body and prepare it as I ask. This lever here will start the current. I hope. Once I've checked the wires. Oh, this is all so rushed! Then, sound. Vibration. It need not be Bach. A drum, a gong. Any loud, musical note . . .'

'You aren't about to die.'

'I wish I had more sense of that.'

'We have a plan. *I* have a plan. You know that. And once it's done, your troubles will be over. Yes?'

'I'm happy, Hans.'

'There is a plan. You understand?'

'I should have come here years ago. You know the way it is? You fear something. You put off facing it. Then, when finally you must confront the thing, at once a load lifts from your soul, and you discover it's the very matter which you should have dealt with years before. And—well. Here we are.'

'I have a plan. I will explain it shortly. It will work,' I said, an affirmation I was making with a dreadful regularity—as if mere repetition were enough to make it true.

'We all die here, you see. The Lavenzas, the Frankensteins. We die here, or are born. . . .'

'You will not damn well die!'

But he turned from me, speaking softly, as to a rather backwards child. 'I have always had two notions in my head, Hans. Two . . . *plans*, as you might say.'

'Indeed.'

'The first was simplest, and, if successful, offered least risk to myself. That was, I do what had been asked of me, satisfy the brute, accomplish what my ancestors had failed to do, provide him with a mate and thus appease him. I set off with such confidence. Such fervour. But in time. . . .

'The other course was more involved. Assuming he would kill me—which I do assume, friend Hans, no matter what you say—I need to find some means of surviving. Surviving death, you understand.'

'We've talked of this before. Medical science might increase our life expectancy, of course, but any further—'

'I believed, for many years, that this necessitated bodily survival. Today, I'm not so sure. Seeing the twins again. . . . Why should the body be the be-all and the end-all, eh? This flimsy, filthy carton.' He plucked the skin of his own arm. 'What do we have, without it? Nothing, as may be. Or mere energy, loose upon the universe . . . wave and frequency, the scattered elements of personality, adrift, unanchored. . . .'

'This,' I told him, 'is mere simple-minded mysticism.'

'Nonetheless. You'll do this thing I ask, won't you? You swear?'

'If need be,' I assured him. 'Which it won't. I swear.'

※

I was exploring. Searching. Roaming. Through this honeycomb of rot and dust. . . . Here, in the cellars of the monster's Eden, the dungeons of his Paradise, I picked my way by lantern light through rooms half-blocked with ancient storage, crates and boxes, drums and sacks and pieces of machinery, from farm tools to capacitors. In one room stood a printing press, the floor scattered with little metal cubes of letters. . . . And always, just ahead, behind, or to the side, the endless drip-drip-drip of water, like someone dropping pebbles down a well.

I had not lied to him.

Oh no.

I had a plan.

Only the mechanism of it still eluded me. The how, the what and where. And even they were slowly coming clear, it seemed: resolving in my head with all the pure, inevitable slowness of a photograph developing.

I would do what must be done. I would achieve my goal.

In times past, I had made plans, grand schemes, only to have them thwarted by some unseen element, some random factor twisting my whole system out of true. But not this time. This time I would succeed. Because I had to. Because I had no choice.

Because I could.

I was no toy of fate, no blind fool drifting in the wind. If I should choose to force my will upon the world, then I would do it. Oh yes. Oh yes, indeed.

I paused, refilled my pipe. Even my tobacco was now running out. I cursed myself for not having the foresight to stock up.

And then, a few steps on, I found it.

Among countless little storerooms, heaped with dust and coal and pottery and endless half-forgotten things, here was the one place I had sought, without so much as knowing.

It was a stone-built cell. Long enough to lie in, not much more. A broken box lay in the corner. Debris crunching under foot.

A ragged hole punched in the ceiling gave the look and feeling of an oubliette. I heard Lavenza pacing in the workshop overhead. I heard the clatter of his tools. I heard him wheeze and mutter to himself.

It made me smile, thinking of him there, oblivious to me, and I doused the lantern, lingering a while, and listening to him work.

Frankenstein's Prescription

❋

'Ho, Karl! What news?'

He stiffened, but was slow to look at me, as if expecting someone else, someone he did not care to see. His frown lines and the bags beneath his eyes marked a great X upon his face.

'News, Master?'

'How goes your day?'

'The entry pipe is clogged. There is oil here, and here, and the plugs are thick with filth. I notice also—'

'It was a general enquiry, Karl, no more. So—generally well? Or poorly?'

'. . . fairly well, Master. There's dirt, but I think everything must work, once clean.'

The generator was a massive, antiquated thing, a relic of another age, like some huge tortoise hidden in a cave.

'And fuel?' I said. 'Plenty of fuel?'

'Think so, Master. Haven't checked. It's over there.'

'Well. There's no use for a machine without the fuel. That's like . . .' But my cheerful patina soon failed me, and no simile came forth.

There were drums stored to the rear of the chamber. Like the machine itself, they were rusted, caked with dirt. I shoved at one. It seemed heavy enough.

'Friend Karl. Do you have a wrench?'

He passed me an adjustable wrench. The place was well equipped, at least. I fitted the tool around the drum's stopper and twisted. For a second it seemed jammed beyond all help; then, at once, it turned. I smelt the fumes.

'That's good, that's good.' I looked to Karl. 'Can you find—oh, say, a lidded container—about so high? Easily carried? Fill it, then set it aside for me, will you? There's a good chap.'

'Yes, Master.' Karl nodded. Then he put his head on one side, watching me. 'Master?'

I was already half way out the door.

'Am I your friend?'

'What?'

'You called me "friend". Am I your friend?'

I laughed, but something in me made me pause. 'Yes, Karl,' I told him. 'You're my friend.'

And I went on my way.

Chapter Fifty-three

Someone had moved the lumber.

I had gone into the yard for water only hours before, and all had been in order then. Now lengths of wood, cut from the tallest trees, lay spilled over the flagstones, and the grey tarpaulin that had covered them was flung back, gleaming in the sun.

I gazed round warily. Saw no-one.

It might, of course, be a simple accident—a rotted guy-rope, sudden strain, the covering snapped back, the timber rolling—but I could not believe it. These beams would take at least three men to lift. I clambered over them, feeling I was spied on the whole time.

In a stone shed built against the outer wall, I found carpentry tools, most still ordered neatly on their shelves, wrapped in oil-cloth, beautifully preserved. A few lay on the bench—saw, clamp, ratchet—as if recently inspected, and a scattering of nails had spread across the floor. I moved quickly, still not certain what I wanted; picked a hatchet and a small saw, several other items. Then hurried back into the house.

The door was heavy, oaken, and I felt a great deal happier once it was shut and locked behind me.

Knowing, nonetheless, that it would scarcely keep him out.

※

He was back. Wherever he had been, whatever preparations he had made, now he was back with us.

He brought us food.

He fed us.

Like caged beasts, or like prisoners, he fed us.

A crash of glass, up in the rooms above. A crash, then silence. We froze. Foremost in my mind was the awareness I was not yet ready, that he had come for us before my preparations were complete. I cursed, drawing my guns. Lavenza, seeking to help, pointed me towards the stairs; but I was well ahead of him.

Still no further sound. The monster could move softly, as I knew; but now the silence puzzled me. I moved from room to room, opening each door with trepidation, my finger tense upon the trigger.

And so I found it, in a study on the first floor, a picture window punched straight through, the floor all glittering with broken glass.

And in the midst, the body of a fallow deer, a fair specimen, its fur all sparkling with a hundred points of crystal light. . . .

Outside, an empty and unmoving landscape. No sign of him. And yet, what force must he have used to pitch the beast so high and with such violence, as if from a ballista . . . ? Just thinking of it made my blood ran cold.

'Venison,' I said, as Karl and Lavenza joined me. 'At least he doesn't plan for us to starve.'

Lavenza said, 'That isn't dinner.'

'No? It looks like it to me. Karl, if you'll prepare the beast—'

'It's a reminder,' said Lavenza. 'The kind he always gives. An animal, this time. The next. . . .'

'You're saying, like before? Some hapless peasant woman?' I glanced out once more at the wild lawns, the tangled orchards, and the forest far away. 'That's something I'd prefer us to avoid, if possible.'

'Not a peasant woman, no,' Lavenza said. 'No-one lives near.' My relief must have been visible, for he added then, 'His next victim, I fear, is in this room. We've had this conversation previously, I believe, or one much like it. So I remind you that he deems me of some use to him, and therefore I am much afraid that. . . .'

'Yes. I see.'

I found a box to stand on. I worked by lantern light. From time to time Lavenza would break off his own exertions and appear, framed in the hole above my head, frowning, chewing at his lower lip.

'Your plan,' he said, 'is clear insanity.'

'My plan,' I told him, 'is expedient. Yours, on the other hand, is obviously insane.'

'Oh yes,' he mocked. ' "My plan will work." Isn't that right?'

'I don't think I shall answer you. Or have you learned the art of humour? If so, I might perhaps manage a smile.'

I hacked into the joists, then used the saw to cut them almost through. It was a gruelling job, forever reaching up above my head, and pushing upwards. I had been strong, but the dissipations of Paris and the deprivations of the coast had both taken their toll. My arms ached. Once, I grew so dizzy that I almost fainted, and only just stepped from my perch in time. I let myself drop to the floor, slumped in the corner till my head cleared and I forced myself to carry on. Yet in my mind I had an image of my scheme in action, as if it had already taken place; I saw it clear as day, and the vision, endlessly repeated in my thoughts—it spurred me on.

I had Karl bring straw down from the stables. Dry wood and tinder. We piled it in the room. There was no door, but we found a heavy cabinet and dragged it into place, barraging the corridor outside with sacks of coal and other items, till both corridor and doorway were entirely blocked.

'He's an animal,' I told Lavenza, 'and we'll trap him like an animal.'

'No animal,' Lavenza said. 'Oh no, no, no.'

'For my purpose, an animal. That's all he is. All we are, too. Just animals.'

'You don't believe that there's a spirit in us, then? A soul? I'm not speaking religiously, of course, but scientifically—an essence, if you will, which under proper circumstance, may possibly survive—'

'It isn't that I don't believe in it. More, that I don't care.'

Lavenza tutted. 'It will resume its relevance,' he said, 'if our friend should ever get his hands around your throat.'

I brushed the wood chips from my face and beard, spat sawdust on the floor. 'More vital in that instance,' I announced, 'will be how fast I can unload a bullet in his face. Not spout this pious nonsense, eh?'

That night, we dined on venison.

And waited for him.

Still he did not come.

Chapter Fifty-four

'Where?'

'The tall tree with the ragged top. See that? Then down, a little to the right. No—left. See?'

Morning once more. Staring from our castle, or our prison, whichever it might be. Lavenza had a telescope, a dusty, rust-marked thing, but like all else here, clearly of the finest workmanship. I took it from him, held it to my eye.

The view was upside down.

'Under the tall tree.'

'To the left. . . .'

I moved the glass, getting my bearings only with some difficulty. It was an astronomical telescope, not meant for work like this; but presently I found our quarry, hanging from the top of the scene, shadowed and yet unmistakable—his weight, his bulk, his sheer solidity. . . .

I scanned to right and left, from tree to tree. Then something stopped me.

'What?' Lavenza said.

'Not sure. . . .'

I shifted back. The creature was still there, as immobile as a rock.

'Is he alone?' I said.

'Why?'

'I thought . . . a movement. Probably an animal. Another deer, maybe. Our lunch.' I smiled, rather an effort in the circumstances. 'Can he see us?'

'At a guess . . . better than we see him.'

'I wish,' I said, 'that one day, when I ask a question, you could bring me good news. Just the once, eh? Just the once.'

⁂

I made changes in the big hall. Lavenza grumbled, for I broke into his work regime, but I hardly cared. From an upstairs room, I took an artist's easel, placed it in the middle of the floor, a schoolroom touch. I shifted furniture, narrowed the entranceway. The weak spot in the floor, the hole which would become my snare, I covered with a dusty carpet of North African design. A further rug, I threw down just beforehand, over solid floor, thus to allay suspicion.

I did everything I could, and still new opportunities appeared. My mind was in a whirl. I chanced to glance up at the ceiling. Here, just at the entrance to the chamber, it was half-made, or half-unmade; beams and joists exposed in parts, some little space between these and the floor above; and it struck me, with a few boards carefully placed, a man might readily conceal himself up there, safe, yet perfectly positioned to wreak havoc on whoever stood below. . . . Yes. It was a moment when the world seemed to have fallen in my grasp, and schemes begun in desperation, rendered hastily out of whatever came to hand, revealed their true strength, proving themselves not flimsy, as I feared, but strong as iron.

I was ready now. Oh, I was more than ready.

Let him come. Just let him come.

⁂

'Vienna, I would say. Spare capital, a lot of money to invest. Progressive, forward-looking medical establishment. What more could we require?'

'More . . . ?'

'Oh, come on, man. Let's think about the future. A better workshop—better than any you have had to date. A proper, authorised supply of bodies. Straight from the city morgue. You'll have support, approval. Ratification. . . .'

'And why should I want that? Or any part of it?'

'Because—because it's your work, man. It's your mission in the world.'

'And if *he* no longer bothers me? Why would I need it then?'

Was he joking with me? After all this time, had he actually acquired a sense of humour? It was hard to tell.

'Because you need to eat, for God's sake! You need warmth and shelter! Unless you have some other trade you haven't spoken of till now?'

'Oh yes. I am the keeper of a lunatic asylum. Is that not good enough?'

'You were. You were.'

'Good enough, indeed.'

'Lavenza,' I said. 'Your spirits were improved by our arrival here. I fear they have improved so much you are becoming irresponsible. We must make plans, look to the future.'

'And so I do.'

'Good! Then—'

'He's going to kill me. That's the future. Very simple, when you come to it. Has he explained? Has he described it to you? I'm sure it will be carefully planned out. He is . . . methodical, after his own manner.'

'He isn't going to kill you. I will admit, though, he may try.'

'I recall my father . . . he ordered all the shutters closed. At noon, the rooms were lit by candlelight. He thought that he could keep him out, you see. He thought the castle strong enough. . . . But then, as I suppose you pointed out, the memories of childhood can be less than accurate. Can't they?'

'I want to know why he's not here yet. What he's waiting for. What he's been doing all this while. . . .'

'His sense of time is different. After the first hundred years and more . . . and he dislikes the house.'

'Fears it?'

'It carries memories for him.'

'No doubt. Well. He's given us the time we needed. Much to his own misfortune.'

'And to ours,' Lavenza said. He produced a bottle of schnapps. 'Here,' he said. 'Let's drink a toast. To the last of the Frankensteins.'

His lips curled up. It was a moment till I realised he was grinning; I had never seen him grin before, seldom even smile. It should have been encouraging. Yet with his clothes dishevelled, hair all out of place, moustache untrimmed, it gave him the disturbing, manic look of a psychotic clown.

•.•

I paced. I fidgeted. I smoked.

And then, a little before noon, Karl came to the door.

'Master,' he said.

His voice was small. He held on to the door jamb, as if he needed to support himself.

'Master,' he said again.

'Well? What is it?'

'Master. . . .'

'He's coming, isn't he, Karl?' Lavenza said, quite calmly as he bent to his machinery, made final readjustments, final checks. And then he looked at me, said, 'Happy now?'

And I went up, to meet my fate.

Chapter Fifty-five

I watched him, striding through the grass, as I had seen him striding through the surf a few nights gone. A lope, more than a walk. The movement of an animal, a wild beast. The wind picked at his hair and lifted it in trails. His greatcoat swung about him, thick with dirt. I could read nothing on his face, no hint or glimmer of emotion, or clue to his intent.

His eyes were blackened hollows. Emptiness, devoid of life.

I swallowed, stepped out from the doorway, spreading my arms wide.

'Good sir! We are expecting you!'

He made no sound.

'It's all prepared. We're ready. If you'll follow . . . ?'

I retreated some way down the hall; but he paused upon the threshold, blocking out the light.

'Surely,' I said, 'surely you don't fear to come inside?'

It was a calculated taunt. His mouth tightened, his lips down-curving, like a toad's.

And he came on.

'This way,' I said, as lightly as I could, and turned my back on him.

It was a fearful thing to have to do. I could almost feel him, his hands about to reach out, seize me. . . . My very flesh was tingling with the sense of him. I had to force myself to slow my pace, to seem at ease . . . to stop my very posture giving me away.

I led him to the cellar steps. I chatted—idly, nervously—trying not to think how hollow it all sounded.

'. . . ready now since yesterday. We were expecting. . . . One of the rooms has been prepared to teach in. It will all go well. Don't be afraid. If this had happened at the start—'

But he broke in on me then, his voice a dog's growl.

'Why down here?'

'This is the way—you know. To the great hall. To the—the universe, you called it. Where you were made. Were . . . born.'

'Why here?'

He had stopped walking. I turned, beckoning, as if he really were some large and stubborn beast refusing to be kennelled. 'It's the right place. You understand—it needs a certain shape. A certain resonance. Come now! Come. Dr Lavenza will explain.'

He stood, filling the corridor.

'You have to come with me,' I said, 'I'll show you. Follow me now. Follow.'

'There is an odour.'

'I daresay.' I knew which odour, and more, knew what it was; but I said, 'Machinery—old machines. They must be oiled, and fuelled, and . . . the place has changed somewhat, since you were last here, I'd imagine. Come and see.'

It was all that I could do not to start pleading with him; to have myself so well prepared, then meet such obstinacy, such, such—it was not suspicion yet, but it might easily become so.

'Well,' I said, 'this is your chance. Take it or leave it. He's waiting for you. If you're interested.' I brought my pipe out, made to light it, then stopped myself. I'd save the fire till near the time. If he delayed, and it went out. . . .

'The passage to the workshop,' he said.

'Yes.'

'Where I was bound and caged.'

I made a laughing sound. 'No cage there now, sir. Come and see.'

'Something's amiss.'

'I assure you, it's exactly as it ought to be.'

'The small one. Where is he?'

'You mean Karl? Preparing dinner, I should hope. We've some venison remaining, thanks to you. He's not a bad cook. You may wish to join us after, if you would.'

'I smell no venison.'

'Just follow me. There's no need for concern, I can assure you.'

I took a few steps backwards. I felt the edges of the rug beneath my feet and shuffled sideways, nearer to the wall.

'My senses are much sharper than your own. Sight. Hearing. Smell.'

'You were well-made.'

But I could smell it, too.

Above me, in the little space between the ceiling and the floor above, Karl had uncorked the gasoline.

I moved backwards, pipe in one hand, matches in the other.

'Come if you will,' I said. 'If not. . . .' I made an airy sort of gesture, half turned as if to go. . . .

He ran at me.

Not like a man running. No warm-up, no gathering of speed. A single stride propelled him, and he came at me like an express train. There was no time for fear. I staggered, scrambled back, still with the good sense to stay by the wall rather than fall into my own trap.

And I had him. I saw it, plain as day: I had him where I wanted him.

I fled into the great hall. Lavenza ducked away from me. My footsteps echoed round the walls. The creature was upon me. Almost, almost—

The carpet slid beneath him. He reeled and swerved, somehow gained his balance, reached up. . . .

Karl shrieked. The monster dragged him from his hiding place and whirled him through the air. The canister of fuel went flying from his hand, smashing to the floor. The air shook. Liquid spilled, the stench of it suddenly everywhere.

'Master, Master!' screamed Karl, though whether he addressed Lavenza or myself, or the brute who swung him like a pendulum, it was impossible to tell. The creature glared at us. As if without exertion, it lofted the poor madman, made to hurl him at us—

And the floor began to break.

I heard it crack. The monster tried to step back. The carpet slipped, vanished as if sucked into the ground, and for a fraction of a second it seemed that he might follow. Boards snapped. One leg went through the floor, yet somehow—I could not see how he did it—somehow, with his other foot, he kicked himself away, tumbling backwards, crashing to the safety of the uncut boards behind. With a single movement he was up again, and on his feet. Karl still dangling in his grasp.

I drew my pistol.

'Put him down,' I said.

'So you can shoot me?'

'Put him down.'

The creature's eyes were on Lavenza, where he hunched beside a cabinet of stored retorts. He looked as if he would have crawled into the half-inch space behind it if he could.

'Shoot him,' he begged, his voice a rasp. 'Don't wait. For God's sake, shoot—'

But the creature still held Karl, swinging before him, thin legs kicking feebly. I had no clear aim.

I feinted to the left, flung myself right, hoping I might get under his guard, trusting my talent as a marksman.

And I fired.

The shot boomed, echoed; in that place, meant to resonate with all the frequencies of life, the sound of death roared like a thunderclap, seeming to rush away from me, returning like a tidal wave, re-echoing, its pitch straining, twisting upwards, striking new and terrible harmonics. The monster reeled. I had hit him, but he did not fall. His face was like a face of stone, some hideous, carved idol.

Frankenstein's Prescription

Karl chattered frantically. He waved his arms. And with the smallest gesture—no more than a flick—the creature flung him, lightly as if brushing off a flea.

It was not a throw that any normal man might have survived.

He smashed into the far wall, and the awful thump of it was magnified just as my shot had been; the sound went creeping round the hall, seeming to grow, its overtones dividing, multiplying, splitting into ever finer notes that trembled in the air a while, and died.

The monster was across the pit. My hands fumbled like lumps of clay. I could not aim. Yet all he did was look at me.

'Witness,' he said.

And seized Lavenza.

It was done in moments. He swept the man up, tucking him beneath his arm as if he were a child. Then turned, and he was gone.

My heart roared in my ears. I could barely breathe.

Poor Karl lay heaped against the wall where he had fallen. He looked so thin and feeble, like an old man. One arm was twisted under him; I tried to move him, and he moaned once more, and the walls and ceiling groaned in mockery.

'You'll be alright,' I said.

A bloody spittle burst upon his lips.

He made a sound like, 'Dead.'

'No. You're not dead. I'll come for you. You'll have to wait, but I'll be back, I promise. You're not dead, Karl. Not dead.'

But, 'Dead,' he said again. Then, 'Been dead. Now . . . being born. . . .' With the fingers of his free hand, he clutched my shirt-front, barely able to sustain his grip. 'Hurts,' he said, 'more than I thought. . . .'

I left him there.

Chapter Fifty-six

A bullet in the head, I thought. Up through the eye, or through the mouth. If I could find the skill. The luck. . . .

I moved into the hallway, cautious now, wary of the slightest sound. A bell-pull tapped against the wall, swayed by the breeze . . .

The door gaped, broken from its hinges.

Sunlight shivered on the fields, gleamed in puddles and on stones, picked out in bright half-moons the hoofprints left from our arrival; it rippled through the grass, only to die against the black wall of the forest, blunt and final as the wall of an arena.

He had not gone far, the beast. I saw him, just a little way beyond, crouched in the grass, intent on some activity which I could not discern. Of Lavenza, I saw nothing. The coldness tightened in my gut. The monster's great back rose and fell, his shoulders heaved. . . .

Lavenza screamed.

I ran. I feared a rape, some violation scarcely thinkable to man. Yet as I closed upon the brute, I stopped. The gun hung in my hand, but went unused, and I tried to take in what I saw.

Laid out upon the ground was timber from the house's yard; a spar of maybe fifteen, twenty feet, a lesser beam nailed crosswise, to which Lavenza's arms were bound in strips of his own clothes. What caught me though, was not the strangeness of the scene, but its familiarity: an image I had seen a thousand times, upon the altarpiece of churches, in the halls and cloisters of St Peter's, on the necklace of a pretty girl whose honour I might hope to take. . . .

Yet, to see it here, and now—

I tried to aim. I held the weapon in both hands, and still I could not halt the trembling.

I went closer. The brute looked up. 'Witness,' he said, and it seemed that I heard welcome in the tone.

I raised my gun.

'No,' I said. My voice was very small. 'No more.'

Lavenza, hearing me, cried out; the monster dropped a hand over his face to silence him.

He squatted on his haunches, head tipped sideways, watching me.

'Suppose,' he said, 'the legionaries had been called upon to free the Christ. What then?'

'He isn't Christ!'

'Not your Christ, no.'

He turned, and with his free hand, reached into the grass. He held a hammer. My gun was ready. I could not delay. I fired. The jolt ran up my arms, jerking me backwards.

He was at me.

Had he planned my death, I would have died that instant. I have no doubt of this. He seized me, flung me in the air; the world spun, I crashed down hard and could not breathe, yet once again he took me up, wrenching my arm half from its socket, hurling me aloft as if I were a trinket, or a child's toy.

My voice was gone. I tried to beg, to plead with him. I would have offered anything, simply to save myself, but there was no more air left in my lungs, no way to stop the onslaught.

For a moment then he left me. I was still conscious; I still lived. I forced myself to move. I pushed myself up on my arm; a fierce pain stabbed at my shoulder, and I fell gasping to the ground, my arms and legs still moving like a beached swimmer's. And he had me. Once more he threw me in the air. He pummelled me. Toying with me, playing with me; and this time, when he left, I scarce knew who I was, or where. I lay upon the ground, half numb, feeling the aches and spasms of my limbs as if they had belonged to someone else, some broken puppet from another life, another world.

And I heard hammerblows.

He hammered. Hammered, chanting, softly, all the while, as to a close yet unseen friend: 'Blessed! Blessed, blessed, blessed! Blessed are the meek! Blessed are the poor! Blessed are the lonely, the forgotten, and the dead! Blessed!'

※

The cross was up. He had raised it by himself, into some pit he must have dug in readiness. The figure on it I no longer recognised, shaking and dancing in its pain; the melancholy doctor, man of intellect and learning, rendered down now to a squall of bodily responses, a web of agony eclipsing all that he had ever been, might ever be.

Pain makes us animals. It shuts out thought and rationality; reminds us we are beasts at heart.

The monster strode around him. For he *was* a monster, this I knew, no matter how he spoke about himself; no victim, or lonely sensibility trapped in a world indifferent to his needs. He was a creature without empathy. Without compassion. Oh, how proud he looked! He swaggered, strutted. Sometimes he peered up at his victim, frowning, as if to read some secret in his agonies, some key within his fear, his whimpering, his jagged, broken dance.

He turned his back on me. He stared out at the woods, that great black barrier he once believed to mark the frontier of the world. He raised his arms, and a sound came from his lips, a long, peculiar ululation, and words, words in German, words I understood: 'Oh little brothers! Little sisters!'

I heard the wind among the leaves, its rush and rustle, like a sudden indrawn breath.

And then the woods called back.

Chapter Fifty-seven

Not one voice, but many. Not one sound, but a host: a low, uncertain murmur, mingling with the music of the wind, rising to a single awful roar no human throat could ever have produced. Sheer panic beat inside me. I dragged myself along the ground, straining to escape, dragged myself exhausted to the nearest of the outbuildings, then set my back against the hard stone, pressing myself into it, wanting no more than to sink straight through the wall and vanish. And the voices came again, the babble of some distant multitude, while the monster waited, arms held wide, mirroring the cross above his head. Inviting, beckoning. Lavenza squirmed; I saw the ghastly heaving of his chest, the way his head rolled, and I felt round for my guns, thinking I would kill him rather than prolong his pain; but my guns were gone, nowhere to be found.

Deep shadows cut across the land. The sun was down upon the treetops, and there were creatures coming from the woods, singly or in pairs, or groups of three and four, from all parts of the forest. Some were people, some were animals, still others, in the half-light, seemed to me to have the qualities of both. Yet in their movements there was something dream-like, jerky and uncertain, like the motion of malfunctioning machines. Each was different. Many, as I saw, were crippled, lacking hands or arms, or hobbling on defective limbs. One stumbled, weaving blindly in among its fellows, a parody of human form, its legs stretched out to slender stilts. I cringed from them, these creatures neither living nor yet truly dead, though they took scant interest in me; and when the first few reached the cross, they stopped, like an audience at the theatre, strangely decorous and calm. Their breath hissed, spat. It steamed upon the evening air. And all the while he paced before them, counting off their numbers like a schoolmaster, his dreadful handiwork a shadow on the sky behind.

This monster.

Killer.

First born.

Brute.

I had imagined him unique, and in some ways so he was. No other here possessed his grace, intelligence, his sense of purpose and volition, nor his near-resemblance to a man.

Unique, perhaps. But not alone.

They had been his thralls for decades, the Lavenzas, every generation forced to do his work. And if none could match the genius of Victor, their great ancestor, even so, they had not failed entirely.

These, then, were the mishaps, sat before me now; the almosts and the nearlies and the test runs; immortal like the first-born, immortal for in no true sense alive, as you and I and all God's creatures are alive; and neither, by the same token, were they bound to death. The bastard children of the Frankensteins, called from their dens, back to the ruins of their Eden. These were the blunders, errors and mistakes. Like Lavenza's clever puppets, though they needed neither wires nor trolleys to sustain them.

Some seemed almost human in the twilight—almost; others were misshapen and grotesque. One carried on its shoulders the enormous, prow-like head of a horse, its scabby hide all peeling, one ear gone, the whole thing like some huge, burdensome helmet. Only by twisting its whole torso could it swing the head around to view the scene, giving it a mad, hopeless kind of twitching, like the fidgets of the damned.

Broken, damaged, still the spark of animation clung on in their withered forms, driving them to answer to their eldest's call. Cripples, half-things. To look on them evoked both fear and pity.

Slowly, as by pre-arrangement, they settled in a semicircle round the cross, some standing, swaying in the dim light, others sinking to the ground. There were—I don't know—four, five dozen of them altogether, sad, pathetic, ugly things. The first-born stood in front of them, king before his court. I could only wonder at the interest he took in them. Had he cared for them, over the centuries? Nurtured them? Sought their companionship?

He raised his hand.

'Behold,' he said. A hush fell instantly upon the onlookers. 'Behold the Christ, the Saviour. See.'

It was a strange moment—though I was weary now beyond all measure, and mad myself, I think, from all that I had seen—but I was eerily reminded of my father's sermons, on a Sunday morning, as he inveighed against the drink and lewdness, laziness and lack of productivity, to a congregation made up largely of his own employees. There was, too, something theatrical in the performance, the monster's slow and studied moves, as he turned abruptly, faced the crowd, and raised his head.

'God made us. Made our world. And now we unmake Him.'

I pressed myself into the cold stone, my face against the rock. My arm hurt. My leg hurt; the crawl across the ground had set it throbbing. For a time, if I lay still, the ache would ease, but always it returned. If I moved, sharp spasms stabbed up through my thigh, into my chest.

'He sent His son to save us. He sent His son, and His son's son, and His son's son's son. Into the wilderness. Into this semblance of a life.'

The creature spoke. I may have blacked out; in memory, events all shift and merge one with the next. But presently, I was aware of something nuzzling at my leg.

It was a dog. Long, thin face, sad eyes, it whimpered when I looked at it. Instinctively, I reached out. 'Here, now. Here, boy.' Nervous, it tottered back, and I saw then it was not a dog, or not as I knew dogs; it balanced on two awkward forelegs, taking little, scampering steps, as if to stand still would be to lose its balance and go down. It had, perhaps, once been a whippet or a greyhound. Now it made a kind of parody of man, wobbling on its two front legs, an odd, truncated thing, which perhaps should have been blessed with arms, and yet was not. Repulsed, I made a throwing motion, and the creature skittered off, though not too far. It put its head down, watching me. I regretted my own cruelty; and to make amends, I called to it, *tch-tch-tch*. It took a few uncertain steps, still wary, keeping out of reach. It was such a dog-like act, this need to seek approval of a man. The creature's shape was ugly and unnatural; its instincts, commonplace.

I recalled the monster's story of his first months, his efforts to secure affection from his God. My own attempts, though long since gone, to win my father's praise; and my rebellion, when no praise came.

The little creature sniffed at me. I opened up my arms, embraced it, hugged it to my breast. It wriggled, shivered, fearful of affection as it had been of my scorn. Then it snuggled up against my side, and put its head down, and went to sleep.

Chapter Fifty-eight

'The world was dark, and void, and formless. My eyes opened; the world began. All things sprang into being: light and texture and the forms of matter. Thus was seen the flaw in the Creator's scheme, that He believed He made me, when before I was, was nothing. In the beginning, at the start, was this: my eyes opened. No more.'

He preached. He preached to this bizarre and loathsome congregation; raised himself before them, spread his arms.

'So it was I who made the world. And I who made the God of this world. Where else was He, before my eyes beheld Him? Where did He live, and move, and have his being? Where *could* He live, before I was? Creation has become Creator; Maker, made. My eyes opened. The world began.'

His siblings watched him, faces turning as he strutted, back and forth; for he was one of them, both one and not one. The one of whom they all were only flawed, failed copies.

'The snake that swallows its own tail,' he said. 'The god become man. God sacrificed to God. See. See here: the last of the Frankensteins.'

Lavenza, on the cross, moaned, and the monster mimicked him, held his arms wide, wriggled and coughed.

It seemed like mockery, and a fierce resentment rose in me. Yet now, I wonder, was it something more? Some sign of oneness, as if in some way to identify himself here with the dying man?

At my side, the dog-thing stirred. I smelled its matted, stinking fur, its wet-dog smell, an oddly comforting familiarity.

'Christ will die. Christ will die for all of us. For you, and me . . . For Christ is dying, Christ is risen. He will never come again.'

I did not sleep, not as we think of sleep; and yet for periods my senses left me, and my consciousness grew hazy, even while I fought to keep it. Ages passed. I can remember looking up, abruptly—jerking awake—to see two great stars spinning through the heavens, stars that whirled in darkness, and I reached my hand towards them, pleading, begging them for help, but they were far beyond my reach. They circled, spun, filling my vision for a moment, before soaring off at speed.

The twins had left the castle. Come to bid farewell.

They wheeled, orbited the cross in an ornate and complex dance that had, it seemed to me, a stateliness about it, sombre and intensely mournful. By turns, they swept up to Lavenza, pausing only inches from his face, then fell away once more, their graceful dive a motion without sound. Their presence seemed to soothe him. He struggled less, his breathing, though still laboured, became noticeably slower.

The creature stood beneath them, watching, stock-still.

In the east, the sky grew grey.

The two lights circled once, twice, three times more, and then, as one, they lofted high into the air, swerved left, and right—as if seeking direction, sniffing for some scent upon the wind, perhaps —and sailed away together, far from the house, over the woodlands and the hills, till I lost sight of them.

The creature too stared after them, then seated himself, tailor-fashion at the cross's foot.

Dim light began to creep across the scene. Shadows cut their way into the crowd, the throng of beings, all still watching, shuffling sometimes, stirring in their places. The snuffle of their breath, the odour of them, borne upon the morning breeze . . . a mix of sweat and chemistry, the odour of a tramp's den, yet somehow not quite human, not quite natural. . . .

I lay there among gargoyles. I had sunk beneath the company of vagrants and of common criminals, to this sub-human horde. And strange to tell, I found myself at ease. It was as if a weight had lifted from me; some burden placed in childhood, but now gone. My aspirations and ambitions, my pretensions—meaningless. I would no longer seek to change myself, or make myself in any manner other than I was. And what I was, it seemed to me, was nobody. A no-one among nobodies—among creatures too decrepit and outrageous to be real.

Some time during that long pre-dawn, Lavenza died.

He was my friend, for all that I had sometimes cursed him. He was the only human being within miles around. And I dreamed still that I might rescue him, that I would find my pistols, kill his enemy, and take him down. . . .

I have no notion how long normal crucifixion lasts—if I can even use the term. Once the body suffers so much torment, any of a dozen different traumas might induce an end—shock and cardiac arrest, tissue loss and dehydration. . . . The Biblical three days stuck in my head. But Lavenza lasted no more than a night.

Was this a mercy? I can hardly say. I know that at the time I was reluctant to believe him gone. I put his stillness down to sheer exhaustion, one of the periodic faints that had relieved his final hours. The realisation came, I think, to everyone at roughly the same time. A kind of ripple seemed to pass among the crowd, a murmur, less than words yet more than breath. A faint rustle of movement. . . .

With difficulty now, I stood. Off in the east, above the trees, the sky was paling into blue. The dog-thing clambered to its feet beside me, rubbed itself against my leg, and whined at me. I scratched its head. The hairs came off on my hand.

I cannot convey the complex of emotions surging in my breast. A dozen different thoughts, tugging me all directions. I might have simply run—or hobbled—hoping that the creature had no further use for me. I might have looked round for my guns. But I did

Frankenstein's Prescription

neither. These feelings were emotions at a distance. They had no hold on me. I recognised them; I did not, in any real sense, feel them any more.

The pain in my leg seemed to push me into wakefulness. I had to walk with care, but slowly, I approached the cross, and the monster, squatting at its foot.

What I intended, I no longer know. He did not look at me. I stared up at the body, hanging, twisted, bent up. It resembled not at all the gold and silver crucifixes of the church, so smooth and clean, devoid of agony; the posed Christ, half-naked, body elegantly curved, as if the model for some male pornography. But this was meat that hung here. A carcase dressed in rags. Grey, touched by the morning light.

Lavenza was long gone.

I said at last, 'Enough. It's done. Now take him down.'

The creature's face was like a slab of rock, lifeless as the figure up above. Then, I heard the soft sigh of a breath. He raised his head, surveyed the sky.

'I thought the stars would have gone out.'

'They will soon. It's near sunrise.'

He sniffed the air, as if to ascertain the truth of this.

'The sun, also,' he said.

'Take him down.' My voice cracked as I spoke, and what was meant to sound commanding turned into a plea. The creature merely glanced at me, his looks unreadable. With just a single motion he could reach out, swat me from existence like a gnat. But I said again, though in a voice now tiny, openly begging: 'Take him down, please. Please . . . ?'

'You order me?'

I shook my head, lowered my gaze.

'No,' I told him. 'No.'

'Then I must order you.'

I looked around. The grotesques were gathered at a distance from us. Even the dog-thing scuttled back and forth, unwilling to approach. I cast about forlornly for my weapons, hoping to see them in the growing light, but they were gone. If any of these gargoyles understood their use, they would most certainly have seized them for their own.

The creature was still watching me.

'Do what you planned to do,' he said. The first rays of the sun shone in his eyes like flames. 'Do it. Destroy the world.'

Chapter Fifty-nine

I leaned against the doorframe. My chest heaved and my leg was throbbing; I could scarcely find a stance in which it did not hurt. My heartbeat seemed to pulse in rhythm with the pain.

I stood upon the threshold of the house, and once again, I thought to flee. Yet it seemed that I, too, had become a monster now, in every way as crippled and grotesque as those upon the lawns behind. Here I belonged; I had lived with death, and now death drove me on. I forced myself to stand and, holding to the wall, moved slowly down the hallway. In the dim light, there were swathes of gloom like pools, and the floor was strewn with debris. Once I stumbled, and a spasm shot up through my injured leg, so dreadful and so sudden that I cried out. But I pressed on. I counted to myself—a trick I had employed since childhood, to distract the mind with mere banality—*one, two, three, four, one, two, three, four.* . . . And at last came to the cellar steps. I grasped the stair-rail, thankful that it took my weight. In the cellars it was pitch dark. I struck a lucifer, to get my bearings; noting, also, there were precious few left in the box.

When I emerged again the sky was almost light, though washed out, pale. Chill air touched my skin. The dog-thing skittered back and forth, excited by the sight of me; incredibly, it had waited, just beyond the shadow of the house, till I returned. But it would not approach me, only run and chitter round about. Perhaps it sensed my purpose. Perhaps it smelt the gasoline, heavy in the can I dragged behind. So too, then, must its cohorts. And perhaps guessed what I planned.

They watched me, their ragged and distorted features seeming quite without emotion. In daylight they presented an appalling hotchpotch of monstrosities, of things cobbled together, cruelly saddled with this mimicry of life. I did not dare to think of them, nor how they might respond to what I was about to do.

Lavenza's body gleamed like gold under the morning sun.

One last cruel joke of fate.

I walked up to the cross. And to the monster, hunkered at its foot.

He seemed scarcely to have moved since I had left. A creature made of rock, of dirt, of stone.

I said to him, 'Be ready.'

He looked up without turning his head. His dry lips cracked. His voice was like the rustle of the leaves caught in an autumn breeze.

'The world half-gone,' he said. 'I thought that it would be enough.'

I unstoppered the can. A sharp stink oozed into the air. I saw the creature's nostrils twitch.

'I want the world to end.'

I raised the vessel with some trouble, and I held it over him.

'End it.' He looked at me. 'Burn it. Burn the trees, the fields. Burn the house. Burn the sun and sky. Do it. Do it now.'

'Your dream,' I said, 'that you'll be one with the world . . . ?'

'When I am gone, there will be no more world.'

I saw his eyes then, for perhaps the first time. They were yellow, almost golden in the dawn, and there was something in them infinitely distant, infinitely far removed from man.

He might resemble us, but he was never one of us. Never meant for our world.

Knowing that, it made my task a little easier.

Not easy. Easier. No more than that.

I balanced myself carefully, fearful that my leg might suddenly give way. The canister was heavy and I raised it only with the greatest effort. I let the liquid splash upon his coat, upon the back and on the sleeve. When he failed to move or try to stop me, I grew bolder, anointing his shoulders and his hands. 'Shut your eyes,' I said, and poured it on his chest, his head. The thinning hair lay slick, the ancient, battered scalp quite clearly visible beneath. In the pattern of its injuries one might read years of history, of suffering. I poured, and the canister grew lighter, and at last, somewhat to my surprise, I upended it, and we were done.

I stepped back. I glanced round at his brothers, his sisters. They were watching, but they made no move.

I took my pack of lucifers. I had but three left, and the first failed to ignite, the sulphur simply scraping off and falling in the grass. That gave me pause, and for a moment my intention faltered. I cursed myself for the lights I had expended in the house, finding my way about, mere minutes earlier; for the profligacy of my pipe-smoking over the last few days. I lit the second, threw it, and it died before it reached its goal.

It would be a final irony—unbearable—were I to fail at this last moment, for want of just an ordinary, common flame.

I took my last match, and now with great care, struck it, huddling close in to the monster, sheltering this tongue of fire with my body. Gently, I touched it to his coat, first here, then here, then here.

There was a time it seemed that nothing happened. I touched it elsewhere on his person, till the flame burned at my fingers and I had to let it go. Then, whoosh! The rush of heat was like a stone wall hitting me. I tumbled back, half-blind, threshing on the ground. I rolled, struggling to get away. I looked up, blinking.

It happens sometimes that the first explosion of a fire will seem to blow the flames out and extinguish them. So here. The creature sat beneath the cross, its back half-turned to me. I blinked away the dazzle and the after-image floating in my eyes, and only gradually grew conscious of a kind of nimbus, creeping slowly up the shoulders of his coat, an oily light of burning vapour. It was a magical thing—like a living creature tenderly enfolding him, sheathing him in light.

And then he burned.

The fabric of his coat began to scorch and rupture, peeling from his body, threads unwound from threads, dissolving in the flame. The light crept up, onto his shoulder. It was no longer cloth and wool that burnt. His hair caught, flaring like a firework, and then vanished. His flesh was aflame. A thick grey smoke rose in the morning air, and I could smell him now—like roasted meat, but sickly, too. And still he did not move. The flames began to eat at him—for that was how I thought of it—devouring, taking tiny bites, tiny bites in infinite profusion, slowly tearing at his clothes, nipping at his cheek, as the skin puckered and peeled, pulling it away, piece by piece. . . .

Suddenly he moved. He arms came out, spread sheets of flame like angels' wings. He lurched forwards, upwards, but clumsily, his old grace gone, got to his knees then staggered to his feet. The flames swirled round him, whipped alive by sudden movement. I felt the heat. I moved back without thinking, till I found myself once more among that company of gargoyles that he called his brothers. They stirred, shied like nervous animals. The fellow with the horse's head brushed past me, snorting, swinging his great skull from side to side.

Blazing now, a sheet of flame from head to foot, the monster moved towards us. It seemed to float across the grass, to drift as if no longer anchored to the world. A ball of fire, a salamander, loosed upon humanity.

Burn it, he'd told me. Burn the world.

But he could not burn the world. It lay beyond his reach, as it had always done; and instead he fell. The smoke coiled, dancing round him.

He had dreamed that he would melt into the Earth.

Yet in the end, he merely burnt, like any of us.

I saw it all. I watched his carcase smoke and blacken, saw the flesh peel back, the ribs poke through the chest. By now the sun was high. I had been watching him so long that I had scarcely noticed when the brothers—shy of daylight—slunk away, into the shelter of the woods, and left me there.

They had not harmed me.

I had expected it. I had anticipated threat, and more. Yet none had come.

The dog-thing rubbed against me. It muttered to itself, then ran away towards the trees; stopped a moment, tottered back and forth, and whined for me.

'Go on,' I said. 'Go on. Get out.'

It took a few steps backwards, paused again and dithered, looking right and left, until I yelled once more for it to go. The monster smouldered on the grass. The dog-thing put its head down, long face peaked and sickened. Then it let loose an extraordinary howl. High-pitched, lonely in a way that I could scarcely bear. I turned my back on it. Next time I looked, the thing was gone.

I had a promise to Lavenza to keep.

It took a great part of the day for me to fetch his body down.

I found a ladder in the stables. Now in almost constant pain, I brought it to the cross, and climbed it. I pulled the nails out from his palms, I cut the bonds upon his wrists.

He dropped, and almost took me with him.

I dragged him to the house.

Away upon the field, the monster's body sent a thin grey plume into the air, so still it might have been a solid thing; a monument, a testimony to his life, whatever that might be.

Lavenza, in his final hours, had laid a charge on me. It took me an unconscionable time to carry out. But I shall tell it briefly.

I fired the generator. I placed Lavenza's corpse upon the apparatus, as instructed. I clamped the electrical devices to his skull, and pulled the switch. Nothing discernible took place. I tried again. Again. I had no hopes of a success, only of following his orders, to the letter, to the word. But I had dreamed there might be something. Some sign, some brief acknowledgement. . . .

For a time, I lay upon the ground, and consciousness departed me. An hour, perhaps. Or more, or less.

I woke, and pressed the switch once more.

There came a scent of cooking meat. . . .

I slept then, in an inner room, a place without windows. I heaped a barricade against the door.

Next day, the monster's corpse still smouldered, though the grass around was wet with dew. I took a length of timber and I walked out in the morning, and I struck at the remains repeatedly, again and again and again, till there was nothing left but ash.

Of the creature's siblings, I saw no sign.

I called to them. I tried to imitate the sound that he had made, the wail that drew them forth. My throat was cracked and dry. I waited, but they would not come.

Our mounts were in the stables still, restless and hungry, and I gave them fodder, and fetched water from the well. Then I saddled up the horse that I had ridden here—a struggle, for it pained me just to stand—and roped the others to him.

I left behind two graves. One for Lavenza, one for Karl. In truth, more piles of dirt than graves. But I could do no more.

For the monster, I left no mark.

The wind scattered his ashes. The sun blazed down on him. The rain came, washing him away.

I did not allow myself to sleep, much as I wanted to. I had to be away from there. I forced myself to ride, to keep on riding.

I had nowhere I could go. No home, no destination. So like Lavenza, like the monster too, I did the only thing remaining. I went back to my father's house.

Chapter Sixty

No fatted calf awaited me.

My father frowned, my pitiable state merely confirming his worst fears. My mother and my sisters fussed around. Even the servants came to ask about my health, and in the days to come, my brothers, both away from home, sent letters, wishing me well, both saying how glad they were to find me safe at last.

Only Herr Schneider Senior stayed aloof. Ledgers to tally, orders to put through, clients to meet.... Some days, as I sat out in the garden in a pile of blankets—fresh air was deemed good for me—I saw him watching from his window, though if he caught my gaze he would most often turn away. Encountering him in the house he offered me a curt 'Good day,' before his business took him elsewhere. In truth, I worried little about this, for there was too much else upon my mind.

My family knew nothing of my life over the last few months, nor was I willing to enlighten them. My looks alone bore testimony to the horrors I had seen. I had left them as a dandy, smitten with the pleasures of the world, and come home ragged, starving, filthy. More, as I myself had diagnosed, my leg was broken: a fractured femur, just above the knee. Had it been tended to immediately, it would probably have healed without the slightest harm. As it was, bone had ground and gouged at bone, and I have spent the best part of my life with a limp.

I was aware my life seemed to conform to one of father's nasty little moral lessons—a rake's progress of misery. But I would give no explanations, nor excuses. It was not a strategy I planned. More, I found it practically impossible to speak of anything that I had undergone. My head still whirled; I woke each night from dreams which I could not recall, yet left me in a panic, sweating, searching for a light. I was often heard to cry out, and a servant was positioned by my door, should I require assistance in the night.

My mother made it known my father asked after me daily. (He did not, however, bother to ask me.) One afternoon, he brought me tea, setting it down beside my chair and remarking some small pleasantry about the weather. From then on, we were able to trade words, at least on harmless matters. I assume my mother played a part in this reunion. Circumspect it may have been, but once done, he seemed much relieved. I also.

I had thought he bore no love for me. Yet there was duty, and it may be duty is a kind of love, or near to it, perhaps the best of which his heart was capable.

(Years later, when I learned that he had died, I wished we could have spoken more, and striven for that intimacy usually enjoyed by sons and fathers. Still, I must confess the fault was mutual; a kind of shyness keeping us apart, a fear our truce, if breached, would crumble into nothingness. Just one of many things which, had I chance, I would go back and change.)

In due course, I returned to Heidelberg.

For the most part, I lived quietly, outside town; rooms in a family house, with no daughters, and the frau too old and ugly even for my broad tastes. My father paid the rent. A year ago, I would have moved out in a week, returning to the heart of town life; now, I stayed. Not that my days were altogether pure. I revisited old haunts, though found them somewhat changed. Only a scattering of faces proved familiar (of bodies, too). Yet it may be that my attitude had changed the most of all, and the prospect of a few hours' pleasure, simply to wake up with a headache and an empty purse, seemed now a stale adventure, long since drained of novelty.

My life grew narrow, shuttling between digs and lectures, like some penny-pinching scholarship boy. I suffered a prolonged grey melancholy. Nothing pleased me. Thus life continued for some months; but gradually, I found comfort in its stark routines, until there came a moment when I realised, to my great surprise, that I was not unhappy. There were matters in my past I did not care to think about. By sinking into study I was able to avoid them. In more light-hearted moments, I would wonder if perhaps some reckoning were due; if one day I would undergo a terrible religious upsurge, become a monk or priest or missionary. . . . I did not, of course, although my life's course has proved almost as unlikely.

On graduating, I sought out a position. I retained in some vague way my former goals, but posts at fashionable spas were hard to find, and I had lost touch with those folk to whom I looked for help establishing myself. So, as an interim arrangement, I took a little rural practice, among the peasants and the farmers, planning to stay a year at most, gain some experience, and then move on.

Here I remain, these decades afterwards. And glad to be here, too.

My later life, eventful in so many ways, has little bearing on my narrative. Some six or seven months into my stay, I made acquaintance with a local schoolmistress, a young woman like myself new to the district. She had a gramophone and a passion for the works of Wagner, which she played in snippets of a few minutes each from her great stack of recordings. So we began to meet. It was a dalliance for me, no more; a little educated talk, some female company, little I regarded with much gravity. Strange, then, among much strangeness: we are now great grandparents.

Once caught up in the chaos of a country doctor's life, I found little time to think of self-promotion, or to hanker after luxuries, beyond a meal, a hot bath, a bottle of wine, and a warm, companionable bed. There is no predicting what one's work will be, or when; and all too often physic proves merely a choice of evils, in the hope of doing good. Our limits in the face of sickness and mortality are all too plain, and many times Lavenza's words would echo in my head, his efforts to transcend the confines of our mortal selves. I understood his craving, as people I knew well, some of whom I loved, sank in their final illness, and I was forced again to recognise my helplessness. Oh, how I longed then for Lavenza's gifts, his hubris and refusal to submit to nature! Yet still: as I remarked near to the start of this account, my own gifts are but modest ones. I have sought to mitigate my clients' pain, to save where I can and heal where I can; to comfort and relieve where healing is no longer possible.

I served as a physician in the Great War. I was noted for my calmness in the face of terrible events, a calmness I did not, in truth, much feel. Yet I had seen my share of horrors, and it had steeled me for the devastation of the trenches. I survived; but I cannot forgive.

In youth I had caused misery to many, not so much through malice as through selfish, narrow-minded chasing after my own interest; and in the War I saw whole nations take that self-same course, and governments treating their subjects with the kind of callousness I, too, once treated my fellows. Though with consequences infinitely worse.

There is a monstrous egotism manifest in war, pompous, empty and unthinking, like the dictates of a child.

I have tried to be a good and loving father. And grandfather. And more. I have tried in every way to be the father that I lacked when I was growing up.

If there is value in the lives we live, it lies in small things: an act of kindliness, a smile, a little practical assistance, or a caring touch . . .

I still see ghosts.

The same ghost, these days. Always the same.

It is a phenomenon I can account for in no scientific way: a prickling in the back of the neck, a twitching of the hair upon my arms; a sense of someone standing, just behind my shoulder, offering advice, direction, though I hear no voice, no words. . . . In surgery, I have felt this presence. Other times as well.

Just weeks ago, I woke up in the grey dawn light, my wife

sleeping beside me, and breathing in a soft, slow rhythm; outside, the intermittent clanking of a cowbell. All was as it should have been, all as usual.

Except the figure standing in the corner of the room.

I saw him quite distinctly. Nothing vague or immaterial. No haziness. Indeed, he was familiar to me, with his straggly hair, untrimmed moustaches, and his rumpled clothes. . . .

He merely looked at me, as he has other times. He did not speak, although it may be that he smiled a little. I felt a sense of quite extraordinary stillness, as if the world had briefly ceased to turn; and knew instinctively he wished me well. I reached a hand in greeting, said, 'Good morning—'

He was gone.

There are hallucinations which occur upon the edge of sleep, left-over dreams which for an instant gain the lustre of reality. There are errors made in judgement, and freaks of brain activity leading the mind towards all sorts of strange conclusions. I have worked with the insane; I have seen this taking place. And I myself, deranged on alcohol, ether and cocaine, have held conversation with the spectre of a man I killed.

But I wonder, sometimes, if Lavenza's mechanism might have worked, in spite of all appearance. If he might even now be watching me, going about the world as wave, or particle, or frequency; and I confess, I feel a friendship for him I could never bring myself to feel in life. And more, I owe him: owe him for the years of happiness I have enjoyed, the years that once I would have scarcely dreamed might have been mine.

The monster asked to be redeemed, though in whatever twisted way he meant the term. Lavenza, too, sought redemption, from mortality, and from a legacy he could no longer bear. And yet the truth is this: that only one man was redeemed at Castle Frankenstein.

It was a gift most undeserved, and one for which I am, and will be, always grateful.

Finis